52 Steps to Murder

Steve Demaree

Steve Demaree

This book is dedicated to the two people I love the most and whose love I deserve the least, my wife, Nell, and my daughter, Kelly. May God continue to bless me with their presence in my life.

This book is also dedicated to those people who come to me personally to get my books at bookstores and libraries where I'm doing book signings, art and craft fairs, town festivals, and book fairs, as well as to all my friends on Facebook. If you are not yet a Facebook friend, send me a request to become friends.

May each of them and each of you enjoy this book.

Books by Steve Demaree

Dekker Cozy Mysteries

52 Steps to Murder
Murder in the Winter
Murder in the Library
Murder at Breakfast?
Murder at the High School Reunion
Murder at the Art & Craft Fair
Murder in Gatlinburg
Murder at the Book Fair
Murder on a Blind Date
A Body on the Porch
Two Bodies in the Backyard
A Body Under the Christmas Tree
Murder on Halloween
A Valentine Murder
A Body on April Fool's Day
A Body in the Woods
A Puzzling Murder

Off the Beaten Path Mysteries

Murder in the Dark
Murder Among Friends
A Bridge to Murder
A Smoky Mountain Mystery

Stand-Alone Mysteries

A Body in the Trunk

Aylesford Place Series

Pink Flamingoed
Neighborhood Hi Jinx
Croquet, Anyone?
Scavenger Hunt

Other Fiction

Stories From the Heart

Non-Fiction

Lexington & Me
Reflecting Upon God's Word

Steve Demaree

1

I don't like exercise. I tell people my favorite form of exercise is lying in the bathtub, pulling the plug, and fighting the current. But I only take baths on occasion, so, I guess my favorite form of exercise is falling into bed each night.

But on one particular day, that presented a major problem. I pulled up in front of a house that hovered over where I was parked. The number of steps leading up to it was a greater number than I could count to in the first grade. Probably at least third-grade level. But I needed to get inside that house. See, I'm Lt. Cy Dekker, the head of homicide for the Hilldale Police Department, and I had received a call that we would find a murdered woman at this address, along with her granddaughter and a rookie cop. And because our burg isn't large enough to have more full-time homicide detectives, the case fell in my lap. Well, mine and my partner's.

I looked over at my partner in crime-solving, Sgt. Lou Murdock, who detests exercise as much as I do. Lou and I traded shrugs, then opened two car doors and hoisted ourselves out of Lightning, my yellow VW bug, that is my choice of transportation. No gunmetal gray tank for me. Like the one parked in front of us.

I looked up at the house. Or was it the summit. I'd seen mountain ranges that were closer to sea level. Well, actually I hadn't, but I was sure there were some.

I turned to Lou. We waited until we were sure no one was sending a tram down to get us.

"Lou, we've got some greenhorn upstairs, and the department wants us to check this out. The old woman probably keeled over of a heart attack after climbing these steps, but we need to find out. Are you ready, Tonto?"

"Ready when you are, Lone Ranger."

"Remember, don't look down, and try to think of it as Mt. Everest without the snow and the wind."

"You really know how to make a situation sound better, Cy. I think I've already spotted the place where I plan to pitch my tent tonight. If I can drive the stakes in far enough that we don't get blown down the hill, I think we can make it all the way to the summit tomorrow."

"Just look at the bright side, Lou."

"There's a bright side?"

"Yeah, neither you nor I have to carry the old lady down the steps."

Lou laughed and then commented.

"That's comforting, although if we dropped her I doubt if she'd complain."

I wondered how many steps it was to the top and decided to count them. Halfway up I lost count, but there was no way I was going back to the bottom and start counting again. I didn't care. When it came time to tell this story to those who were not there, I would double the number of steps, invent a howling wind, and recall how our hands stuck to the frozen railing as we fought to keep our feet from sliding down the icy steps. Should I also add how I saved Lou's life as I protected him from the two gunmen who shot at us from above?

What seemed like an hour later, after multiple stops to curtail the latest wheezing, two homicide detectives made it to the front porch, tried to catch our breaths, and reached for the front door. I opened the door and entered the house. Lou followed. Another doorway stood a few feet in front of me. I assumed it led to the back of the house. The living room was to my left. As soon as we entered, the rookie police officer rose from a chair. He looked worse than I expected. He could not have been any wetter behind the ears if water had dripped down the back of his neck. Could it be that unbeknownst to me the department had started hiring extra men when our workload was heavy, much like construction companies do? I merely nodded at him. Was this another case of a minimum wage for minimum age? I didn't want to scare him out of the house before I found out if he knew anything that had happened there that day, so I nodded to him and smiled briefly to calm his uneasiness.

I turned and looked at the young woman, hoping she had held up better. She hadn't. Her eyes were red. Her cheeks were tear-stained. And her wringing hands had already shredded a handful of tissues. All of this overshadowed her beauty.

I saw the need to lighten the moment and took advantage of the opportunity.

"We would've been here sooner, but it took the Saint Bernard a while to find us. We got lost on the north face."

The young woman gave me a look that seemed to say that these two clowns are no better than the first one. I turned to Lou, who was doing his best to suppress a grin, then turned to face the young woman.

"I'm Lt. Dekker and this is Sgt. Murdock. And who might the two of you be?"

The young woman looked at me and then turned to the young officer, giving him the first chance to answer. My guess was that she was curious, as was I, to see if he remembered his name.

"I'm Officer Dan Davis. This is my first day alone."

Officer Davis looked like he wished he could have taken back the last sentence as soon as he uttered it.

"Well, you don't look so alone to me," I replied. "And who is your friend?"

From the looks on their faces, "friend" did not appear to be the word either of them would have used to describe the other. Obviously, it had been a trying morning for both of them.

"I'm Angela Nelson. That's my grandmother upstairs," she said as she pointed to a staircase that led upward from the other side of the living room as if Sgt. Murdock and I might have trouble discerning the meaning of "upstairs." The thought of her dead grandmother changed Angela Nelson's mood from indignation to sadness, and she began to cry.

"Miss Nelson, why don't you stay here and calm down while Officer Davis shows Sgt. Murdock and me where we can find the deceased." The word "deceased" added sobs to her tears.

I realized my bad choice of words and tried to comfort the young woman.

"I'm sorry, Miss Nelson. Would you like for Sgt. Murdock to keep you company?"

She shook her head and then replied. "No, I'll be fine," she said as she removed another tissue from her purse.

"Okay, well, come on, men. We'll be back in a few minutes, Miss Nelson."

Lou and I let Officer Davis lead the way, and the three of us climbed the stairs. As I sneaked a peek back at Miss Nelson, it appeared that Lou and I were doing a poor job of hiding our labored breathing. The steps creaked as we mounted them, not as if they found our weight painful, nor to scare us from continuing, but more to let us know that we were not welcome.

+++

Lou and I looked briefly at the woman who lay on the four-poster bed, her face badly bruised, her body heavily bandaged. A cast covered one arm and one leg. The obvious injuries happened many days before her death, but I wondered if they had anything to do with it. Did someone try to murder her before and return to complete a botched job? I made a mental note to find out. The sergeant and I planned to examine the body extensively after Officer Davis and Angela Nelson left.

Once again, I tried to put the young officer at ease. I asked him about his trek up Mt. Hilltop. He lied. At least, I think he lied. Either that or he had already forgotten the difficult climb. Officer Davis turned and looked at the dead woman. He still seemed ill at ease in her presence.

"Officer Davis, have you ever known anyone who died?"

"Y-yes, Lieutenant."

"Well, have you ever been to visitation at a funeral home or to a funeral."

"Sure."

"Well, just think of her as those dead people you've seen; only the casket is missing. Don't let the bandages fool you. This is not Lazarus. This woman will not come back

11

to life. If she does, Sgt. Murdock and I will protect you. Okay?"

Officer Davis managed a sheepish grin.

"Now that we've established this much, tell us what happened here today."

"I don't know, Lieutenant. I wasn't here when it happened."

I looked at the young officer and wondered how he had passed the tests necessary to become a policeman.

"Let, me rephrase that, Officer Davis. Tell me what happened to you, beginning with the time you received the call to come to Hilltop Place. You do remember receiving the call, don't you, Officer Davis?"

"Of course, Lieutenant."

With a little prompting, Officer Davis related his story. Dispatch had contacted him and directed him to proceed to this address. A young woman had phoned, concerned because her grandmother did not answer her front door. He arrived and found Miss Nelson on the front porch. She seemed frantic and wanted him to break in so she could see if her grandmother was okay. Because he was afraid to call headquarters in her presence, he went back to his cruiser and called in. Headquarters granted permission for him to break into the house.

I tried to suppress a smile and wondered if he would admit to calling in three times, which I knew is what had happened.

Officer Davis continued his narrative. He forced the window to gain entry to the house. Once inside, he checked the front door while Miss Nelson checked the back of the house. A couple of minutes later, the two of them headed upstairs where Miss Nelson found her grandmother. Officer Davis needed to report Mrs. Nelson's death. He convinced Angela Nelson to go downstairs with him. As they descended the staircase, both of them heard someone running through the living room and out the front door. By the time Officer Davis got to the front porch, the intruder had vanished.

Officer Davis ran down the front steps and looked both ways. He did not see anyone, so he ran a little way up and down the street, but still did not locate the intruder. He called the department and reported what had happened. After he called in, he waited by the cruiser for a few minutes and then returned to the house.

Officer Davis finished his version of what had happened. I suspected that he'd left out a few details, but I hoped that Miss Nelson would fill in the cracks. I led the way as the three of us left the bedroom and rejoined Miss Nelson.

2

As we returned to the first floor, I glanced at Angela Nelson. She seemed to be somewhat composed. At least she hadn't added to her used tissue pile. I waited for everyone to get settled, looked down at the young woman seated before me, and began my questioning. Even though this young woman had just lost her grandmother, I somehow thought that she might be of more help to me than Officer Davis had been.

"Miss Nelson, I know this has been a trying morning for you, but I need to ask you a few questions."

"Go ahead, Lieutenant. I'll do my best."

I subconsciously reached into my coat pocket and pulled out a Hershey Almond candy bar, still slightly cold from resting in my refrigerator overnight. I wouldn't have noticed what I'd done if I hadn't seen Miss Nelson's eyes follow my actions.

"Would you like a bite?" I asked, trying to be hospitable.

She shook her head. Her mannerisms told me that this had offended her as much as if I had licked the candy before offering her a bite.

After she declined my offer, I unwrapped the paper from my candy bar, took a bite, carefully rewrapped it, and slid it back into my pocket. I never go anywhere without my Hershey Almond candy bars. Well, nowhere except church. I never know when a case will prolong lunch, and anyone knows a good detective works better when his stomach's full. But I never eat a whole candy bar at one time. Well, almost never.

Call me meticulous, if you like, but I follow a pattern when eating my candy. Each time I remove the candy bar from my coat pocket, take one bite, rewrap the candy bar, and return it to my pocket until it's time for another bite. People laugh at me, but each time I carefully eat only one almond at a time. I determine the size of my bite by how close one almond is to the next. If two almonds are separated by only a minute amount of chocolate, I reach into my pants pocket, remove my pocketknife, and carefully cut my next bite, so as not to overstep my bounds and bite into the next almond. Sgt. Murdock and I like to have fun at each other's expense. More than once he has told me he plans to buy a Payday, which he plans to eat one peanut at a time.

Evidently, my actions disturbed Angela Nelson, because I noticed her looking at Sgt. Murdock, fully expecting him to have a Hershey Almond candy bar, too. Lou does carry candy, but he opts for M&Ms instead of Hershey Almonds.

"Miss Nelson, what do you do for a living?"

"I'm a buyer. I travel around the country buying merchandise for McAdams Department Store. You're familiar with McAdams, aren't you, Lieutenant?"

"I am. It's a fine establishment. Do you enjoy your job, Miss Nelson?"

"I do, but sometimes I'm away from home more than I like. Still, buying in person gives me a better feel for the merchandise than buying online."

"And that takes you away from your grandmother. Tell me, Miss Nelson, how many grandchildren did your grandmother have?"

"I was the only one."

"Did your grandmother have any other living relatives?" I asked as I settled into a chair across from Angela Nelson.

Sgt. Murdock continued to stand, as did Officer Davis. The sergeant rested against one wall, while the rookie leaned against a breakfront. Angela Nelson looked at both of them, offered each of them a seat, which they both declined. Then, she faced me again and answered my question about her grandmother's family.

"My father died of a heart attack, and my mother died of cancer. My grandmother was my only living relative, as I was hers. She had two sisters and a brother, but all of them have been dead for quite a few years."

"Miss Nelson, can tell me how you came to be here today and what happened after you arrived."

"Well, I returned early this morning from a three-week buying trip. I hadn't seen my grandmother in all this time and I wanted to check on her, so I decided to take a taxi here and see her before I went home. As tired as I was from the last three weeks, I knew that if I went home first I would fall into bed and not leave the house again today."

"You didn't call your grandmother while you were gone?"

"I never get back to the hotel until late, and by then she's already in bed."

After answering my question, the young woman looked away from me as Sgt. Murdock reached into his pocket and removed a package of M&Ms. He ripped open the corner with his teeth and swallowed a few from the bag. The fact that both of us chose to eat candy while I questioned Miss

Nelson seemed to bother her just a little. I still was not convinced that she didn't want any candy.

I wanted to learn what else Angela Nelson knew about what had happened earlier that day, so I continued my questioning.

"So, you took a taxi here after your plane landed. Don't you own a car?"

"I do, but I prefer not to leave it in long-term parking at the airport, so I always leave it at home and take a taxi any time I travel."

Angela Nelson had stopped wringing her hands and had placed them in her lap, but her sad look remained.

"What time did you arrive, Miss Nelson?"

"I'm not sure exactly. The cab company might have a record. Anyway, I got out and instructed the driver to take my luggage to my home. I didn't want to lug it all over the place."

"You trusted the taxi driver with your luggage?"

I could not believe someone would do that in these times. Maybe it was just the policeman in me coming out.

"Oh, sure. I've done it several times before, and my luggage always gets home okay. They take much better care of it than the airlines do. Of course, if I had known that you were going to be here, I would have kept it with me and let you carry it up when you arrived," she said as her face broke into a smile for the first time.

Try as he might, Officer Davis was unable to suppress a grin, although he turned away from me to hide it.

I wasn't about to let anyone get the best of me, so I replied, "Oh, I'm sure any good, well-meaning taxi driver would've carried your luggage up the steps, and Sgt. Murdock and I would have been willing to sit on your suitcases and slide down the hill when you left."

Angela Nelson laughed and replied, "And I would've let you do that as long as I could've watched, especially if you'd aimed for a tree."

I'd already noticed how beautiful Angela Nelson was, but I noticed that her smile improved her looks even more.

"We have digressed, Miss Nelson. Please tell me what you did when you arrived here this morning."

Angela Nelson's smile disappeared.

"I rang the bell. My grandmother didn't answer, so I rang it again. When she didn't answer the second time, I went to check with Miss Penrod to see if she had any news of my grandmother."

"Miss Penrod?"

"Yes, Irene Penrod. She lives next door at 121. She checks on my grandmother occasionally and more often if I'm out of town."

"Don't you have a key to your grandmother's house?"

"Yes, I have a key, but the door was bolted."

"But won't your key unlock the bolted door?

"Miss Nelson?"

"I'm sorry, Lieutenant. What was that again? Never mind. I remember. The door was double bolted. My key will unlock the dead-bolt lock, but not the second one. You can check it out."

She reached into her purse, removed her keys, and flipped them to me. "It's that one," she said, indicating the key to the front door.

I got up from my chair, walked over to the door, and looked at the double bolt. I slid the key into the lock and turned the key. I looked at the other keys. None of them fit. I finished my experiment, returned Miss Nelson's keys to her, and resumed my questioning.

"Miss Nelson, do you have any idea who else has a key to this house?"

"Well, of course, my grandmother had a key and Miss Penrod had one, too. I'm sure of those two, but my grandmother told me she gave keys to other neighbors, as well. Oh, and come to think of it, Mrs. Murphy, the cleaning lady had one, as did Bobby, the grocery boy, Mr. Hornwell, her attorney, and Mr. Hartley, the mailman. But it really doesn't matter who had a key. See, even if someone had a key, there's no way they could have gotten into the house unless my grandmother pushed the button or went to the door and unlocked the sliding bolt."

As Miss Nelson mentioned the names, I jotted them down in my notebook.

"Back to Miss Penrod, Miss Nelson. What did she have to say when you went over this morning?"

"Miss Penrod didn't answer her bell, either, so I came back here and rang again, figuring that maybe my grandmother had been in the bathroom, or had fallen asleep on the sun porch and hadn't heard the bell. When she didn't answer the second time, I called the police and they sent out Officer Davis."

"I assume you used your cell phone."

"That's right."

"Why didn't you use it to call your grandmother or Miss Penrod?"

"I figured if my grandmother didn't answer the door, she wouldn't answer the phone, either."

"And why didn't you call Miss Penrod?"

"I have no idea what her number is."

"And how long after you called did Officer Davis arrive?"

"Oh, probably ten minutes or less."

She laughed.

"What's so funny, Miss Nelson?"

"Well, for a minute there I thought I was going to have to call the police to report an accident."

Officer Davis looked down and hid his eyes. I suspected Sgt. Murdock and I were about to learn more than Officer Davis had told us upstairs.

"Go on, Miss Nelson."

"Well, I heard tires screech and looked up to see this police cruiser barreling down the street. Just when it looked like it was going to crash into the two trees at the end of the street, the officer must have returned to reality, because he applied the brakes and came to an abrupt stop."

I could see why Officer Davis hadn't told me everything.

"Please continue, Miss Nelson."

"Maybe I shouldn't have been so candid."

"No, we want to know everything from your perspective."

I said "we" wanted, but I knew that one of us didn't want the other two to know what had really happened.

"Well, he backed into a driveway, turned around, and pulled up in front of this house. He seemed to call in as if to let someone know that he had gotten where they told him to go. Then, he got out and stood there, as if the climb was too much for him."

I wanted to smile, but I couldn't. This was definitely a different version than the one Officer Davis shared upstairs.

"I did my best to put him at ease. I told him that I was the one who called, that there were only fifty-two steps, and he could hold on to the handrail as he climbed."

How could telling someone they had fifty-two steps to climb comfort them? At least, I had found out how many steps Lou and I had conquered.

"And then what happened, Miss Nelson?"

"Well, I told Officer Davis why I'd called, and told him that we needed to break in to see if my grandmother was okay. First, he insisted on trying my key, even though I'd already tried that. Then, he said he couldn't do anything unless he called in first."

This time I couldn't suppress my grin, and Miss Nelson grinned, as well. So, she too figured Officer Davis couldn't do anything unless he called in first.

"He seemed to take forever, but finally he returned. He insisted on ringing again before he cut a hole in the glass. Then, he reached in and unlocked the window, and opened it. Then he crawled through, helped me through, and told me to watch my step."

"And what did you do next?"

3

Angela Nelson had become more comfortable with the questioning. She had her hands folded calmly in her lap and had crossed her legs. Angela Nelson's legs were long, shapely, and tanned just enough that they neither resembled Addams Family white nor did they look like she had fallen asleep on a tanning bed. I wished I were ten to fifteen years younger. As a detective, I'm paid to notice things. I'm paid to notice people, too. Because I'm a man, I pay particular attention to beautiful women. The more Angela Nelson shifted in her seat or crossed her legs, the more I noticed that I was in the presence of a strikingly beautiful woman.

I even began to notice her clothes. Other than a lightweight jacket, I had no idea what I was wearing that day, but I checked out her outfit. Instead of traveling in a business suit or a casual pants outfit, Angela Nelson wore a white skirt, a knit green-and-white top, and white sandals with a thin strap between the big toe and the second one. Later, when I relayed this information to Mary, one of our police dispatchers, she replied, "A white skirt and sandals this late in the year?" As far as I was concerned, Angela

Nelson could wear a bikini in December and I wouldn't mind.

Because God gave me the handicap of being a man who has lived alone most of my adult life, I had no idea what colors a person should wear in what season. I do well to button my shirts the right wa so that both sides end at the same place at the bottom. But I did notice that the white in Angela Nelson's clothing contrasted with her tan. The green in her top highlighted the green in her eyes. Her thick, straight, auburn-colored hair fell to her shoulders and framed her face quite nicely. She wore only a little make-up. She didn't need it. She was quite beautiful without it. Everything about Angela Nelson, her tan, her hair, her eyes, her clothing, complemented everything else.

Miss Nelson must have been able to read my mind because she cleared her throat. My thoughts returned to the matter at hand. I glanced at Angela Nelson once more and gained further evidence that the young woman was easy on the eyes. Then I raised my eyes to make contact with Miss Nelson's eyes and waited to hear her answer to my question. I was thankful she remembered what I'd asked; I wasn't sure I could have at that moment.

"I told Officer Davis that my grandmother has, uh, had a heart problem and that it would be best if he let me look for her so that she wouldn't become scared when confronted by a stranger. I told him I'd call him if I needed him."

I raised my eyebrows and interrupted Angela Nelson.

"Pardon me for breaking in, Miss Nelson, but wouldn't your grandmother have been frightened by seeing you, as well?"

"I don't understand, Lieutenant."

The look in her eyes echoed her statement.

"Your grandmother didn't admit you to the house, so wouldn't she have been frightened if she saw anyone?"

"I never thought of that, Lieutenant. I guess that's possible, but more than likely she would've been less frightened of me than a stranger."

"Please go on, Miss Nelson. I didn't mean to interrupt."

Angela Nelson knew that I did mean to interrupt her, but didn't pursue the point and continued with the details of her search.

"Sometimes my grandmother sat out on the sun porch and watched the birds fly in and out of the yard, so I headed to the back of the house to see if she was there. When I didn't find her, I came back and told Officer Davis that I was going to look upstairs. He followed me halfway up the stairs."

"Officer Davis didn't accompany you?"

"There was no need. He was just on the stairs a few feet away."

I made a note that Officer Davis didn't tell us he didn't accompany her.

"And how long were you gone?"

"Probably not more than a minute."

"Thanks, Miss Nelson. Please continue."

"Where was I? Oh, yes. I went upstairs, started with the rooms closer to the stairwell, and eventually found my grandmother in her bedroom."

I interrupted again.

"Sorry to break in again, Miss Nelson, but when you went upstairs, why didn't you go to her bedroom first? Wouldn't you think that would be the most likely upstairs room to find your grandmother?"

"Not necessarily. My grandmother spent some time in her sewing room, and anyway, when you're looking for someone, it just makes sense to start in the room closest to where you are."

I reached into my pocket and again removed the Hershey bar. By this time, I'd eaten almost half of the chocolate bar. Lou followed my action, pulled out his bag of M&Ms, and gulped down a few more.

"Go ahead, Miss Nelson. Pick up where you left off with your upstairs search."

"After I saw my grandmother wasn't in the sewing room and the bathroom door was open, I thought maybe she was asleep and that was the reason why she didn't answer the bell, so I rushed to her bedroom. When I first saw her, I figured I was right, and I just stood there a few seconds looking at her. As I drew closer to the bed, I couldn't hear her breathing, so I picked up her arm to check her pulse. I'm not sure, but I think that when I couldn't feel her pulse, I screamed and Officer Davis came running up the stairs."

Angela Nelson did her best to keep from breaking down again, and while she didn't cry, her expression showed that she was becoming emotional once more. I paused for a moment to let her regain her composure and then continued.

"Miss Nelson, how long was it from the time you first went upstairs until you screamed and Officer Davis came running?"

"I don't know, Lieutenant. Officer Davis could probably tell you better than I could. I assume just a few seconds, but things were pretty fuzzy for me at that point."

I didn't tell her that I didn't agree with her assertion that Officer Davis could probably better tell me.

"Please go on, Miss Nelson. I know you're anxious to get this over with."

"Well, when Officer Davis came into the room, I explained to him what had happened. He said he needed to report it, and we headed to the stairs. As we made our way down the stairs, we heard someone running through the house and out the front door."

"Did you get a glimpse of this person?"

"No. Officer Davis tripped over my feet trying to get around me, and we both tumbled down the remaining stairs. By the time we got up, whoever it was was gone. Officer Davis went outside. I don't guess he saw anyone."

I made a note of still another item that Officer Davis had failed to include.

"Do you have any idea who it was, Miss Nelson?"

"None whatsoever."

"Do you have any idea how he or she got in?"

"The only thing I can think of is that they came in the front door after Officer Davis and I went upstairs."

"Don't you think that this person could have already been in the house?"

"I guess they could've been if someone had let them in or if they had had a key, but if so, they would've had to have rebolted the door because it was bolted when we tried it. That's the reason Officer Davis and I had to come in through the window."

"Isn't there a back door, Miss Nelson?"

"Yes, but it wouldn't matter if the back door was unlocked. There's a twelve-foot-high wall all the way around the back yard of each of the homes on this street. It would be almost impossible for anyone to scale that wall."

"Miss Nelson, did you by any chance see anyone else this morning?"

"Anyone else?"

"Yeah, you know, like any of the neighbors?"

"Well, I noticed Stanley Silverman looking out his window, if that's what you mean."

"Who's Stanley Silverman?"

"He's the guy across the street. He knows everything that goes on around here. I saw the creep down the street, too. He was hiding behind a tree."

"The creep down the street?"

"Yeah, Jimmy Reynolds. He lives two doors that way," she said as she pointed toward the dead-end part of the street. "He scares me."

"Why's that, Miss Nelson?"

"He's crazy. That's why."

I added these names to the others. Could it be that I had begun a suspect list? Of course, I wouldn't need one. If my guess was right that Mrs. Nelson had been murdered, I would only have to walk across the street and talk to Mr. Silverman. Because he knew everything that went on, he could identify the murderer.

"You say you arrived here by taxi, Miss Nelson."

"That's right."

"Well, why don't I have Officer Davis give you a ride home?"

Both Angela Nelson and Officer Davis tried to keep from showing how uncomfortable they were with my suggestion, and Miss Nelson offered another possibility.

"If you don't mind, I'd like to remain here with my grandmother for a little while. I can always call a cab when I'm ready to leave."

"I'm sorry, Miss Nelson, but that won't be possible. Sgt. Murdock and I have some work to do here."

"I don't understand, Lieutenant."

"Anytime Sgt. Murdock and I are called out on a case, we have to file a report. Besides, we need to look around and see if we can find out how the intruder got in and when."

"You don't think the intruder caused my grand-mother's heart attack, do you, Lt. Dekker?" Angela Nelson asked, eager to find out what I thought of the situation.

"Probably not, but don't worry. We'll look things over. It's merely routine. Now, you go with Officer Davis, and I'll let you know as soon as we release your grandmother's body."

"Does that mean I can't go ahead and make funeral arrangements?"

"Oh, feel free to make them, but we have to finish our report before we can release her body to the mortuary. As I said, it's merely routine. There's nothing to worry about. We'll probably be out of your way before the day is over. Uh, one other thing, Miss Nelson. You say that your grandmother had no other family?"

"That's right."

"Does that mean that you'll inherit this house?"

"I don't think so. I told my grandmother a while back that I wasn't interested in the house or her money, but that I'd like all of her family photographs and a couple of keepsakes to remember her by. I'm sure that Mr. Hornwell can supply you with all the details."

I consulted my list.

"Let's see, that's her attorney."

"That's right, Harry Hornwell. He'll know all about my grandmother's estate."

"Oh, yes, one more question, Miss Nelson. I noticed your grandmother had several bruises and broken bones. Can you tell me how and when this happened?"

The thought of her grandmother's injuries made Angela Nelson's eyes tear up again. In a few seconds, she recomposed herself and then answered my question.

"I don't know, Lieutenant. I noticed them when I found her. I don't know what happened to her, but it had to have happened in the last three weeks. She was fine when I left."

"Thanks so much, Miss Nelson. I know this has been a rough day for you, so you go home and get some rest. I'll call you as soon as I can."

I turned to face Officer Davis. I wondered if he would make eye contact with me. He did, but the look in his eyes said it was difficult for him.

"And thanks to you, too, Officer Davis. I'll let you know if we have any more questions for you."

Officer Davis walked over from the corner where he had been standing, and Angela Nelson got up from her seat. Both of them nodded and said goodbye to Lou and me, then walked toward the front door.

As Angela Nelson stood and faced me, I noticed that the beautiful woman could almost look me straight in the eye, so I guessed her height at five foot nine. The handsome, light-brown-haired rookie officer was slightly taller than me, so I guessed him to be around six feet.

If my mother were still living and she could lean me up against a doorway and mark my growth spurt with a ruler, she'd find out I topped out at five feet ten and a half inches, give or take a fraction. Lou and I can look one another in the eye, so I'd say he topped out about the same place.

4

As soon as Officer Davis left with Angela Nelson, I called and reported in, asked for an SOC team and Frank Harris, our medical examiner. Then Lou and I trudged up the stairs to see what the crime scene could tell us, without either of us getting close enough to disturb any evidence.

"Come on, Lou. Let's go take another look at the old lady."

I entered Mrs. Nelson's sewing room on the right as we completed our climb. Lou followed me. We stayed a moment and then found two more bedrooms down a hall toward the back of the house. We glanced quickly at each, then came back, passed a bathroom just past and opposite the stairs, and then a linen closet before we came to Mrs. Nelson's bedroom. We entered the room, looked at the body.

"Well, what do you think, Lou?"

"You mean, do I think the old lady died of a heart attack?"

"That's exactly what I mean."

"I'm not sure, but I can tell you've got a strong feeling. Was it murder, suicide, or natural causes?"

"Murder, Lou."

Sgt. Murdock raised his eyebrows, not so much in disbelief, but because my comment piqued his interest.

"Go on, Cy."

Before I continued, I reached into my pocket and withdrew a Hershey wrapper that now engulfed the minuscule remains of a once robust chocolate bar. I smiled as I saw that there were mounds of chocolate surrounding the next tasty almond. My next bite would be a large one. I didn't have to use my fingers to break off a piece, so I wouldn't need to lick them, just my lips. After I sampled my delicacy, I carefully rewrapped the chocolate bar before I continued. Being used to my meticulous nature, at least as far as eating candy was concerned, Sgt. Murdock waited patiently until I continued.

"Look at the clues, Lou."

Sgt. Murdock studied the room to see what I had seen. It was a large bedroom with an adjoining bathroom. The deceased lay on the bed. There was a bedside table with a brass lamp and a telephone, a chest, a dresser with a mirror, a bentwood rocker, and another chair beside a marble-top table with a floor lamp beside it. A couple of books lay on the table. Other than the deceased, bedcovers, and a bedpan on the bed, and the books on the marble-top table, there was nothing on any of the furniture, not even dust. The hardwood floor was spotless, except for a goblet that lay on its side.

"All I see is a little old lady lying on the bed and a glass on the floor. Those wraps covering her broken bones and bruises make her look like a mummy whose head has broken out of her cocoon."

I chuckled.

"Well, I'm not sure I'd call her encasement a cocoon, my friend, but those are the same clues I see."

"I know I'm only a Dr. Watson to your Sherlock Holmes, but my guess is that you think she was poisoned, Cy."

"That I do, Lou."

Lou smiled, having correctly guessed my thoughts.

"Because of the glass on the floor?"

"Partly."

"Is the other partly that you see no poison anywhere and the old lady was in too much pain to get up and get it?"

"That's right, Lou. This old lady has taken a mighty tumble recently. The presence of a bedpan tells me that the lady next door came over a few times a day and emptied it for her. Mrs. Nelson wasn't going anywhere on her own."

"But what's to keep the next-door neighbor from assisting her in suicide?"

"Nothing, as long as the next-door neighbor put the glass on the floor, too, because this bed sits up too high for the glass to fall out of the old lady's hand and not break. Plus, I'll bet they won't find a single fingerprint on the glass. No, she was murdered, Lou, and our murderer doesn't mind us knowing that she was murdered. Otherwise, he or she would have done a better job of making it appear to be a suicide."

"Unless the murderer had to make a quick getaway because someone was entering the house."

"Come on, Lou. Even a murderer making a hasty retreat has enough time to grab a glass. Besides, it could serve as a weapon in case someone confronted the murderer on his or her way out of the house. He or she could have thrown it at someone to gain a few seconds, or broken it in order to cut someone. Now, let's go outside and wait for Frank Harris and the SOC team to get here so we can see what else we can find out."

The two of us had investigated many murders over the years. So had Frank Harris, the medical examiner. During those many years, the three of us had seen a lot of each other and had become good friends in the process.

No sooner had Lou and I walked outside until the SOC team pulled up. We wanted to stay out of their way. I noticed a swing and a metal chair with two arms and motioned for Lou to take his choice. He selected the swing. I should have picked first.

If you haven't already figured out that I'm not a typical cop, you soon will. I carry only the customary gun. I carry no communication devices on my person, whether I'm working or not. I don't even own a pair of sunglasses, mirrored or otherwise. Neither do I require a method of transportation that goes one hundred sixty miles per hour and burns a gallon of gas for each mile it travels. Why do I need to hurry? Murderers never remain at the scene of the crime to make my job easier, and corpses never recover, even if I hurry.

I looked up and scanned the houses that hovered above the street. No trees blocked my view except those at each end of the street. All the houses were made of brick, most of them a shade of red, and all of them had front porches that ran from the left side of the house to the left side of the garage which sat below on the same plane as the street. Many of the porches had swings, and a few of them had other furniture as if to encourage visitors if someone was in good enough condition and so inclined to make the climb.

The SOC team had already gone inside. Someone else slammed a car door and interrupted my thoughts. Frank Harris had gotten out of his vehicle and stood there looking up at Lou and me and smiled.

"So, Cy. How did you and Lou get here? Someone airlift you in?"

"No, Frank, Lou and I came up the same steps you're working on right now. Actually, we made it in record time."

"Oh? How many days did it take you, Cy?"

"Oh, not many. If it's any trouble Frank, we can slide the old lady down to where you are. I don't think she'd complain."

"I appreciate it, Cy, but I think I'll carry on. What I might do, however, is get you to go back down to the wagon and pick up anything I might have forgotten."

"I'd be glad to do that, Frank, as long as you're willing to visit the neighbors to see if they saw anything out of the ordinary here today."

Lou smiled as he watched the two of us volley repartees. He enjoyed our verbal tennis match. None of this was new to him.

"I had a feeling you'd ask, Cy, so I already checked. No one saw anything out of the ordinary except for two middle-aged men having coronaries on the way up these steps. Oh, by the way, Lt. Huff-and-Puff, do I need oxygen up where you are?"

"Not where we are, Frank, but up where the old lady is. As a matter of fact, I think your report might show that she died from a lack of oxygen. Of course, if you don't hurry up, the body will start to decompose before you get up here to check it."

Only a medical examiner could listen to a comment like that and visualize it without his stomach doing flip-flops. Frank Harris leaned his head back, laughed, and then resumed his climb.

I watched my friend who wore glasses that darkened in the sunlight. I knew how much he wished he had seen us climb those same steps.

+++

A few hours later, after Frank examined the body and the others dusted for fingerprints, nothing out of the ordinary had been found. The medical examiner's preliminary finding was that the victim was poisoned, but he wouldn't know the details until further tests were done.

When an ambulance showed up to take the victim for an autopsy, I noticed two interested bystanders who were not the police. A nerdy man, who appeared to be in his forties, stood across the street taking in the proceedings, not caring who did or didn't see him. Lou got my attention and pointed out a young man, probably in his mid-twenties, hiding behind the only burr oak tree on the block. When the young man noticed that Lou had spotted him, he darted away in a nervous manner to the next tree away from the house.

5

Lou and I stood on the front porch, glad that the two men who carried the body out of the house didn't drop it on the way down. After the ambulance left, I noticed the nerd from across the street approaching the house. Lou noticed him too, and the two of us headed down to intercept the man before he set foot upon the crime scene.

If I'm honest, I have to admit that it irritated me that this unbecoming man, who appeared to be only a few years my junior, had no trouble navigating the steps. His stride coming up the steps equaled our jaunt heading down them.

We encountered our visitor about half-way up the steps. I stood and eyed the stranger, Dodge City style. None of us spoke immediately. The man had thin light brown hair and a wimpy mustache. At least there was a wisp of hair on his lip. He wore glasses with ugly yellow-brown frames, a white sport shirt with geometrical figures on it, and an unbuttoned, tan cardigan sweater which allowed us to see all six, cheap, ballpoint pens that were stuffed into the protector that protruded from the shirt's pocket. I could see nothing to distinguish our visitor from any other wimp. The new arrival appeared to be around five-foot-eight inches tall, and his light brown wingtips seemed to be a size eight or thereabouts. The fact that he stood two steps below me made him seem even shorter.

Finally, our unwelcome visitor broke the silence.

"Do you have any idea yet who killed her?"

"I beg your pardon," I replied.

"I said, 'Do you have any idea yet who killed her?'"

"Sgt. Murdock, did I say anything about someone being murdered here today?" I asked as I turned to face Lou.

"Not that I recall," my friend replied with a smile on his face.

"Make a note, Sergeant, we must let the medical examiner know Mrs. Nelson was murdered. It will save him lots of time."

"Oh, come on, detective. A passel of police doesn't show up when an elderly woman drops dead of old age," our perceptive intruder interjected.

I focused in on the little man who stood before me, a contrast if I ever saw one. His eyes twinkled as if everything was a game to him. His nervous mannerisms told me this was a man who had something to hide. He stood with his left hand in his pocket, jingling keys and coins as he listened and talked.

"I think there was a period of many days between the time when Mrs. Nelson dropped and when she died," I replied.

The nerd laughed at my statement.

"I assume you're talking about when she fell down the stairs," the stranger said.

"Is that what happened to her?" I asked.

"Don't you know, detective?"

"No, I wasn't present when it happened. Were you here for the occasion? You weren't by any chance standing behind her when she fell, were you?"

The man laughed again.

"Not guilty, your honor."

"By the way, I don't think we've been properly introduced. I'm Lt. Dekker and this is Sgt. Murdock. And you are?"

"I'm Stanley Silverman. I live across the street," the man answered as he turned and pointed to his house with his free hand.

Lou and I watched as our visitor quit jingling the coins and keys, removed a quarter from his pocket, and put it in his right hand. He slid it between his thumb and index finger and began to flip it under one finger and over the next without looking at his hand. The man is ambidextrous, I joked to myself. He jingles left-handed and flips with his right.

I observed Stanley Silverman for a moment and then continued my questioning.

"And Mr. Silverman, do you have any answers about anything that went on here today or are you only full of questions?"

"I'll scratch your back, Lieutenant, and you scratch mine."

I shuddered at the thought.

"I don't think that would be quite fair, Mr. Silverman. After all, my back is much larger than yours."

Stanley Silverman laughed again. Obviously, he enjoyed my humor. I studied the interesting man who stood a couple of steps below me. I labeled him a paradox. On the one hand, the neighbor seemed to be in total control and as calm as a windless night. On the other hand, he seemed to suffer from paranoia. I was anxious to find out more about this man and what he had seen.

"So, Mr. Silverman, why don't you go first? Tell me anything you can think of about what went on here today."

Mr. Silverman began to tell Lou and me about what he had observed at Mrs. Nelson's house that morning. He told us that when he first looked out of his front window that morning he noticed Irene Penrod leave Mrs. Jarvis's house and head to Mrs. Nelson's. I interrupted him and asked who Mrs. Jarvis was. He pointed to her house on the other side of Miss Penrod's. Then I let him continue. He told us that Miss Penrod had an envelope in her hand when she left Mrs. Jarvis's. Mr. Silverman said that it was quite common for Miss Penrod to visit Mrs. Nelson. He had no idea if Miss Penrod was Mrs. Nelson's first visitor of the day, but he did know that Mr. Hartley entered the house with the mail before Miss Penrod left.

I asked Mr. Silverman who left the house first, but the nosy neighbor didn't know because he'd left the window.

When I asked Mr. Silverman why he left the window, I got the impression he was lying when he told us his phone had rung. As Mr. Silverman said this, he looked at his feet. I looked at them too and noticed the dust on his shoes. From the looks of his shoes, the dust had not been there long, and I doubt if he got his shoes dusty as he looked out his window or talked on the phone. But why would the man lie to us?

Mr. Silverman told us he later returned to the window and saw Miss Penrod leave her own house in a taxi. Mr. Silverman chuckled as he related this to Lou and me.

"What's so funny, Mr. Silverman?"

"Oh, it's just that I noticed that the cab driver stared straight ahead so he wouldn't have to help Miss Penrod with her luggage."

"So, Miss Penrod left with luggage?"

"She had a bag."

"So, I assume you went over and carried it down for her."

"No, I have a problem with my back," Stanley Silverman said as he reached back and rubbed his lower back.

"Yes, I noticed that, Mr. Silverman, when you ran up the steps to meet us," I answered sarcastically. "Anyway, go on. So you returned to the window after finishing your phone call."

"That's right."

"I don't want to take up much more of your time, Mr. Silverman, but did you see anyone else at the house today?"

Mr. Silverman told us about Miss Nelson's arrival, and nothing he said varied from her version.

"Oh, and there's something else you might want to know about. As far as I can recollect, it happened about the same time that Miss Nelson arrived."

"And what is that, Mr. Silverman?"

"I know it sounds creepy, but someone was peering out the blinds at Irene Penrod's house."

"Are you sure it wasn't Miss Penrod?"

"No, this was after she left."

"Maybe she had company?"

"And left them? I don't think so."

"So, how long after Miss Penrod left did you see this person?"

"Well, I never actually saw a person."

"Then, maybe it was a cat."

"Miss Penrod doesn't have a cat. This is probably the only street in the county where no one has any pets."

"So, tell me what you saw, Mr. Silverman."

"Well, I noticed some movement in the blinds, so I zeroed in my binoculars to take a look. I couldn't see anything except a parted blind and some fingertips. Then the person must've turned and seen me looking in that direction because he or she moved away from the blinds. They came back, though."

"Could you tell what this person was doing?"

"Not for sure, but my guess is watching Miss Nelson."

"And what do you base this on?"

"On what part of the blind he or she looked through. See, it was the bay window," Stanley indicated, as he pointed to the house next door, "not the other one. As you can see, it juts out a couple of feet from the rest of the house, so if someone wanted to look at Mrs. Nelson's house, they would look out the left blind. If they wanted to see across the street where I live, they would look out the front blind, and if they wanted to look up the street, say to where Mrs. Wilkins lives, they would look out the right side."

I was thankful for his first-grade explanation and had another name to add to my list.

"Mrs. Wilkins?"

"Yeah, she lives in that house there," he said, pointing to a house up the street on the same side of the street as the Nelson house. "And part of the time whoever it was did look up that way. It was as if he or she didn't want to get caught."

"Let's get back to the Nelson house. Other than Angela Nelson or the police officer, did anyone else enter or exit the house?"

"I don't know, Lieutenant."

"Another phone call?"

"No, it was getting close to my lunchtime. Other than a glance out a couple of times, I didn't look out again until just before they removed the body."

"Lunch! I knew that we were forgetting something, Sergeant."

My stomach growled, as if on cue.

"Oh, one more thing, Mr. Silverman. Do you have a key to Mrs. Nelson's house?"

"Now, why would I have a key?"

"Does that mean you don't have a key?"

"No, I don't. Mrs. Nelson had few visitors. I've already told you about Miss Penrod. Of course, Mr. Hartley delivered the mail every day, and occasionally he went inside or visited with her on the porch. Her granddaughter Angela stopped by from time to time. Harry Hornwell, Mrs. Nelson's attorney, stopped by every few weeks. Mrs. Murphy, the maid, came every Friday to clean, and Bobby, the grocery boy, delivered to her every week or so. Then, there's Mrs. Reynolds. She used to go over. I suppose all of them could have had keys."

"Mrs. Reynolds?"

"Yeah, she's the old bag down there," Mr. Silverman said as he pointed to the last house on Mrs. Nelson's side of the street. "She used to go over and see Mrs. Nelson some before Jimmy came home."

"Who's Jimmy?"

"He's her son, and he happens to be the wacko standing behind the third tree watching us. He went crazy in the war. Oh, come to think of it, I saw him this morning, too, hiding behind a tree, just like he is now."

I had already decided that Mrs. Nelson had had some interesting neighbors. I just had to find out if one of them killed her. That meant meeting some of them, and to do that it meant Lou and I would have to climb some more steps. Probably somewhere around fifty-two of them at each house. Why couldn't the victim have lived on Flat Street instead of Hilltop Place?

6

I called the department and asked for someone to keep an eye on Mrs. Nelson's house while Lou and I went to our usual haunt to grab a very late lunch. A few minutes later, I winced as Officer Davis arrived. I quickly dismissed my lack of belief in his ability. Surely he could watch a house. Couldn't he? I gave him instructions and Lou and I left.

I parked the car in front of the Blue Moon Diner and neither Lou nor I wasted any time getting out of the vehicle. The counter where Lou and I always eat has eight vinyl-covered stools, plus there are five tables, three along the front wall next to the jukebox and two on the side of the restaurant farthest from the entrance. The place has an old-fashioned cash register, and black-and-white checked linoleum flooring. Lou and I don't go there for the ambiance, whatever that is. We go for the food.

We entered the establishment, took a whiff of the blended smells emanating from the kitchen, grabbed hold of the counter, and plopped down on the same two vinyl-covered stools where we always sit. Lou and I are probably the diner's best customers. As usual, we were approached as soon as we had landed on our perches.

"Hello, Rosie."

"Well, if it isn't Dick Tracy Squared," the waitress replied. "What can I get for the two of you before you drool all over my counter?"

"I'll have the 'old-fashioned newfangled special,'" Lou blurted out. He referred to a half-pound cheeseburger with lettuce, tomato, pickles, onions, and Thousand Island dressing, topped with two, large, fried onion rings. The special came with an order of French fries with gravy. Lou and I never count calories, carbs, or fat grams. That would be more depressing than counting steps.

"How about you, chief?" Rosie asked as she turned my way.

"Give me the 'swimming in gravy bonanza,'" I replied, which translated meant chicken-fried steak smothered in gravy with mashed potatoes submerged in even more gravy. I couldn't help but smack my lips as I ordered.

"And what can I get you to drink with that?"

Lou opted for a large mug of root beer, while I ordered a glass of iced tea.

"Back in a flash, boys," said the woman with brown hair that came courtesy of a bottle and eyelashes that had to be reattached each day. The short, plump woman, who wore a light brown uniform covered by an over-the-head, food-stained apron, turned around and hung our written order on a revolving carousel and spun the carousel so the cook could rip it off and read it. Rosie approached retirement age, but she moved with the grace of a much younger woman. While I never pay attention to how she greets the other patrons, my guess is that she has a smile for everyone and feels quite at home among anyone from business executives to street people. She puts on no airs and works at what she enjoys doing each day.

+++

44

Lou and I had done our part to feed the hungry. We returned to Hilltop Place. I drove down the street and was pleased to see that no one had stolen the house or Officer Davis's cruiser while we were gone. I was sorry to see that no one had lowered all the houses to the same level as the street. I let Officer Davis know he could leave. I wanted to begin our door-to-door investigation with the houses farthest from Mrs. Nelson's house, so I turned the car around and drove to the house nearest the cross street. I parked the bug and both of us extracted ourselves from the car. When we left for lunch, Lou counted the number of houses. Nine houses towered above each side of the street, and nine long sets of steps led up to them. One house was the victim's house and Stanley Silverman had already been interviewed, so only eight houses remained on each side of the street. Lou and I realized that Jesus had sent his disciples out in twos, but we also remembered that none of those disciples ventured as far as Hilltop Place. Lou and I decided that eight sets of steps were less than sixteen, so we agreed to split up and each of us took one side of the street. While both of us know that there is strength in numbers, each of us realized that if he encountered difficulty, he could call out to his friend who would be there within an hour, provided he didn't have a coronary on the way.

Lou took the even-numbered houses, and surprisingly found everyone at home. As he moved down the street, each climb became more difficult than the previous climb, and each new house meant more stops before Lou reached the front porch. He held on to the railing because his tired legs didn't always lift his feet as high as necessary, and he scraped his toes against the front of a step more than once. I know because I turned and watched him at many of my rest stops on the way to each summit. A street-level driveway that led to the basement of each house separated each set of houses and caused him to ascend and descend at each house. In case the resident answered the doorbell quickly, Lou had his identification in his hand and showed it to each resident until the good sergeant had finished wheezing and was able to speak again.

+++

Because of poor planning, I failed to bring a pickax or any other means to aid me in my conquest of Hilltop Place. I contemplated my options. I thought of rubbing butter on my hands to help them glide up the railing. I quickly discarded that option when I realized that if the rest of my body did not follow suit, I would wind up with a cut chin, scraped knees, and possibly an arm pulled out of its socket. My next thought was to shoot some sort of projectile and land it against the door. I scrapped that idea when I envisioned broken doors or irate residents who sicced their dogs on this roly-poly man. I'd forgotten that Stanley Silverman said that none of the street's residents had pets.

After much grunting and groaning, I arrived at the first house only to find that no one was at home. If I had known that, I wouldn't have bothered to climb all those steps. I ambled down the steps with a few more aches and pains, but no more evidence. When I found no one at home at the second house, I gave a little more consideration to my first two ideas. Well, at least the second one, but I had no projectile. Besides, I hurt too much to project anything sufficiently enough to land with a thud to summon the household.

At my third house, I encountered the "Mrs. Wilkins" Mr. Silverman had mentioned. She told me why my luck was bad. The first house was vacant, and the second house might as well have been. Someone had rented it but chose not to live there.

46

"Mark my word, Lieutenant, there's something illegal going on in that house."

I smiled and promised to check it out. Already I could tell that if I gained no new information at this house, it would not be because of Mrs. Wilkins's unwillingness to talk. This was not a woman who sat idly by while the neighbors went about their business, nor was this the person I wanted to share my secrets with.

"I always try to be a concerned citizen. Not enough people do that, nowadays. Anyway, you're not going to find anyone home next door. They've gone to Florida for a month."

I couldn't help but wonder if they took the trip solely to get away from Mrs. Wilkins.

"Mrs. Jarvis lives next to them, but I doubt if you can raise her. She's in a wheelchair and almost never answers her door. Of course, feel free to try if you want to. Miss Penrod lives in the next house. Claimed she was leaving on a trip this morning, but I don't trust that woman. Lies more than a lazy dog."

As I listened to Mrs. Wilkins, I wondered why the murderer hadn't already been identified, considering that Mrs. Wilkins and Mr. Silverman lived on the street and probably took turns doing sentry duty. Surely, no fortress in history had had better lookouts. Mrs. Wilkins continued her job as the immobile tour guide. I listened in case she said something that would later prove helpful.

"I suppose you know that poor old Mrs. Nelson lived in the next house. God rest her soul."

"How do you know that Mrs. Nelson is dead?" I asked, as I carefully hid the smile that loomed just inside.

"Well, I was sitting on the porch when they carted her out. Her face was covered, and when someone's face is covered there's not a lot of chance for recovery."

"Except for Lazarus."

"You have a point there, Lieutenant. Maybe you shouldn't bury her for a few days. You know, Jesus was a few days late getting to Lazarus. Anyway, Lieutenant, let me finish quick so I can get to my beans. I'm canning the last of my beans today. Miss Overstreet lives on the other side of Mrs. Nelson. Good Christian woman and she should be home. She can tell you all about the old biddy with the psychotic son who lives in the last house."

Mrs. Wilkins did not mention Mrs. Reynolds by name. When Mrs. Wilkins began to tell me about everyone on the other side of the street, I interrupted and told her that I had a man talking to those people. I decided to ask her one more question before I left and was glad that I did.

"Mrs. Wilkins, did you happen to see anyone on the street today that doesn't live on this street?"

"Mr. Hartley, of course. I saw him when he handed me my mail."

"Does he have a habit of knocking on your door and handing you your mail, or did you just happen to see him coming?"

"Neither. I was sitting on the porch then, too. He went down the other side, started up this one, checked in on Mrs. Nelson, and a few minutes later brought me my mail."

"You were sitting on the porch all that time?"

"Longer than that, Lieutenant."

"Wasn't it a little cool to be sitting outside this morning?"

"I had my sweater on. I enjoyed the breeze."

"So, did you see anyone other than Mr. Hartley this morning?"

"Oh, my, yes."

"Mrs. Wilkins, maybe you'd better start at the beginning and tell me who all you saw this morning."

"Well, first was Irene Penrod. Right after I poured my coffee and came out on the porch, she came out of Mrs. Jarvis's house."

"Do you have any idea what time that was?"

"Yes, because Irene asked me if I had the time, and I looked and told her it was 9:13."

"Do you have any idea why she went to see Mrs. Jarvis?"

"None whatsoever."

"And what did she do when she left Mrs. Jarvis's?"

"Went right to Mrs. Nelson's house."

"Did she have any trouble getting in?"

"No, I suppose she just pushed the buzzer and Mrs. Nelson let her in."

"You didn't see Mrs. Nelson let her in, did you?"

"Of course not, Lieutenant. Mrs. Nelson was confined to her bed ever since her fall. Of course, I still think she was pushed. Anyway, Mrs. Nelson had to buzz Miss Penrod in."

"Any evidence Mrs. Nelson was pushed?"

Mrs. Wilkins smiled. I could tell she was glad her comment piqued my interest.

"I didn't see it happen if that's what you mean."

"Any suspects?"

"My guess is the loony did it."

"You mean the guy in the last house? The Reynolds boy?"

"That's right, the loony."

"And why do you say that?"

"I was sitting on my porch that morning when he came running out of Mrs. Nelson's house hollering like a hive of bees were after him."

"You're talking about Jimmy Reynolds?"

"That's right, the loony."

49

"I ran in immediately and called Irene Penrod and told her she should check on Mrs. Nelson."

"And did she?"

"She did. Even Stanley Silverman got in on the act. I guess his binoculars don't see through brick walls."

"Who got there first?"

"Irene. She found Mrs. Nelson on the floor at the bottom of the steps, called an ambulance, and they came and took her to the hospital."

"Did Mrs. Nelson say what happened?"

"She said she fell. I'm not so sure. All I know is the old biddy kept the loony in the house for the next three days. Even after that, she kept him on a shorter leash."

"Back to today, Mrs. Wilkins. All of this happened before you saw Mr. Hartley?"

"That's right. Mr. Hartley pulled onto the street just after Irene went into Mrs. Nelson's house."

"And how much later was it when he entered the Nelson house?"

"Oh, I'd say five or six minutes."

"And how long did he stay?"

"A few minutes. It was 9:35 exactly when he handed me my mail. I know because I'd turned the radio on. I like to listen to those call-in shows in the morning, and they were just coming back from a news break."

"Who left the Nelson house first, Mrs. Wilkins? Mr. Hartley or Mrs. Penrod?"

"Mr. Hartley. Irene left about five minutes after he handed me my mail."

"And did you see anyone else this morning?"

"Yeah, the old biddy opened the door to check on the loony several times. He'd come out of his house and was hiding behind a tree. He was there most of the morning. She probably came out to make sure he didn't hang any squirrels."

I suppressed a laugh and asked my next question.

"And did you see anyone else?"

"Well, Stanley Silverman was looking out his window watching what was going on."

"Did you notice how long he was there?"

"Well, the first time I noticed him was when Mr. Hartley delivered his mail. He sat there awhile, then he left for a few minutes, and then he came back again."

"Do you know when he came back?"

"He might've been gone fifteen minutes or so. He was sitting there when Irene left and was still there when Angela's taxi pulled up."

"Tell me about that, Mrs. Wilkins."

"Not much to tell. Irene left in one cab and Angela came a few minutes later in another one."

"What did Angela do?"

"Went up to the house. Looked like she rang the buzzer. She waited a couple of minutes and then went over to Irene's and rang the bell. Naturally, no one came to the door. Then, she went back to her grandmother's and stood on the porch. Looked like she called somebody and then a few minutes later a police car pulled up. Just about that time my phone rang, so I went in to get it."

"So, you didn't see anyone else?"

"Well, after I got off the phone I remembered that I left my coffee on the front porch. Came out just in time to see Bobby, the grocery boy, running up the street. Jumped in his car and took off. A minute or so later, this cop comes running out of the Nelson house. I picked up my cold coffee and headed in the house to put my beans on."

"When did you first notice Bobby's car?"

"When he left. Wasn't there when I first came out on the porch."

I thanked Mrs. Wilkins for her help and turned to leave. I was sure that before she got to her beans she would call at least one friend to tell her how she had helped the police department solve a murder.

Like Mrs. Wilkins predicted, I found no one else at home until I arrived at Miss Overstreet's house. While it was obvious that Miss Overstreet didn't like Mrs. Reynolds, thankfully, I did not find Miss Overstreet as talkative as Mrs. Wilkins. Mrs. Overstreet hadn't seen or heard anyone that morning.

I had no problem with downhill, but going up steps was another matter. I paused so often that Lou finished his side of the street before I arrived at my last house. We met on the sidewalk and paused to compare notes before beginning our final ascent. I led the way as Lou and I headed upward to question Mrs. Reynolds and her son Jimmy, who likes to hide behind trees.

7

I stared at the woman who stood in front of me. She wore a scarf over her head to cover the bobby pins that adorned her gray hair. She wore a frown on her face. I wasn't sure what the frown was meant to cover. The hardened look on Mrs.Reynolds's face was enough to scare any child, even if her arms were loaded with Christmas presents.

"Mrs. Reynolds, I presume?"

My first impression was to agree with Mrs. Wilkins. At any rate, I wasn't as excited to see her as Stanley was to see Dr. Livingstone.

"Who wants to know?" asked the scowling woman, who was probably younger than she looked. Surely her heart had been extracted from the same quarry as her face.

"I'm Lt. Dekker and this is Sgt. Murdock. We're detectives with the Hilldale Police Department."

Mrs. Reynolds, obviously irritated that two detectives had rung her doorbell, said, "I ain't done nothing wrong," and attempted to shut her door.

"No one has said that you did, Mrs. Reynolds," I replied, as I reached and grabbed the door before she could shut it.

"Well, then, why are you bothering me?"

"Mrs. Reynolds, do you know Mrs. Nelson?"

"Yeah. I knew her. What of it?"

"Knew her, Mrs. Reynolds?"

"Well, she's dead, ain't she?"

"And how do you know that, Mrs. Reynolds?"

"Someone told me."

"And would that someone be your son Jimmy?"

"Leave Jimmy out of this," the woman replied in a voice even louder and less friendly than before.

"Mrs. Reynolds, when was the last time you saw Mrs. Nelson?"

"Today."

"You went over to her house today?"

"No, I saw your men drag her out. I wanted to see if they dropped her on the way down."

Lou tried hard not to smile. I could tell that he figured I had met my match.

"And when was the last time you saw her prior to to-day?"

"I don't know. It's been a while."

"Did you know Mrs. Nelson had a fall?"

"Is that what killed her?"

"I'm talking about her fall a few days ago."

"Heard about that. So what of it?"

"And have you seen her since?"

"No."

"No? No visit to see how she was doing?" I asked as I raised my eyebrows for emphasis.

"She had someone to look in on her."

"And who was that?"

"Miss Penrod, and Mr. Hartley the mailman, but I suppose you already know that."

"Mrs. Reynolds, did you have a key to Mrs. Nelson's house?"

"No."

"Are you sure, Mrs. Reynolds? Someone told me they thought you had a key."

"Must have been that no good Mr. Silverman. He had a key, or at least his mother had one. Imagine he has it now."

I made a mental note that I must invite Mr. Silverman and Mrs. Reynolds to dinner on the same night. If I did, I could charge admission.

"And where can I find Mr. Silverman's mother?"

"At the cemetery, I guess. That's where they usually put people when they die. She died suddenly a couple of months ago. Imagine he killed her. Maybe he used her key to kill Mrs. Nelson, too."

"Back to you, Mrs. Reynolds. Are you sure you don't have a key to Mrs. Nelson's house?"

"Used to. Don't anymore. Gave it back to her."

"By her, do you mean Mrs. Nelson?"

"No, I meant her grandmother. Of course, I meant Mrs. Nelson. Who did you think I meant?"

"Well, you could have meant her granddaughter."

"Angela. She has a key. She's probably the one that did it. Probably killed her to get all that money."

Totally perturbed with Mrs. Reynolds's comments, I couldn't resist my response.

"Do you think she and Mr. Silverman did it together?"

"Wouldn't put it past them."

I noticed a small movement behind the door and realized that Jimmy hid behind dead trees as well as live ones.

"What about Jimmy? Where's he been today?"

"Been here with me."

"All the time?"

"Well, he was here when the old lady got murdered."

"Oh, and who told you she got murdered?"

"I did."

"Mrs. Reynolds, you might be of great help to us. I need to know the time of the murder."

"Sometime before they carried her out."

"Mrs. Reynolds, I need to talk to Jimmy."

"I told you to leave him out of this."

"I just need to ask him a couple of questions."

"He isn't here."

"He's been with you all day, but he isn't here now. Are you sure?"

"Well, he's too sick to talk right now."

"He's not too sick to stand behind the door and listen to us. Let's see how sick he is."

"No."

"Mrs. Reynolds, we need to talk to Jimmy. Now, I can talk to him here, or I can take him downtown and talk to him. Whichever you think is better."

Mrs. Reynolds shrugged and realized that she couldn't win. "Okay, but go easy on him."

Mrs. Reynolds motioned for Jimmy to come out. I looked at Jimmy and realized that he was not in the same world as everyone else.

"Jimmy, I'm Lt. Dekker."

Jimmy snapped to attention, saluted, and said, "Yes, sir, Lieutenant, sir!"

"Jimmy, do you know Mrs. Nelson?"

Jimmy didn't answer.

"Jimmy, where have you been today?"

"On maneuvers, sir!"

"And Jimmy, did your maneuvers take you to Mrs. Nelson's house today?"

Again Jimmy did not answer.

"Jimmy, where were you on maneuvers today?"

"I was spying on the enemy, sir!"

"And who's the enemy, Jimmy?"

"Everyone, sir!"

"Please, Lieutenant. Don't you think you've put the boy through enough?" asked his pleading mother.

I stopped my questioning but told Mrs. Reynolds that I might have more questions later. She quickly closed the door. I nodded at Lou and the two of us walked down the steps and back to the car. As we walked, we discussed Mrs. Reynolds's disposition and wondered if she had always been that way or if it was a result of the trauma her son received in the war. At one time, she did have a key to Mrs. Nelson's house, which led me to believe that the two women were on friendly terms at one time. Yet none of Mrs. Reynolds's neighbors had anything good to say about her. Is she merely a lonely old woman who has trouble handling her loneliness and her son's illness, or is she someone to be feared?

As Lou and I walked back to my car, both of us looked up at 125 Hilltop Place and saw plywood covering a front window, a front door that was once again locked, and the yellow tape that blocked the porch, yellow tape that read, "Crime Scene - Do Not Cross."

8

Lou and I sat in the car, both of us deep in thought. Lou has known me long enough to be quiet when I'm quiet. He also knows I'm only quiet when I'm thinking, eating, or sleeping, although sometimes I'm quite noisy when I'm doing all three.

I turned and glanced up and down Hilltop Place. Everything was quiet, peaceful, and elegant, much like the cover of a magazine enticing people to choose a bed-and-breakfast for their next vacation. I thought about the people we met that day. They were a strange group. Each of them sneaked up close enough to find out whatever he or she could about any of his or her neighbors but hid in the shadows to keep from being discovered. Maybe they weren't a strange group after all. Maybe they are like most everyone I've ever met. I thought of the ones I'd met who never seem to leave Hilltop Place, and then I contemplated those who invaded it from time to time. I struggled to find a murderer. All of them seemed too kind, frail, or stupid to fit the profile. And then I remembered all the kind, frail, or stupid murderers I'd helped convict over the years.

I turned to Lou. It was time to compare notes. When he noticed me looking at him, he knew the game was on.

"Well, Cy, what do you think?"

"Well, it's too early to tell, but from what we've found out so far, it seems like Angela Nelson has an alibi since two people say she never entered the house until Officer Davis arrived. Also, Mr. Hartley appears to be in the clear, since he arrived at the house after Irene Penrod and left before she did, and resumed delivering his mail. And Mrs. Wilkins saw Mrs. Reynolds and Jimmy, and I'm not sure either of them had time to do it. Mrs. Wilkins and Mr. Silverman seem to give everyone an alibi since one or both of them appear to have been on guard duty until after the old lady was murdered. But of course, you and I both know that things are not always as they seem. Who knows? Maybe one or both of them were merely providing an alibi for himself or herself. Then there's the grocery boy. When did he enter the house, or did he? But Mrs. Wilkins seems to rule him out too because his car wasn't on the street earlier. Of course, he could've had an accomplice bring the getaway car."

The fact that Mrs. Wilkins had stood guard seemed to eliminate all the suspects but one. After all, no one entered or left Mrs. Nelson's house after Irene Penrod left. That made things too simple. Usually solving a murder is not that simple. But then maybe that's what Irene Penrod wanted us to think. Why did she leave town so soon after Mrs. Nelson was murdered? But then, if Irene Penrod wasn't the murderer, how could she have known she was leaving so soon? And did she leave someone behind when she left home?

Lou and I quickly decided to talk to everyone who had a key to Mrs. Nelson's house, as well as anyone who was rumored to have a key. This meant there would be further talks with Angela Nelson, Stanley Silverman, and Mrs. Reynolds, as well as first-time talks with Irene Penrod, when we could locate her; Mrs. Murphy, the maid; Bobby, the grocery boy; Harry Hornwell, Mrs. Nelson's attorney; and Mr. Hartley, the mailman. Also, we hoped to locate Mabel Jarvis, the wheelchair-bound neighbor, and see if she could contribute anything that would help us to find Mrs. Nelson's killer. That is, provided there was a killer. I hoped to hear something from Frank soon, but then sometimes it takes medical examiners a while to sort through their evidence.

The next day was Sunday. It would be more difficult to question some of the people on our list, so Lou and I decided to put off further questioning until Monday. We agreed to spend Sunday going through Mrs. Nelson's house to see if we could find any clues we might have missed earlier. Neither of us liked working on Sundays, and we never did unless we were in the middle of a murder case that warranted immediate attention, and both of us felt that this case warranted immediate attention.

I dropped off Lou at his apartment and headed home. After the day we had, both of us deserved some much-needed rest.

+++

Lou is not married. A long time ago, I used to be married, but I wasn't married long enough. Eunice and I spent five happy years together before she died of cancer. Cops are supposed to be tough, but sometimes I wondered how I was going to be able to make it by myself. Eunice and I were very much in love. Yes, cops are capable of love. Not only was it tough to live without her, but it was also tough to live by myself. For weeks I cried when I woke up each morning and looked over at the vacant side of the bed. It was just as tough coming home to an empty house each night. I made excuses to work as late as possible, so I wouldn't have to spend much time at home. I don't think I would've been able to make it without my faith in God and help from Lou and some of my other friends with the department.

Lou has never married, but he has been dating the same woman for quite a few years. Thelma Lou Spencer is quite a gal. Lou and Thelma Lou are quite a pair. I wonder why they don't just go ahead and get married. I often wonder if Lou is afraid of losing a wife the way I did. Or has he lived by himself so long that it would be too hard to change? Sometimes Lou and I double date. Betty McElroy and I are good friends, but Betty's a widow, and still in love with Hugh, just as I am with Eunice. Both of us are there for the other one for an occasional evening out with the opposite sex. I call Betty if I need a woman's opinion about something, and she calls me when she needs something fixed. I'm always able to recommend a good repairman.

While Betty and I go out about once a month, Lou and Thelma Lou go out on a date every Friday and Saturday night unless we are in the middle of a case.

I enjoy driving and Lou doesn't, so Lou never drives when we're working, but he keeps his red-and-white 1957 Chevy in immaculate condition for his weekend dates with Thelma Lou. Because Lou has never married, his needs are few, so he doesn't spend a lot of money on accommodations. He lives in the lower-right-hand apartment of a brick fourplex. All of the building's other residents are elderly, so noise is never a problem. Lou has both an inside and an outside entrance. Each morning he stands on his small front porch and waits until I pick him up, or, if it's too cold, he watches for me from his living room window. His modest dwelling includes a large living room, a kitchen, one bedroom, and a bathroom. Unless Lou's sleeping, he spends most of his time in the living room. It's sparsely furnished with a well-used, but still usable, couch, a recliner that doesn't match the couch, and a straight-backed chair, which stands in front of a card table that's usually in use. Along one wall of the living room is a built-in bookcase, which includes more books than empty spaces.

I live in a cul-de-sac in a middle-class neighborhood. I've lived there for many years. My wife and I bought the house a couple of years before she died. After she died, I thought about moving but decided not to. While my house isn't large, my place is more spacious than Lou Murdock's. My home includes a living room, dining room, kitchen, and two bedrooms, one of which I use for storage. I also have an unfinished basement, which I do not use at all.

I like to do things my way, but some things I don't like to do at all. I also pay someone to come in once a week to clean my house. See, dust comes in even if no one is home. Clutter needs someone to help it along. I interrogated seven cleaning women until I found one who would do it my way. Mrs. Watson is willing to do what I want to be done when I want it done. She comes after I've left and is finished before I return. She does only what I want to be done and does it the way I want it. After all, I'm the one who lives in my house. If Mrs. Watson wants to clean her house differently than she cleans mine, I have no problem with that. I'm easy to live with as long as I live by myself. Three months after Mrs. Watson began cleaning my house, I gave her the Dekker seal of approval. That satisfied Lou Murdock, and she's been cleaning his apartment ever since. Ever since has been nineteen years.

Cooking and cleaning are not the only things I don't like to do. Since I'm seldom home, I pay someone to mow my lawn and shovel my snow, two things I detest doing. I'm not as picky about the outside of my house, as long as everything looks neat. If my yard boy wants to mow in circles or diagonally, that's okay with me.

+++

Because I know Lou well, I know his habits. I know what he's going to do before he knows it. Like any two people, Lou and I look forward to unwinding after a hectic day on a case, but we don't share the same interests. I love classic comedy TV shows of the '50s and '60s, and own several videos and DVDs of my favorite shows, most of them birthday or Christmas presents from Lou. *I Love Lucy* is my all-time favorite TV show, but that night I was too tired to watch anything. Instead, I opted for a soothing, hot bath and an early bedtime.

While I'm a classic TV man, Lou unwinds with crossword puzzles, jigsaw puzzles, or a good book, most received as presents from you know who. Lou and I started using his hobbies as a method of measuring our time between murders. As best I can recall, when we found the old lady's body, it had been two jigsaw puzzles, four crossword puzzle books, and four novels since our last murder.

I continued to think of Lou as I parked in my driveway, then stumbled into the house. As I tried to rid my mind of the Nelson murder, I pictured Lou falling into his recliner and kicking back. My guess is he remained there a few minutes before easing over to the card table, which always contained a jigsaw puzzle in progress. I could see Lou looking over his newly-begun mountain cabin scene. So far, he had merely completed the border and most of the cabin. The fifteen hundred-piece puzzle, with a myriad of pine and brightly-colored trees, would take some time to complete, possibly even more time than solving the mysterious death of Mrs. Nelson. Lou is a man who enjoys his work, the time we spend together, his weekend dates with

Thelma Lou, and his hobbies. Few people enjoy what they do as much as Lou.

+++

After a few minutes in the tub, my head must have slid down the back of the tub and into the water. Either that or our murderer was trying to add another victim to his or her conquests. At least, I was underwater when I awakened. I woke up, grabbed for the sides of the tub, and pulled myself to a seated position as I spit water in every direction. The soapy water in my nose left an unpleasant taste in my throat. This middle-aged man got out of the tub, yanked on the towel until I'd pulled it from the bar, dried myself, and got dressed for bed. I'd had enough struggles for one day. I went to bed.

9

I had no idea how long the phone had been ringing before it woke me. I turned over and glanced at the clock. Its hands pointed to 8:12. Sunday morning. I did not remember turning over being such a painful exercise. I sprang from the bed as quickly as I could, stumbled into the living room, and knocked my phone off the hook. Whoever was there stayed on the phone until I picked the receiver up off the floor.

"Dekker, here," I mumbled into the phone, proud that I could remember who I was after such a rigorous day the day before.

"Cy, Frank here. I guess I woke you. Luck is with us. I have the results from the autopsy and figured you'd want them as soon as possible, but I knew you had a rough day yesterday, so I didn't want to wake you too early."

"And I thank you for that. So, what's the news? Were we right?"

"Have you ever known us to be wrong, Cy? Okay, don't answer that. Anyway, it was poison, all right. Codeine to be exact."

"Codeine. So the pharmacist did it?"

"The who is your job, Cy. The how is mine."

"How was it administered?"

"It was added to a glass of grape juice."

"Turn up any other evidence?"

"Sure did. Somewhere between forty-five minutes and an hour before the poison was ingested, someone gave her a heavy dose of painkillers and sleeping pills. I'm not talking a whole bottle or anything like that, but it was double what she needed."

"Any idea why someone would do that?"

"Not unless they didn't want her to holler while she was being poisoned. I don't understand why someone would give her a sleeping pill and then codeine. Codeine makes people drowsy, and then go into a coma before death. There's no need for a sleeping pill."

"Would the sleeping pill make her begin to get sleepy a little at a time, or fall asleep all at once?"

"She would probably start to yawn a few times after a few minutes. She would appear to be somewhat sleepy to anyone who saw her."

"What else do you have?"

"The lab boys got a few prints, but I imagine after we find out who all of them belong to it won't lead us anywhere. From what I can see, there were four sets of prints, but none of them were on the glass."

"What about outside the house?"

"A few smudged fingerprints, which are quite normal. No footprints or ladder marks in the back yard."

"Any idea as to the time of the murder, Frank?"

"Well, other than to say it was sometime yesterday morning, no."

"So, no one could have given it to her Friday night?"

"Well, they could have, but only if they'd put gloves on her, told her to hold it in her hand until Saturday morning, and then came back and removed the gloves before we got there."

"So, Frank, what's your best guess as to how long it took the poison to kill her?"

"Fifteen or twenty minutes."

"Are you saying one minute is not enough?"

"It would be if it was injected, but this time it was administered orally, so instant death is out of the question."

"Officer Davis told me that Angela Nelson arrived at her grandmother's side thirty seconds to a minute before he did. You say that there was no way she could have killed her grandmother in that short of a time."

"Absolutely, no way, Cy. Codeine comes in both liquid and a white powder form. This time the powder was added to a glass of grape juice. Judging from the amount in her system, I'd say that she died fifteen or twenty minutes after it was ingested."

"White powder? Don't you mean cocaine, Frank?"

"No, and I don't mean flour or powdered sugar. It was definitely codeine."

"Officer Davis also said that he and Miss Nelson had probably been in the house three to five minutes when they discovered the body. So, you're saying that Miss Nelson could not have murdered her grandmother during that time?"

"The murderer needed to be alone in the house for at least fifteen minutes, and probably a little longer. Actually, a lot longer if our murderer gave her the medications, too. My guess is the babysitter did it."

"She didn't have a babysitter, Frank."

"Well, then, you're on your own, Cy."

"No, I've still got Lou. Anyway, thanks, Frank. I appreciate you being so prompt about this. Let me know if anything else comes up."

"Sure thing, Cy. Oh, by the way, did the doctor tell you whether you'll ever be able to walk again?"

I laughed a painful laugh, hung up the phone, and went back to bed for a few more minutes of rest.

+++

"Lou, did I wake you?"

"You know me. I've been up for hours."

"And how are you feeling?"

"Fine. I can feel every ache and pain and remember how I got it."

"And I was hoping you would carry me up those steps today."

"Please don't mention those steps. I counted them all night long."

"Listen, Lou, Frank just called. It's just like we thought. The old lady was poisoned. Codeine. Plus, someone gave her some medication to help it go down easier. I'm going to call her granddaughter and tell her and then take a shower. After that, I'll do my devotional reading and reflection. So, I'll probably be over to pick you up in an hour. We won't be going to church today."

+++

I hung up from talking to Sgt. Murdock and phoned Angela Nelson.

"Hello."

"Miss Nelson, this is Lt. Dekker."

"Oh, hi, Lieutenant. What can I do for you?"

"I was just calling to let you know that they've finished the autopsy on your grandmother. The department will be finished with her this afternoon, so you can call the mortuary and make funeral arrangements."

"Thanks for calling, Lieutenant."

"Well, don't you want to know the results?"

"Yeah, sure, but I just assumed she had a heart attack."

I hate to be the bearer of bad news, so I used my most comforting voice to tell the young woman what caused her grandmother's death.

"I'm sorry to have to tell you this, Miss Nelson, but your grandmother was poisoned."

"Poisoned?"

"That's right, Miss Nelson."

"Are you sure? Well, could it have been an accident?"

"No."

"But, I don't understand. Everyone loved my grandmother."

"Everyone?"

"Well, maybe everyone didn't love her, but I can't see anyone poisoning her."

"Not even Mrs. Reynolds."

"She's mean, but not that mean."

"What about Mr. Silverman?"

"He's a snoop, but not a murderer."

"Didn't his mother die suddenly?"

"I'm not sure. But he was devoted to his mother. I don't think he killed her."

"Who would be at the top of your list, Miss Nelson?"

"I can't see anyone who knew my grandmother doing this, and I can't see how anyone else could have gotten into the house."

"Well, someone did, Miss Nelson. You didn't happen to notice a glass on the floor when you found your grandmother, did you?"

"No, but I wasn't paying attention to anything other than my grandmother. You mean you found the murder weapon, so to speak?"

"So to speak. By the way, is there anything you might have forgotten to tell me yesterday?"

"Not that I can think of. Oh, when I got home there were three calls on my voice mail from Irene Penrod. The first time she called was a few days after I left, and she informed me that my grandmother had fallen, broken some bones, and was pretty bruised up. From what I can tell, she called the second time a couple of days later. She phoned to see if I got her message about my grandmother. The third call was Friday night. She said that when she didn't hear from me she called my employer and my employer told her that I was out of town and that I would be back yesterday morning. Normally, my boss wouldn't do that, but Miss Penrod explained that she was my grandmother's next-door neighbor, and I had mentioned her name to my boss.

"Anyway, on Friday, Miss Penrod called to ask me to look in on my grandmother, because she was leaving town Saturday for a week. I guess that's why she wasn't home when I knocked Saturday morning. She'd already left."

"Speaking of leaving town, Miss Nelson, will you be leaving on another buying trip anytime soon?"

"Even if I was, I'd cancel it for my grandmother's funeral, but as it turns out I won't be leaving again for at least a week, and maybe two."

"Well, thanks for your time, Miss Nelson. I'm sorry to be the bearer of bad news. Call me if you need anything or if you think of anything else."

"I will, Lieutenant. By the way, do you have any idea when my grandmother was poisoned or is that confidential information?"

"We're still working on that, Miss Nelson. I'll call you if I have any questions or answers."

"Thanks, Lieutenant."

10

Even though Lou and I attack each case like a hungry Doberman mauls a piece of raw steak, both of us spend some time with God before we begin each day. Each month, I pick up a devotional booklet from my church, and each morning I spend time reading a devotional and the comments that accompany it. I also take time to reflect upon it and spend a few moments in prayer before I head off to pick up Lou.

Lou, who requires less sleep than I do, rises early and spends time in a more-involved Bible study, which includes a booklet with spaces to write answers to the questions that accompany what he reads. He too spends time in prayer before I pick him up each day. This helps both of us get through the trying times that confront us.

+++

I stepped out onto my front porch, which is much smaller and sets much closer to the street level than the porches on Hilltop Place. I noticed that the sun was a little higher in the sky than when I usually leave for work before turning to close and lock the door.

"Good morning, Cyrus," said the voice that made the hair on the back of my neck stand up.

The all-too-familiar voice sounded like fingernails on a chalkboard. I turned to face my next-door neighbor, Heloise Humphert, and her white toy poodle, Twinkle Toes. Surely no one else has a next-door neighbor they despise as much. The woman continues to hit on me, even though I tell her I'm not interested in her.

"Miss Humphert, if I've told you once, I've told you a thousand times. It's not a good idea to sneak up on a cop with a gun. I can see the newspaper headline now. 'Dog Resembles Owner. Miss Heloise Humphert and her small dog were found with bullet holes in their heads. A gangland slaying is suspected. It was ironic that the bodies were found in front of her police detective next-door neighbor's house.'"

"Oh, Cyrus. You say the funniest things. Are we on our way to church?"

"I have no idea about we, but one of us is on his way to work."

"Oh, has someone else been murdered?"

"I'm supposed to keep this quiet, see, but it was a nosy woman with a dog. We suspect the next-door neighbor did it. If so, we're going to let him go free. Because you answer the description of the dead woman, my suggestion to you would be to become a part of the Witness Protection Program and relocate to Point Barrow, Alaska. You might be safer there."

I lowered my voice a little with each word until I was whispering at the end. With my last declaration, I turned toward my car and hastened in its direction.

Heloise and her sister Hortense were the unbecoming daughters of the president of the bank, Horatio Humphert. Horatio tried his best to find husbands for his daughters, and let it be known that both daughters would come with a sizable dowry. No man in Hilldale ever got drunk enough to accept Horatio's offer of either of his double-chinned daughters. Because Horatio found no takers for Heloise, he bought her a house and a bulldog. When each dog died or ran away, Horatio bought Heloise a new one. Each time, he bought a different breed, hoping that someday he would find a suitable dog for his daughter. Because sisters are usually opposites, I imagine that Hortense joined a convent, even though the family was not Roman Catholic. I just know that she did not buy the house on the other side of mine, and for that I am thankful.

+++

Each time Lou and I work on a murder case, he gets a thought that has something to do with the case we are working on. Because they are helpful, although most times not initially, I call them Lou's messages from God. I thought of Lou's "message" from the day before. It was, "Today you will rise above." Boy, did we rise above! I was anxious to find out what Sunday's message was for us.

"Lou, what's God's message for today?"

"Strange happenings in the night."

"So, you're still sleeping with that inflatable doll?"

"I never started. You told me you couldn't part with it."

I wondered what strange happenings and pondered them as I steered the car toward Hilltop Place. Before we arrived, I filled Lou in about the conversations I had with Frank Harris and Angela Nelson. As I turned and headed the car down Hilltop Place, Lou and I noticed Jimmy Reynolds hunched over and running away from the Nelson house. By the time we pulled up in front of the dead woman's house, Jimmy had started climbing the steps to his sheltering mother.

As soon as I'd climbed out of the car, I heard my name being called. I looked up and saw Stanley Silverman running down his steps. I waited for him.

"Oh, hello, Mr. Silverman. What can I do for you today?"

"Someone's been here."

"You mean someone came to see you, or someone's been on the Nelson property?"

"Not only has someone been on the property, but someone went into the house."

"Could you tell who it was, Mr. Silverman?" I asked, still not sure if I believed the man.

"Whoever it was was wearing a long yellow raincoat, black galoshes, and a yellow rain hat."

"And you're sure they went into the house, Mr. Silverman?"

"I sure am, Lieutenant," the neighbor answered, nodding as he replied.

"Through the front door?"

"No down the chimney. Of course through the front door. How else was someone to get in?"

"Well, they could always pry away the plywood. When did this happen?"

"Last night."

"And you're just now letting the police know?"

"Sorry, Lieutenant, I didn't have your phone number, and I find a person always saves time when he starts at the top and works down."

"Well, I'm not exactly the top of the department, Mr. Silverman. But enough about that. How did you happen to notice this person?"

"Well, I just happened to be walking by the window when I saw someone wearing a raincoat walking down the street. It surprised me because it wasn't raining, so I decided to look and see which way they went."

I had to keep from smiling when Stanley Silverman told me that he just happened to be walking by the window. I was sure that Stanley Silverman happened to walk by the window any time he thought there was something to see outside that window. I brushed away my thoughts about the nosy neighbor and continued my questioning.

"Did the intruder immediately turn at the Nelson house and climb the steps?"

"That's right."

"Did this person seem to labor as they climbed the steps, or did this person climb them like they were used to the ordeal?"

"Whoever it was had no trouble climbing the steps. They hurried up the steps."

The thought that anyone could hurry up those steps reminded me of my sore legs. Immediately I deduced that neither Lou nor I had been walking in our sleep. Besides, sleepwalking takes far more energy than dreaming.

"And what did you do after you saw this person?"

Mr. Silverman smiled sheepishly before he replied.

"I sat down in my chair and watched through my night-vision binoculars."

I couldn't suppress a smile.

"And I assume that eventually, someone came out of the house."

"About thirty minutes later, but that was the strange part."

"Do you mean it didn't look like the same person?"

"No, it definitely looked like the same person, but they didn't come out of the same house. Whoever it was came out of Mabel Jarvis's house."

"You mean the woman in the wheelchair?"

"That's the one."

"Well, maybe you were gone for a moment when this person left one house and went over to the other one."

"I swear, Lieutenant. I never left my chair. I saw everything," Stanley Silverman replied, holding up his fingers as if taking an oath of a Boy Scout. I doubted if Stanley Silverman was ever a Boy Scout.

"Well, could it be that we're looking for two people, Mr. Silverman?"

"You tell me, Lieutenant. All I know is the outfit looked the same and both people looked to be the same size."

"And what size was that, Mr. Silverman?"

"Average."

"Average for a man or a woman?"

"I don't know. They weren't really tall and they weren't really short. They were average."

"You said that you were looking through your night-vision binoculars, but since you cannot identify the intruder I assume you didn't get a look at his or her face?"

"Whoever it was had on a ski mask. I couldn't tell a thing."

"Well, could you tell anything or eliminate anyone you know from the size of the person?"

"I guess you're talking about people I know. The only one I might be able to eliminate is Jimmy Reynolds. He's too big. Or at least, that's the way it looked to me. Anyway, while this person seemed strange, they didn't seem as strange as Jimmy. They walked normally but kind of fast."

"Mr. Silverman, think of the walk. Is there anyone you know who walks as that person did?"

Mr. Silverman paused, rested his chin in his hand, and pondered my question.

"Well, come to think of it, the person in the raincoat did walk something like our mailman, Mr. Hartley, but what would Mr. Hartley be doing on our street on a

76

Saturday night? And anyway, Mr. Hartley doesn't wear a yellow raincoat. I believe his raincoat is clear."

"What about Miss Penrod's house? Have you seen any more activity there?"

"You mean someone peeking through the blinds?"

"That's right unless you've seen anyone coming or going at her house."

"Nothing. Only at the two houses I told you about."

"Well, thanks for letting us know, Mr. Silverman. We might get you that detective job yet."

+++

Lou and I turned away wondering if we were looking for one person or two and if it was only one person, how that person could have gotten from one house to the other without being seen. Or could it be no one at all? Maybe the mysterious person was a figment of Mr. Silverman's imagination or someone he created to draw suspicion away from himself. Lou and I crossed the street and began our climb up the Nelson steps, only to be confronted by a second surprise.

11

I reached in my pocket and pulled out the key I'd removed from Mrs. Nelson's handbag, inserted the key into the lock, and turned the key. When I pushed on the door, I found the door still securely locked. Either Mr. Silverman was right, or Mr. Silverman was playing games with us. The sliding bolt was in place. Someone had been in the house since we left it. Neither Lou nor I wanted to make another trip up and down the steps. The two of us went over to the window to see if we could pry the plywood far enough away from the house to open the window. It wouldn't budge, so we flipped a coin to see who went to the car to get a crowbar.

What seemed like a day or so later, I returned and passed the crowbar to Lou before I collapsed on the porch. It was as if I was handing off the baton and it was Lou's turn to run the next lap. A few minutes later we'd accomplished our mission, although we had to remove all but two nails in order to admit two stout men.

We stepped over the window sill and entered the house. We took a moment to look around to make sure we were alone. If anyone was nearby, he or she had taken on the look of a piece of furniture. Neither of us heard anyone, so Lou slipped on a pair of gloves and walked over, slid the bolt, and opened the front door, while I called the department to let them know about the newest developments. Before long, the house was crawling with a cornucopia of cops which closely resembled the passel of policemen who were there the day before. One man checked the front door for fingerprints, while Lou and I went through the house to see if anything looked different from the previous day. All we found was a pair of men's size eleven galoshes. They were in the pantry just off the kitchen. The bottoms of the boots were dusty.

Other men headed to the back yard to see if it looked like anyone had gone over the wall. Once again, there were no footprints or ladder marks. Another man was sent to call on Mrs. Jarvis, but like the day before, no one answered the door. All the work went for naught. We found no new clues other than the galoshes, so we reattached the plywood and everyone left, except Lou and me.

+++

Lou and I stepped out the back door. The thick grass cushioned each step as we walked around the well-manicured lawn. I made a note of how flat the backyard was. If only we could find a way into the house via the backyard, but the door was locked on the inside. I noticed that the patio had been enclosed to form a sun porch. I imagined the many days Mrs. Nelson must have spent sitting on her sun porch watching the birds splash in the multi-level, fountain-like birdbath and eating the seeds in the bird feeders. I don't know much about birds, but Mrs. Nelson had several bird feeders, so they must have contained different types of food for many species. I twisted my head and looked at the large wall that enclosed the backyard and the large trees that towered above it on the other side. Was it possible that this wall played some significance in the mystery, and if so, would it make our job easier or harder? Was it possible that someone climbed one of the trees on the other side of the wall and dropped down into Mrs. Nelson's yard? It was possible, but the drop would have been far enough that someone could have sprained an ankle in the process.

In case someone had leaped, he or she would have encountered another problem. Flowers grew all along the wall inside Mrs. Nelson's backyard. What kind of flowers I did not know. Some were red. Others were yellow. Still others were pink, blue, and lavender. Other than roses and tulips, I learned to identify only two types of flowers. Funeral home flowers and clothing flowers. Years ago I learned to tell the difference between mums and gladiolas. As far as clothing was concerned, people usually wore carnations or orchids. I know that men sometimes wear carnations, if the occasion is fancy enough, like a wedding or prom. I think someone bought one for me to wear when I got married. Orchids are what guys buy their prom dates if they want to impress them. Used to, there was only one kind of orchid corsage. A woman wore it on her dress. Then, women started wearing dresses that started at the bottom and ran out of material before they got to the top. Then, someone invented a corsage they could wear on their wrists. I had no idea what a man is supposed to do if the woman wears a dress that does not come up to the neck, and she wears a wristwatch. It's a good thing I'm no longer dating.

I saw that no one had tramped any of the flowers that I couldn't identify, then turned to my partner.

"Well, Lou, what do you think?"

"I'd say they're some kind of annuals."

"What are?"

"These flowers you're looking at."

"Which ones?"

"All of them. Of course, there might be some perennials mixed in."

"But there are several kinds of flowers here. How could they all be the annuals or perennials? Anyway, I wasn't asking you about the flowers. I was talking about the case."

Before Lou answered, he looked at me like I was the one who was stupid.

See, occasionally Lou will waste some of his time gathering knowledge about things we need to know only if we plan to appear on *Jeopardy*. I don't plan to do that, and I don't plan to buy any flowers. I can see all the flowers I want in someone else's yard. Evidently, somewhere along the line, Lou learned a thing or two about flowers.

"I'm not sure what to think, Cy. If Mr. Silverman was telling the truth, and the presence of a pair of boots say he is, evidently someone entered the house last night, but who and why? And was it the same person Mr. Silverman saw coming out of Mrs. Jarvis's place, or does someone want us to assume that? Or was Mr. Silverman the intruder?"

"Let's look at what we know so far. Mrs. Nelson was poisoned, and it doesn't look like she poisoned herself. Therefore, we can assume someone murdered the old lady. But who did it, and why? Also, there was someone in the house at the same time as Miss Nelson and Officer Davis. Did he or she get here first, and if so, did this person commit the murder or discover the already-murdered woman? It could be the reason the mysterious person was hiding was that Miss Nelson arrived as he or she was about to leave, and the victim's granddaughter cut off his or her only means of escape. Also, what can we assume about this latest intruder? Did the murderer return to the scene of the crime, and if so, why? Did he or she leave something that we failed to find and came back to retrieve it? Is someone else trying to solve the murder? Or is someone playing games with us?

"We have lots of people to check on, but the only ones who could conceivably have a motive are Angela Nelson, who probably inherits the place despite what she told us, and her grandmother's attorney, who could be crooked. Still, all of Miss Nelson's time seems to be accounted for, and no one saw Mr. Hornwell on this street on the morning of the murder."

"Well, Cy, maybe the old lady caught the mailman stealing her social security checks or the next-door neighbor taking something from the premises? Or, while I doubt if Jimmy Reynolds is capable of poisoning Mrs. Nelson, he could've been the one who pushed her down the steps and sent her to the hospital, and his mother might have poisoned her if she felt Mrs. Nelson was going to call the authorities and have her son taken away."

"Who knows? You may be right, Lou. At any rate, it's too early to eliminate anyone, especially since we haven't talked to all of them yet."

"What about last night's intruder, Cy? Do you think it was the murderer returning to the scene of the crime, someone trying to solve it, or merely someone who is nosy?"

"Maybe someone had left something that they didn't want us to find."

"Or, maybe they brought something they wanted us to find."

"You mean the galoshes?"

"Possibly. Why didn't we look in the pantry when we were here yesterday?"

"I did. If these galoshes were there then, I sure didn't see them, but then I guess my mind was elsewhere."

"Like checking with the other neighbors to see if any of them could tell us something."

"And none of them did. Well, none except Mr. Silverman, who told us a lot, and Mrs. Reynolds, who thinks that everyone but Jimmy did the old lady in."

"Don't forget Mrs. Wilkins. She told me a lot, but will any of it help us? So, Lou, do you have any suggestions as to what we do next?"

"It's been only an hour since breakfast, so it's too early to eat lunch."

"It's never too soon to eat, but I mean do you have any ideas about the case?"

"I don't know. It's almost as if someone is trying to help us find something in this house. I just don't know what. Also, I'd like to talk to Mrs. Jarvis, if we can ever get her to come to the door."

"And let's not forget Miss Penrod, who seems to have left town."

"So, what's next, Cy?"

"I say we go through this place again. Then, let's try one more time to raise Mrs. Jarvis. It bothers me that Mr. Silverman said he saw someone coming out of her house last night. If that's true, and the person Mr. Silverman saw was the murderer, then something might have happened to Mrs. Jarvis, too. If she doesn't answer the door, then I'm calling to get an okay to break in and check out her place."

+++

Another look around Mrs. Nelson's house proved fruitless. The two of us scoured the main floor. Like the houses of many elderly people, Mrs. Nelson's house was crowded with furniture. The house was clean, but who moved all the furniture and swept? Surely not Mrs. Nelson. Maybe Mrs. Murphy did it. I expected to learn more after we spoke to her.

Lou and I traipsed upstairs again, mainly to give the bedroom another going over and to look on and around the four-poster bed where the woman was found dead. We checked the basement too but found nothing unusual. Once again, I locked the front door, and Lou and I headed down the steps and up the street to Mrs. Jarvis's house. As we walked two doors up the street, Lou noticed that we were being watched. As far as he could tell, no one was hiding behind any of the trees, but someone across the street was sitting by a window studying us through a pair of high-powered binoculars.

12

As we walked to Mrs. Jarvis's house, Mrs. Wilkins returned from church. At least, she was dressed as if she had been to church. Because she qualified as a member of the neighborhood watch program, I walked on by Mrs. Jarvis's house to see if Mrs. Wilkins had seen anyone wearing a raincoat the night before. No luck, but she did recommend that I check with Mr. Silverman, who sees everything. I asked her how much she knew about Mr. Silverman. I knew I would get a lengthy reply. I found out that Stanley Silverman worked as a bookkeeper until his mother got sick. Then, he quit work to stay home and take care of her. Also, he has never had a hobby. His mother was his hobby, and since his mother's death, he has had no way to pass the time. He talked of going to her grave each day, but Mrs. Wilkins wasn't sure of that. She seldom noticed Mr. Silverman leave his house. Even if he did visit her grave, he could sit and talk to her only so long each day. He needed another way to occupy his time. Otherwise, he would go crazy, or had he already gone crazy?

We learned that neighbors seldom saw Mr. Silverman before his mother's death. He would go to work, come home, and disappear into the house never to be seen again until early the next morning. He never raised any type of garden. He never sat on the front porch. He merely came home each night and did who knows what. His mother was a little more visible, but she never talked about Stanley, except to say what a good son he was and how good he was with figures. On those few occasions Mrs. Silverman sat on her porch, she sat alone. Shortly after her passing, one neighbor and then another saw Stanley sitting by the front window staring into space. Each day, he sat there staring at nothing in particular. It became his way of passing the time between getting up each morning and going to bed each evening. In a way, I could identify with his situation.

After Mrs. Silverman's death, several of the neighbors began to cast an eye in the direction of the Silverman house. An eye, not a visit. An eye, not a dish of food. A few neighbors noticed that Mr. Silverman had bought a pair of binoculars. At first, they noticed he watched the squirrels that scampered from tree to tree at the end of the street. Maybe watching squirrels became monotonous to Mr. Silverman, because more than one neighbor admitted opening her front door only to find Mr. Silverman's binoculars focused on her. Some of the neighbors got angry, while others merely felt sorry for him. Word got around the neighborhood that Mr. Silverman had bought a second pair of binoculars, one designed to see things at night. This caused a couple of people who had not been used to locking their doors and closing their blinds to start doing so. Of course, that was before Mrs. Nelson was murdered. I doubt if there's an unlocked window or door now. Hilltop Place has been changed forever.

I was sure Mrs. Wilkins knew of Mrs. Murphy, so I questioned her to see what she knew. Again, Mrs. Wilkins was "helpful." Mrs. Murphy lived with her husband on Magnolia Lane. She cleaned houses for a living and worked five days a week. She cleaned for two of Hilltop Place's residents, Mrs. Nelson and Mrs. Jarvis. She came once a week, on Friday, and every other week she brought her daughter, who helped her move all the furniture to clean underneath and behind everything. According to Mrs. Wilkins, Mrs. Murphy was a good woman who knew her place, kept to herself, and could be trusted. Mrs. Wilkins saw Mrs. Murphy on Hilltop Place on the day before the murder, but not on the day of the murder.

+++

Lou and I labored our way up the steps to Mrs. Jarvis's house. I rang and banged, but no one answered the door. Either Mrs. Jarvis was intent on not answering the door no matter who was there, or she was incapable of doing so. It was time to find out which.

I emphasized Mrs. Jarvis's safety when I pleaded for permission to break into her house. When a phone call from the department to Mrs. Jarvis provided no more success in locating the occupant than Lou and I had had, we received approval to break into the house. Mrs. Jarvis's house had only a single lock, with no deadbolt, so the two of us were able to force open the front door with little difficulty.

We entered the house. I called out Mrs. Jarvis's name. There was no response. I noticed that a lamp had been knocked off a table in the hall and a chair had been shoved out of place in the kitchen. Lou looked upstairs while I searched the rest of the main floor. Neither pursuit led us to Mrs. Jarvis or to any other clues of a struggle.

I noticed a set of keys on the hall table. Curious, I picked them up and went over to see if any of them fit the front door. One of them did. I dropped the keys into my pocket.

Only the basement had not been checked. I grabbed the doorknob of the basement door, slowly turned it, and opened it. I reached for the light and flipped the switch. Nothing happened. Lou and I reached for our guns and our flashlights. We turned on our flashlights and shined them down the gray, wooden steps. Lou motioned to me that he would go first. I let him pass. Both of us carried our flashlights in our left hands as we clutched our guns in our right. The top step creaked as Lou stepped on it. The sudden noise that interrupted the silence caused both of us to grip our guns a little tighter. Slowly, we descended into the basement. With each step, we shined our lights on a larger area. We continued in a cautious manner until we stepped down onto the concrete floor of the large, unfinished basement. We saw no one. We continued to flash our lights up and down the walls. Neither of us noticed anything out of order. Light beams moved from side to side as Lou and I looked for Mrs. Jarvis or any clues as to her whereabouts. We spotted a light fixture, but there was no bulb in the socket. Obviously, the wheelchair-bound Mrs. Jarvis hadn't removed the bulb. Of course, I had no idea how long it had been since the bulb had been removed. We peered behind each object. We looked in the storage area. We even examined the inside of the furnace. Our pursuit proved futile.

We shined our lights around the basement floor. Our flashlights met at one spot, much like two spotlights zeroing in on an escaping prisoner, and I whistled at what we saw. In one corner of the basement the dust had collected enough so that two rows of narrow tire tracks could be seen leading up to that corner, and no tracks led away. The tracks were thin and spread apart with footprints between them. The tracks and footprints could easily have been made by a wheelchair and the person who pushed it. After we lingered and studied our discovery for a few minutes,

Lou and I returned to the main floor, and I placed another call. Within minutes, more police arrived to see what they could find. Cautiously, they went over the first floor and the basement. After careful tests, one of the men came to report their findings to me.

"I think we're through here, Lieutenant, but we did turn up a few things."

I smiled and nodded for the man to continue.

"Actually, Lieutenant, we weren't able to find anything except what you and Sgt. Murdock had already found, but we were able to confirm that the tracks do belong to a wheelchair, and the footprints seem to belong to the person who pushed that chair."

"Is there anything in the tracks or the footprints that told you whether this appeared to be someone violently pushing a chair against the occupant's will or merely a leisurely push around the basement?"

"There's not much to go on, Lieutenant, but judging from the distance between one step and the next I would say that it didn't seem to be a violent act."

"Well, were you able to learn anything from the footprints?"

"Yes, I'd say they were made by a man's size eleven galoshes. There are other less obvious tracks near the washer and dryer, mixed in with what I assume to be yours and Sgt. Murdock's footprints, but those come from a smaller shoe. My guess is a woman's size seven."

"Back to the galoshes. There just happens to be a pair of galoshes matching that description two doors down at Mrs. Nelson's, the murder victim's house. Could you check those galoshes and see if the prints match, or not?"

"It's possible, Lieutenant. We don't have a lot to go on here, but there might be enough prints to confirm or rule out a match."

"Did you find anything else?"

"As a matter of fact, yes. We did find a little dirt, both in the basement and on the first floor, but none near the front or back door. To be honest, it's a little puzzling. It's like the dirt didn't come in through either door."

"Any ideas as to how it got there?"

"No, Lieutenant. In a way, it's a lot like the tire tracks and footprints."

"I don't understand."

"Well, the chair tracks and the footprints seem to go right to the wall and disappear. We don't know where they go to from there, nor do we know where the dirt begins. With the wheelchair, it's as if someone picked up Mrs. Jarvis and carried her away. Except for one thing."

"I bet I can guess your one thing. Since the footprints end there, as well, then the person would have had to have flown away with her. It sounds simple to me. Put out an APB on Superman and Peter Pan. We'll hold both of them until one of them confesses."

Everyone enjoyed a good laugh, and then I continued.

"Well, I think we can definitely say someone other than Mrs. Jarvis has been in this house since I don't think she was pushing her own wheelchair. Neither do I think the footprints near the washer and dryer are hers. Nor does a woman who never goes outside put dirt on her floor. Let's go over to Mrs. Nelson's house again and check out those galoshes and see if they match the prints downstairs."

+++

I checked with some of the neighbors to see if any of them knew anything about Mrs. Jarvis when they had last seen her, and whether or not she had any living relatives. Once again, my efforts proved fruitless. Even Mrs. Wilkins and Mr. Silverman had no idea. Or so they said.

+++

"Where do we go from here, Cy?"

"I don't know. I'm puzzled. I need to give this some thought. We'll begin tomorrow morning by talking to Mr. Hartley, the mailman. Let's be here when he delivers the mail. We'll watch him a little bit, and then stop him to see what he can tell us. After that, we have an attorney and a grocery boy to check with. Maybe one of them can tell us which way to go next. Tomorrow night we'll visit with Mrs. Murphy and see what she knows."

We left and I drove Lou to his place. A few more questions, but no more answers. I hoped the next day would begin to provide some of those answers we sorely needed.

+++

I plopped down in my easy chair, took off my shoes. I cleared my head, decided to give the case one more going over before I put it aside for the night.

Today's new developments made things tougher, rather than easier. I had more witnesses than I had suspects. If Frank was right, and I never knew Frank to be wrong when he said he was right, no one had enough time to murder Mrs. Nelson. At least no one appeared to have time. Miss Penrod seemed to be the last person to see the victim alive, but according to the witnesses, and Frank's time constraints, she didn't have time to give the victim the sedative and the poison. She was not in the house long enough. She left in a cab before she would have had time to administer the poison. So, who else was there? Angela Nelson, but she didn't have time, either. She didn't arrive from the airport in time to give her grandmother the sedative and the

91

poison. Plus, two witnesses said she remained outside until Officer Davis arrived and went into the house with her. And Frank said that even though she was out of Officer Davis's sight for a few seconds, she wasn't in the house long enough to administer the poison and kill her grandmother. So, who could have done it? And how did he or she do it? Could someone have entered the Nelson house without being seen by either Mrs. Wilkins or Mr. Silverman? And who entered the Nelson house during the night, and why? And how did this person get from the Nelson house to the Jarvis house without being seen? And what happened to Mrs. Jarvis? Could it be that Mrs. Wilkins and Mr. Silverman were lying? If so, why would both of them lie? Could it be they were in on this together? And if they were lying, why did they give alibis to Angela Nelson and the Reynoldses? You would think that they would want to incriminate as many other people as possible to take away any suspicion from themselves.

I became more confused by the minute. I decided to put the case away until the next morning. Who knows? Maybe the lawyer, the mailman, the grocery boy, or the maid might be able to shed more light on the case.

+++

It was time to relax. Nothing relaxes me more than laughter, and nothing makes me laugh quite like some of the classic TV comedies I grew up with. I bought myself a DVD player last Christmas, and Lou got me a couple of DVDs to play on it. When I celebrated my birthday a couple of weeks ago, Lou came through in grand style. While I don't have DVDs of all my favorite shows, I have a good start. Besides, God willing, I will live to celebrate more birthdays and Christmases.

I rose from the chair and walked to the storage cabinet where I kept my new collection. I perused my choices, selected something to take my mind off my work. I plucked a DVD of *Make Room for Daddy*, starring Danny Thomas. I remember watching the show as a child. Back then, I laughed as Danny's children and his wife got the best of him in each episode. I put in the DVD and sat back to enjoy. It seems not much has changed in all those years. Real comedy never goes out of style, at least not in my house.

13

Sam Schumann is a good friend and a good cop. He's a gentle man who can get tough when he needs to. He has no outstanding physical features, which allows him to blend in no matter what the situation. All of this makes him an ideal investigator for the police department. When I want answers, I turn to Sam Schumann. I allowed Sam to spend a peaceful weekend before involving him in the Nelson murder case. Two days off were enough. It was time for Sam to go back to work.

"Good morning, Sam."

"Hi, Cy. You must have something for me. Otherwise, you wouldn't bother me so early on a Monday morning."

"Your deductive powers are amazing, Sam. That's the reason I always call you when I need to know something."

"I'm your man, Cy. What've you got?"

"A woman named Ethel Nelson was found dead in her home on Hilltop Place Saturday morning. She was murdered. Poisoned. Codeine. Check with Frank if you have any questions regarding the codeine. Then check around and see if anyone with a Hilltop Place connection bought any codeine. A few days ago an ambulance was dispatched to take Mrs. Nelson to the hospital. She had a broken left arm and leg, plus bruises on her body. See what you can find out about that. Also, see if you can find out if her granddaughter Angela Nelson inherits her estate."

"Anything else, Cy?"

"Yeah, keep writing, Sam. Numbers 101 and 105 Hilltop Place are vacant. See if you can find out who owns those houses. And I have some other people for you to check on. There's a Mrs. Reynolds on Hilltop Place. Her son Jimmy lives with her. Jimmy's not right. Supposedly, he lost it in the war. One of the neighbors said Jimmy came running from Mrs. Nelson's house screaming the day she suffered her broken bones. See, what you can find out about the Reynoldses.

"I've got one more for you to check on. His name is Stanley Silverman. He lived across the street from the murdered woman, and he seems to have seen everything except the murder. See what you can find out about him. Also, check on his mother. She died a few months ago. Find out if she died of natural causes and see what else you can tell me about Stanley and his mother."

"I'm running out of paper and time, Cy. I hope this is all."

"It is for the time being. I'm sure there'll be more."

"When do you want this, Cy? Two weeks?"

"Take your time, Sam. No hurry. Tomorrow morning will be fine."

I chuckled as he hung up. I knew Sam well enough to know he was laughing too.

+++

I wondered what the day held for this detective duo. As soon as Lou opened the car door on Monday morning, I could contain myself no longer. I spewed out my question.

"Any messages from God today, Lou?"

"I got some words if that's what you mean."

"Well, go on. Spit it out," I commanded impatiently.

"Twist and shout."

"Come again?" I replied quizzically.

"I said 'twist and shout.'"

"That's what I thought you said. Is that our message?"

"I guess so."

I burst out laughing, turned the radio to the oldies station, and started singing as I twisted in my seat. It didn't matter that Elvis's rendition of *Love Me Tender* blared from the radio.

Lou returned the quizzical look that I had given him just a few moments earlier. He hoped his neighbors were not watching, but, if they were, he hoped they would remember him in their prayers. The sergeant shook his head at my teen-like actions, and commented, "Cy, I've warned you to buy underwear that's big enough for you. When you grow, your underwear needs to grow with you."

I paid no attention to his remark and continued to twist as best my seat belt and aching bones allowed, while Lou merely grinned and shook his head some more. When I regained my senses, at least to the point where they were before Lou got me started, I turned to my partner.

"What's it mean, Lou?"

"I'm not sure, but I think it means you need to have your medication checked."

"No, not my gyrations. What's the message mean?"

"It means we're to be patient until we find out."

"I'm no doctor. I don't do patients."

I hadn't revealed anything my friend didn't already know.

+++

I remembered that Mrs. Wilkins had told me that Mr. Hartley handed her her mail at 9:35 on Saturday morning. I know mail carriers try to keep to a schedule, but don't arrive on a street at exactly the same time every day, and Lou and I wanted to catch him when he delivered to Hilltop Place, which meant we had about a fifteen-minute window to catch him there. We planned to stake out Hilltop Place until Mr. Hartley arrived. I turned the corner onto Hilltop Place and spotted a US Postal Service vehicle parked in front of the first house.

"Our guy Hartley doesn't waste any time, does he, Lou?"

"I think if I had to do this route I'd want to get it over with the first thing each morning, too," Lou replied.

"Do you see him yet?"

No sooner had I asked the question than both of us spotted the mailman quickly descending the steps from the third house on the right. We marveled at his speed.

"Yeah, but let's see how quickly he goes up the steps," I uttered, holding out that the mailman would exhibit the same huffing snail's pace that had become our trademark for climbing those same steps. Lou and I thought we were going to be sick after we saw the mailman quickly mount the steps of the next house.

"What's with this guy, anyway? He's got to be somewhere around our age."

"Yeah, but our belts would go around him twice. He can't have more than a thirty-two-inch waist. It's criminal for a man to be so thin."

I nodded in agreement. I knew that surely this mailman deprived himself of the good food Lou and I needed to get through each day. I had nothing against bread and water, as long as a lot of fine foods came with them. Even yogurt was okay. Well, maybe that's going a little too far.

And I wasn't even going to ask what tofu was. I just knew it wasn't for me. It sounds like some kind of martial arts, but some people claim they eat the stuff. Better them than me. I think yogurt and tofu are for people who go to classes to learn how to wrap their feet behind their heads. I have no intention of signing up for a pretzel class. If I did, I could just see the guys in the department. They would turn out in force to see Lou and me wearing tights.

I focused in on Hartley. He was zipping from one house to another. As he trotted down the steps of the last house and rushed to his vehicle, Lou and I opened our car doors and stepped out to talk with him.

"Mr. Hartley?" I called out as we made our way across the street.

A thin man of average height and straight, dishwater blond hair turned to face us.

"That's right."

"Mr. Hartley, I'm Lt. Dekker and this is Sgt. Murdock. We'd like to ask you a few questions."

As we reached the postman I showed him my identification.

"Let me see that, again. I've never known a cop to drive something like that," Mr. Hartley said as he pointed toward Lightning.

I held my identification closer, so he could see it.

"You're right, there, Mr. Hartley. Far too few law enforcement officers take pride in what they drive."

I could see Mr. Hartley felt he had more important things to do than talk about modes of transportation. He hurried things along with a question.

"Is this about Mrs. Nelson's murder?"

"That's right, Mr. Hartley. How did you know?"

"Well, I saw in the newspaper where she was murdered. I can't believe it, and to think I saw her only

Saturday morning," Mr. Hartley replied with sadness in his voice.

"Tell us about that, Mr. Hartley."

"Well, just a few days before, I'd gotten a notice to re-start her mail delivery. I assumed that meant that she'd gotten out of the hospital and was back at home. I'd been meaning to stop to see how she was doing. I decided to do just that Saturday morning when I saw the front door to her house standing open. I stepped into the house and called out. Since the door was open, I knew someone else was there with her. In a few minutes Miss Penrod, Mrs. Nelson's next-door neighbor, came down the stairs."

"So did you see Mrs. Nelson that morning?"

"I did. The poor thing. She looked in terrible shape. I told her I hoped she'd be doing better soon and handed her her mail."

"What else can you tell me about Mrs. Nelson? For in-stance, did she seem alert when you talked to her, or was she sleepy?"

"She didn't have much strength, but she was wide awake. Is that what you mean, Lieutenant?"

"Anything else you can think of?"

"Nothing comes to mind. Sorry."

"That's okay, Mr. Hartley. After you handed Mrs. Nel-son her mail, did you leave right away?"

"No, I talked to Miss Penrod a few minutes, asked her how she was doing and if she would like for me to give her her mail or put it in her box. Then I left."

"How was Miss Penrod?"

"About like always."

"And how is that?"

"Nice, but businesslike."

"And did Miss Penrod take her mail?"

"No, she told me that if it was all right with me she preferred that I put it in the mailbox."

"So, you left before Miss Penrod left. Is that correct?"

"That's right."

"Mr. Hartley, do you by any chance have a key to Mrs. Nelson's house?"

"I do. Several people have keys to Mrs. Nelson's house."

"And why did you have a key?"

"Well, I'd always check Mrs. Nelson's mail to see if there appeared to be anything important. If so, I'd ring the bell."

"And did Mrs. Nelson answer the door when you rang the bell?"

"Sometimes she did, but many mornings I'd find her eating breakfast on her sun porch as she looked out the window and watched the birds do the same thing. Before she fell, she was in pretty good shape for her age. What time she got up depended on how she felt on a particular day. Some days old people feel old. If she was still in bed, she'd buzz me in. She'd do the same thing if she was in the back on the sun porch, so I used my key on occasion."

"Mr. Hartley, do you have keys to any of the other houses on this street?"

"Just to Mrs. Jarvis's house. I used to have a key to Mrs. Silverman's house when she was living, but when her son took early retirement to stay home and take care of her I gave the key back."

"When's the last time you saw Mrs. Jarvis?"

"Oh, it's been a few days. I'm not sure which day it was."

"Mr. Hartley, did you see any of the other neighbors on Saturday morning?"

"As a matter of fact, I did. I saw Mr. Silverman when I delivered his mail. He was sitting by the window. I waved and smiled. He waved back. Then, I moved on down to the end of the street and that Reynolds boy was hiding behind a tree. He made me jump. He did. He's tetched. He's not really a boy, but he is mental. The war did strange things to him. Not that he was one of my favorites before the war, but I cut him some slack then because he lived with his mother. She's never had a kind word to say to anyone. Anyway, as I turned to leave, his mother opened the door and scared me again. That woman scares me even when she doesn't say anything. After I saw Miss Penrod and Mrs. Nelson, I ran into Mrs. Wilkins. She was sitting on her front porch."

"Mr. Hartley, do you know Bobby Cooper?"

"Yeah, he's the grocery boy."

"Would you recognize his car if you saw it?"

"Sure."

"Did you see it on Hilltop Place Saturday morning?"

"No, it wasn't there when I delivered the mail. Of course, he could've come later. You don't think he did it, do you?"

I avoided the question and asked another one.

"Mr. Hartley, were you by any chance on this street Saturday night?"

"Of course not. I'm never on the street at night."

"Mr. Hartley, what size shoe do you wear?"

"Why, did the murderer leave a footprint?"

"Just answer the question, Mr. Hartley?"

"Nine-and-a-half B."

"Do you own a yellow raincoat, Mr. Hartley?"

"No."

"Have you ever seen anyone on this street wearing a yellow raincoat?"

"Can't say that I have, but then I can't say that I've seen any of these people wearing any kind of raincoat. Are you saying that the murderer wore a yellow raincoat?"

"No, I'm not saying that. Mr. Hartley, can you think of anyone who might want to see Mrs. Nelson dead?"

"I'm afraid not, but my guess is that whoever it was was a stranger. I can't see anyone who knew her killing her. She was just too nice a person. The only thing I can't figure out is how the killer got into the house in the first place. Mrs. Nelson would never let in anyone that she didn't know. You don't think someone sneaked in on Saturday morning when her front door was open, do you?"

"At this point, I don't know anything. Maybe Mrs. Nelson didn't let the murderer in. Mr. Hartley, to the best of your knowledge, is there any other way of getting into any of these houses except by going through the front door?"

He paused and then answered. "No."

"Well, thanks for your time, Mr. Hartley."

I squinted as I looked toward the sun. Then, I used my hand as a visor and noticed the absence of any other activity on the street. Satisfied that no one was committing any new crimes at that moment, Lou and I waved goodbye to Mr. Hartley, who had already jumped into the mail truck.

The two of us returned to the car and found out that someone had phoned headquarters and left an anonymous tip that dealt with the Nelson case. The dispatcher told us to locate a copy of the local newspaper dated October 20, 1948. What would something that happened over fifty years ago have to do with a murder that was committed only two days ago?

14

Lou and I stopped off at the Midtown Market, a mid-size grocery in a mid-size town. It was the type of establishment that carried most of the items its customers considered necessary but didn't stock all brands.

I asked to see Bobby Cooper, but he was out delivering groceries. The manager told us when he expected Bobby to return. I asked him about Bobby's activities on Saturday, and he told me that Bobby took much too long to make his morning deliveries, then complained of being sick and asked for the afternoon off. I made a note of this and planned to ask Bobby about it when we returned. Then, I asked the manager if he could be a little more specific about Bobby's deliveries. He said as a matter of fact he could.

"It was a slow day for deliveries. Especially for a Saturday. Bobby had only two. Our checking device told us he arrived at the first delivery at 9:45 and the second one at 10:07. Despite the fact that he didn't have any more deliveries, he didn't return to the store until a little after 11:00."

Lou and I decided to pass the time while we waited for Bobby to return by asking Harry Hornwell a few questions.

It would be our first time to speak with Mrs. Nelson's attorney.

Hornwell's spacious office occupied the second floor of a two-story, red-brick building in the downtown area. A couch, two chairs on rollers, and a coffee table occupied space on the right side of the room. Two more chairs faced a desk, and another chair stood behind the desk. Each of the chairs and the couch were covered with cordovan leather. Mr. Hornwell's large, mahogany desk matched not only the couch and chairs but the large bookcases that surrounded his office. The Oriental rug beneath our feet looked expensive, and the hardwood floor, visible from the end of the rug to the wall, seemed of fine quality. The entire area screamed that the attorney was well-heeled. Nothing about Mr. Hornwell's demeanor contradicted what the room seemed to say about him. He answered our questions as quickly as possible, and his attitude seemed to say that he felt his time was more valuable than ours. Mr. Hornwell told us that he didn't know much about what had happened to Mrs. Nelson because he spent the weekend at his cabin. He left town late Friday afternoon and didn't return until Sunday night.

We left Hornwell's office and went back to the car. I called DMV and asked them to check on what vehicles Harry Hornwell owned and to give me the license plate numbers. He owned two cars, plus a truck and an SUV. We lucked out. We found a black Lincoln Town Car licensed to Hornwell parked beside his office. There was mud on the tires and the lower part of the car's body. Why would someone who owned a Lincoln Navigator and a Ford F-150 truck take his car into the woods?

We left Mr. Hornwell's office and returned to Midtown Market. Bobby Cooper had returned. He answered each of our questions but seemed nervous doing so. His manner suggested that the young man had something to hide. As I expected, he denied being on Hilltop Place the day of the murder and said that the reason his Saturday morning deliveries took longer than usual was that he wasn't feeling well.

+++

With everyone questioned except Mrs. Jarvis, Miss Penrod, and Mrs. Murphy, Sgt. Murdock and I drove to the newspaper office to see what trinket of information a fifty-plus-year-old newspaper could provide. We arrived and the clerk informed us that we could find the information we wanted on microfiche at the local library. A few minutes later, Lou and I arrived at the library, gave an employee the date of the newspaper we were looking for, and a minute or so later the librarian presented us with a roll of microfiche and instructions as to where to go and how to view it. The two of us scanned the newspaper, found the item we wanted in the local news section under the article "The Secrets of Hilltop Place."

"So Lou, do you think there's any truth in this article?"

"I don't know, but I know there are two guys who are going to do their best to find out."

"One thing's for sure if all of the houses on Hilltop Place really do have secret passageways that lead from room to room and tunnels underneath that lead from house to house; it sure explains how the killer could have gotten into the house without a key."

+++

I braked and eased Lightning in front of Mrs. Nelson's house. Lou and I used one hand for leverage and extracted ourselves from the yellow bubble. As far as we could tell, neither Mr. Silverman nor Jimmy Reynolds was aware that we had returned. We were sure that our reappearance would not remain a secret for long.

"I wish I knew where that tunnel was, Lou. Then we wouldn't have to climb all these steps."

"I don't know, Cy. I'd think these steps might be safer than those leading from the tunnel to the house."

"You never know. This place might be like a mine shaft. There might be an elevator or a mining car leading to the top. Oh, well, we're wasting time. Let's go see if the key works this time."

After a few minutes of heavy breathing, Plump and Plumper reached the front porch. I removed the key from my pocket, inserted it into the lock. The key turned and the door opened. Maybe our luck was about to improve. We looked around like two children on Christmas morning, only this time our gifts had been hidden from us.

"Where do you think we should start, Cy?"

"I don't know. Let's start in the pantry. That's where we found the boots."

To gather strength for our endeavor, Lou and I slid our hands into our coat pockets. I frowned when I noticed the next two nuts almost touched each other. I removed my pocketknife and carefully sliced one almond and a sliver of chocolate away from the remainder of the candy bar. Lou showed no remorse and blew hard enough to make a large opening in his already torn M&M package. He gulped down a satisfactory amount of a rainbow of little pieces.

The two of us studied a well-stocked section of canned goods. Everything had its place. One shelf contained fruits. Another shelf housed vegetables. Miscellaneous items occupied still another shelf.

"Any ideas?" Lou asked.

"Let's slide our fingers across the edge of each shelf and see if we can find a spring that opens one side or the back wall."

We donned gloves to prevent getting a splinter and erasing clues and went to work. A small stepladder helped us to reach the higher shelves. Many minutes later, after a meticulous study of each shelf and corner, neither of us found a spring, lever, or button that identified a secret passageway.

"So, what's Plan B?" Lou asked.

"I don't know. Let's say we remove everything from the shelves and see if we find anything hidden behind them."

We plucked one item from the shelves and then another. After we had removed a few items, we were surprised by the depth of each shelf.

"Why would a single woman living alone have so much on hand?"

"Beats me. Looks like it was definitely enough to last her a lifetime."

"Yeah, and then some."

A few minutes later, we had loaded the kitchen table with items taken from the pantry, and still, the pantry held an adequate amount of inventory.

"Think this stuff is still good, Cy?"

"I don't know. Lou. Open a jar and take a bite. If something happens to you, I'll assume that I should throw out the rest of it."

"Gee, thanks. That's awful good of you, Cy."

"What can I say? That's what friends are for."

"Remind me to recommend Stanley Silverman to be your partner in case I die."

"And I thought you might recommend Heloise Humphert and her walking dust ball."

"Maybe the three of you and your mascot could be our department's first police trio, or would the beast make it a quartet?"

"If so, I plan to use a squad car and lock the others in the back seat."

After what seemed like an eternity, we had removed all the bottles and jars from the pantry.

"Hey, Lou. Looks like you missed one."

"That bottle of olives appears to be stuck, Cy. I couldn't budge it. I guess it's been there so long it's taken up residence."

"Just leave it. See anything that might help us?"

"Not so far."

"Well, let's just push on the wall and see if it moves."

After a few more minutes and no results, Lou surmised, "It looks like this pantry is here to stay."

"I'm still not convinced. Let's take a break and mull it over for a few minutes."

15

We hadn't found a passageway. We trudged through each downstairs room before we climbed the steps to the second floor. Once upstairs, we concentrated on Mrs. Nelson's bedroom and her bedroom closet in particular. Lou and I tried any idea we came up with. I removed everything that hung in the closet. I hoped to find a hidden lever. When my efforts didn't reveal any button, device, or contraption, I removed all the shoes from the closet floor. I wanted so much to find a loose board. Lou located a chair and dislodged all items from the closet shelf. He even pulled on the chain that turned on the closet light, as he hoped some action would cause a wall to slide away revealing a hidden stairway. When the sergeant left the closet defeated, I took a turn and twisted the bar that held the hangers. At least, I tried to twist it. Again, no such luck. Neither of us found anything that revealed a secret passageway. We slumped over and dejectedly made our way back down the stairs.

I plopped down and leaned back in an overstuffed chair and mulled over what we knew. I tried to sort through all the information we had turned up. Finally, an idea came to me.

"We still haven't found Mrs. Jarvis. We don't know where she is or even if she's still living. Maybe if we give her place another once-over we might get a clue. Let's check out her pantry and see how it compares to the one in this house. Could be we'll find a secret passageway and maybe we'll find Mrs. Jarvis in it."

Lou didn't want to rain on my parade, so he failed to remind me of our recent lack of success. Instead, he lifted his tired body from the chair that bore his impression. As he did, the chair breathed a sigh of relief.

We returned to Mrs. Jarvis's house and soon found ourselves in front of a pantry much like the one we had just left. Having already been through the routine, we started removing cans and jars. When we'd finished, we discovered a startling revelation.

"Lou, what do you think the odds are of finding a stuck jar of olives in two pantries?"

"Astronomical."

"I think we have two jars of olives that are trying to tell us something."

I approached the jar of olives not content to let them beat me. Once again I tried to remove the jar but to no avail. Next, I tried to scoot the olives, but they wouldn't budge. I couldn't lift or scoot them, so I tried to push the olives toward the wall. I had hoped to release a hidden spring or lock. Although I couldn't see how it would help, I took both hands and pushed down on the jar. With still no success, I slid my gloved hand across the board below the olives. Once again, I hoped to trip some secret mechanism. Nothing worked. Frustrated, I sat down in a kitchen chair.

"I give up, Lou. Any ideas?"

"How about 'in case of exit, break jar?'"

"I've wanted to break it ever since I found it, but that can't be how it's done. I'm sure whoever devised this didn't break a jar of olives every time he wanted to use the secret passageway."

"Well, we can always go with my other suggestion. Eat them."

A light went on inside my head. At least, Lou's comment gave me an inspiration.

"You know, Lou. You might have something there."

"You're not serious about eating the olives, are you?"

"Not eating them, but we've done everything except twist the lid."

No sooner had the words come out of my mouth until another set of words hit me. *Twist and Shout.* I rushed over and twisted the jar lid counter-clockwise. Nothing happened. The lid didn't budge.

"Maybe it's because it's been so long since someone used it," Lou said, hoping to offer a little encouragement.

"But if our theory is right, it hasn't been that long since someone used it," I replied.

"Well, then try turning it the other way."

Since all jars opened counter-clockwise, I never thought about turning the jar clockwise. Once again, I put my hand on the lid. This time I twisted the lid in the other direction. The lid did not budge, but the wall of the pantry slid to one side. Lou and I jumped up and down like a couple of children who had just spotted Santa Claus.

"Come on, Lou. Let's follow God's directions."

I began to dance. I started twisting and Lou could contain himself no longer. He too began to twist. Until we became exhausted, two middle-aged men twisted, bumped hips, raised both hands into the air, and shouted. The lack of an audience spared us the embarrassment of the moment. After only a couple of minutes, we gasped for air as if we'd just climbed the front steps, again. We staggered over to the nearest chairs, plopped down, and waited until we could breathe normally again. Only two days passed.

Still in a jovial mood, I removed a brand new candy bar from my pocket, unwrapped it, took out my knife, and cut an almond and some chocolate from the center of the candy bar. After I put it in my mouth and savored it like it was a fine wine, I put the chocolate-framed peephole up to my eye and looked at Lou.

He stuck out his tongue and then removed an M&M from his bag. It was a peanut M&M and the one Lou removed was yellow.

He held it up and showed it to me.

"Look, Cy. It's Tweetie."

"The car's name is Lightning."

The sergeant said, "Whatever," and threw the yellow M&M at my peephole. It bounced off my forehead and landed on the floor. I leaned over, picked it up, and threw it back at Lou, who caught it in his mouth. Here we were two grown men acting like little boys as we celebrated our success. When the moment passed, we returned to work, but with a renewed spirit, as if we'd actually accomplished something.

"Before we check out the hidden staircase, let's call the lab boys again."

+++

In a little while, the Jarvis house was once again protruding with policemen. Their search turned up many secret passageways that led to places all over the house, places that appeared well hidden to the naked eye. They found dust and cobwebs, and the lack of footprints ahead of them revealed that they were the first persons to enter those passageways in many years. There was no sign of Mrs. Jarvis.

"I want to try the same thing at the Nelson house. I think we might find another passageway, and I think we'll find that someone has been high stepping there."

16

Stanley Silverman peered out his window. He watched as Lou and I led a posse of policemen up the street to Mrs. Nelson's house. Jimmy Reynolds watched too, but from the safety of his front porch instead of the nearest tree.

Once inside, Lou gave me a look, as if to say, *If this thing works, don't start twisting again. I like my job.* I returned the look as if to tell Lou, *You have nothing to worry about.*

I led the parade to the pantry and was ecstatic when I twisted the olive jar and watched the back wall slide away.

"It's all yours, boys," I said as I turned to face my compatriots.

+++

Many people know Lou and I excel at eating, or grazing, as some call it. Fewer know that we have mastered the art of sitting. Neither of us has a wife to refine us, so each of us had to discover his own method. Most people think we learned from each other. Both of us have learned how to zero in on a chair, lumber over to it, plop down onto it, and sprawl out all over it. It is truly an art that no woman can understand.

On that occasion, even though we didn't have long to sprawl, Lou and I plopped down in a couple of chairs that beckoned to us. We eagerly anticipated more success than we had at the previous house. Sometime later, an expert approached us with his team's findings.

"We've found a little evidence, Lieutenant, but not much. We discovered one set of footprints, which came from the closet in the old lady's bedroom. Our guess is whoever made them went up the steps in the living room but came down through the passageway. There were a few more sets just inside the pantry."

I was puzzled.

"There were no footprints leading up to the bedroom through the passageway? And there weren't any leading to or from any other room?"

"I'm sorry, sir. That's all we found."

"Well, can you tell anything about the tracks near the pantry?"

"That's another strange thing. There are only a few of them, and all of them came from a size eleven pair of galoshes, but not all of them came from the pair you found in the pantry."

"So we either have two people with size eleven feet or one person with two pairs of galoshes."

"Not necessarily, Lieutenant. It could have been someone with smaller feet or someone with slightly larger feet who removed their shoes."

"Anything else, Sergeant?"

"Well, there's one thing that bothers me. The cobwebs have been there for quite some time, but there's some dirt that appears to be a recent addition. The thing is that I've sent men around the exterior of the house, and it doesn't look like the dirt came from anywhere in this yard. Also, there's no dirt in the house that matches the dirt in the passageway."

"Can you tell if it matches the dirt we found at Mrs. Jarvis's house?"

"Not yet. But it looks similar."

"Is it possible that there are additional passageways you haven't found, maybe even ones below the house? Maybe the dirt came from there."

"Sure, that's possible, Lieutenant."

"Well, thanks, and be sure to thank your men. You can go now. Sgt. Murdock and I will lock up when we're finished."

+++

Lou and I sat in Mrs. Nelson's house trying to figure out what we were missing. Surely, there was another clue waiting to be discovered.

"Lou, we have one woman murdered, another woman missing or murdered, and a passageway with dirt but no bodies in it. Any ideas?"

"Someone keeps leaving us clues, but how many of them have to do with this case and how many are red herrings?"

"It makes me think of something else, too. If our murderer's only intent was to kill Mrs. Nelson, he or she could have easily used a pillow. She wouldn't have been able to fight off someone. Also, depending on how good of a job he or she did, it's possible that we might've thought that she'd merely died in her sleep. I still think that our murderer wants to play games with us."

"I see what you mean, Cy."

"Here's what we know. Mrs. Nelson was given some pain medication and sleeping pills, and then, after they had taken effect, she was murdered. The lab agrees that the poison came from the glass on the floor beside her bed. We know that someone pushed a wheelchair in Mrs. Jarvis's basement, probably with Mrs. Jarvis in it, but the wheelchair and the footprints disappeared just like the footprints in the passageway behind Mrs. Nelson's pantry. No one tried to cover his or her tracks after Mrs. Nelson was murdered, so whoever did it didn't mind us knowing that a murder had been committed. My guess is that two murders have been committed because I believe that Mrs. Jarvis is dead. I also believe that there's a tunnel of some type underneath this street. It's just a matter of how to find it."

Lou and I trudged up and down the steps inside the secret passageway for thirty more minutes, but our efforts revealed nothing. When neither of us came up with any new ideas, we left.

I checked my watch. I figured Mrs. Murphy was home by then, so we stopped by to see her. I knocked on the door of the small frame house. A woman with light gray hair pulled back and secured with bobby pins answered the door. Her smile went well with her rosy cheeks. I showed my identification and found out the woman was Mrs. Murphy. I told her I had a few questions for her.

"Of course, Lieutenant, but my feet ache. I've had a busy day today. Would you mind if we sat down and talked?" asked the woman with a voice that sounded like she had just arrived from Ireland.

We agreed and followed the woman with a puzzled look.

"Mrs. Murphy, I understand that you clean houses for a living."

"Aye, that's right. Surely someone hasn't complained about my work."

"Not that I know of," I replied, and then laughed. "Of course, if they did, there wouldn't be any cause for me to be here. I'm in the homicide division."

"Oh, you must be here about poor Mrs. Nelson."

"That's right, Mrs. Murphy. I understand her house was one of the houses you cleaned regularly."

"Aye, that's right, Lieutenant. And I will miss her so."

"When was the last time you saw her?"

"Friday morning, when I did my regular cleaning. I went up and visited with her a few minutes, then went right to work."

"And do you also clean for Mrs. Jarvis?"

"Aye, that I do."

"And did you see her on Friday, too?"

"Aye, of course, Lieutenant. Mrs. Jarvis never goes anywhere."

"Was there anything different about last Friday?"

"Only that Mrs. Nelson was in bed. My daughter and I got to her house at nine. We cleaned. When my daughter is with me, not only do we clean, but we move the furniture and clean and sweep under it and behind it. We finished at Mrs. Nelson's around 11:30, ate the lunch we brought, and then went to Mrs. Jarvis's. Mrs. Nelson is always kind enough to let us eat our lunch at her house."

"And how was Mrs. Jarvis on Friday?"

"Same as always. Has something happened to her, too?"

"I'm not sure. We can't find her."

"Can't find Mrs. Jarvis? Why Mrs. Jarvis never goes anywhere. Maybe she just didn't want to answer the door."

"Maybe that's it," I answered, not wanting to reveal all that I knew.

"Have you ever been in Mrs. Jarvis's basement?"

"Aye, of course, Lieutenant. I do Mrs. Jarvis's laundry. The basement is where she keeps the washer and dryer."

"And did you do Mrs. Jarvis's laundry last Friday?"

"Aye, of course, Lieutenant. Don't tell me someone's stolen her laundry?"

I laughed.

"No, Mrs. Murphy. Was the basement light working last Friday?"

"Aye, of course, Lieutenant. At my age, I wouldn't be able to see in the basement in the dark."

"One other thing, Mrs. Murphy. Where were you on Saturday morning?"

"I was at church all morning. A meeting. There were a lot of women there."

I thanked Mrs. Murphy for her time, and Lou and I left.

Tired from all the work we had done, Lou and I decided to rest until the next day, hoping that a good night's sleep might supply us with new ideas.

17

On our way to Lou's apartment, he and I discussed what we would do when we got home. Lou said he planned to lumber into his apartment, kick off his shoes, plop down, and lean back in his recliner while he decided what he would do until bedtime. For years, Lou had talked about reading some of the great classic novels. He learned about an organization that had compiled a list of what they considered the top one hundred novels of all time.

After we wrapped up our last case, on one of our slow days Lou had me drive him to a bookstore, where he plucked a few titles from the shelves.

I looked forward to hearing Lou's book reviews almost as much as I did his messages from God. Lou began his conquest by reading a novel told from the point of view of one of literature's most beloved characters, Scout, from *To Kill A Mockingbird*. Lou called it "a delightful book," and voiced his disappointment that Harper Lee wrote only two books and wrote the second one many years after the first. So far, Lou hasn't read the second book. But after reading the first book he said no one can make you feel for his or her characters like Lee can, and Lou embraced Scout, Tom Robinson, and Boo Radley, and if Lou had to go to court, he wanted Atticus Finch by his side.

+++

The bachelor sergeant always stayed up as late as he wished. Lou had lived by himself all of his adult life. He had no one to check with. His actions inconvenienced no one. Much like my life, Lou's life revolved around his work. Other than when we worked or ate together, Lou spent most of his time by himself unless he and Thelma Lou were out on a date. Many people told him he should get a dog or a cat for company, but he didn't feel the need for company, nor did he know how long a particular case would keep him away from home. Besides, he had no desire to go outside in a blinding snowstorm just because some dog wanted to go, nor did he want to change a smelly litter box, so a cat was out of the question. He didn't want to move, either, which he would have to do if he owned a pet. His building didn't allow pets. Goldfish excluded.

+++

I dropped Lou at his apartment, then thought about him all the way home. But once I reached my home turf, my thoughts turned to what I planned to do.

I smiled as I entered the house. Not only did I arrive a little earlier than the night before, but I felt we'd made a little headway in the case, though not as much as I would've liked.

+++

I ambled over to my easy chair, picked up the remote. While there are many liabilities from living the single life, not having to share a remote control is one of the benefits.

It felt good to leave the rigors of work behind, and I knew that Lucy, Ricky, Ethel, and Fred always made me feel even better. I was a tired cop that night, so I inserted a DVD, pushed the button on my remote, settled back. By the time I called it a night, I'd watched four episodes of *I Love Lucy*, including the pilot, where Lucy donned a costume and replaced a clown who got hurt rehearsing for an appearance in Ricky's night club act. In addition to the pilot, which never aired on television until 1990, I watched the first three episodes of the show, all of which originally aired in October 1951. I laughed when Ethel taught Lucy how to play poker in two hours. Lucy, who wanted to become pals with Ricky, went to Fred and Ethel's apartment and beat the guys at poker. As I stopped the DVD for the night, I remembered an episode I had seen on television where Lucy wore a yellow raincoat. Whenever Lucy tried to hide her identity, she was guilty of something. Did that mean whoever Stanley Silverman saw wearing a yellow raincoat was guilty of one murder and possibly two?

I let the question slosh around in my brain for a few minutes, then let it rest. I went to the bathroom, brushed my teeth, changed into blue-and-white flannel pajamas, and called it a night. I was just getting used to those flannels again, as the weather had just begun to change.

18

Tuesday morning the alarm went off and jarred me from a comfortable sleep. While I still sported the aches and pains that came with age and a much too unhealthy appetite, my legs felt a little better. As I showered and got ready to pick up Lou, I began to focus on the case. I couldn't wait to hear Lou's latest revelation from God and its bearing on our investigation of Mrs. Nelson's murder. Still, I couldn't see how today's message could be as much fun as "twist and shout."

Before I left to pick up the sergeant, I called Sam Schumann. I hoped that after he and I talked, things would begin to fall into place. From the greeting I received, I assumed he was in a rare mood.

"This is Sam I Am dining on green eggs and ham."

I laughed.

"So, my friend, Sam You Are, what do you have for me so far?"

"Well, Cy, I haven't been able to find out yet if Angela Nelson inherits her grandmother's estate. I'll keep checking on that."

"Please do, Sam."

"I also had no luck finding anyone who had bought any codeine."

"What are we paying you for? Did you find out anything?"

"Of course, I did, Cy. I'm saving the good stuff for last."

"Well, it's last, Sam. What do you have?"

"Well, I can't give you any more information yet, but Harry Hornwell, the attorney, bought both of those houses you asked me to check on."

"How interesting."

Sam Schumann continued and filled me in on what he had learned about Jimmy Reynolds and Stanley Silverman. Jimmy was discharged from the army because he had a mental breakdown. Many people knew that, but what they didn't know was that Jimmy used a shovel to whack another soldier in the back of the head. Word is that Jimmy thought the other soldier was his enemy. It wasn't the only time Jimmy's paranoia and strength got him in trouble. As for Jimmy's mother, she has never been the toast of the neighborhood. Her neighbors feel she can't be trusted.

"Cy, the smart money says Jimmy pushed Mrs. Nelson down some stairs, but we can't prove it. She claimed she merely missed a step and fell. I checked at the hospital. They said she could've fallen or been pushed, but she was not beaten by a blunt instrument. Her injuries were consistent with injuries an elderly person might suffer after falling down or being pushed down a flight of steps."

Not having any more information about Mrs. Nelson's fall, Sam told me what he found out about Stanley Silverman. He never made a lot of money, but Stanley didn't have to make a lot of money. He became wealthy when his mother died. Sam also told me the word was that Stanley dedicated the entire third floor of his house as a shrine to his mother. He decorated it with her favorite furniture, and the jewelry she loved so much. Supposedly, the first thing each morning and the last thing each night he climbs the steps to the third floor, lights candles, and sits around focusing on pictures of his mother.

"You have some strange birds on that street, Cy."

"So it seems."

"Oh, I have something else for you. I understand that the old lady's house had a sliding bolt."

"That's right."

"Well, a strong magnet can slide that sucker and unlock it."

"Really? So anyone who had a key to the front door could get in if he or she knew about the magnet."

"That's right, Cy. I doubt if a lot of people know the trick, but it works. I hope this helps you."

"I'll be on the lookout for strange people with big magnets. Before I let you go, Sam, I've got some other people I want you to check on."

"I was afraid of that, Cy. Shoot."

"Harry Hornwell wasn't too talkative yesterday. See what else you can find out about him. He claims he was out of town at his cabin over the weekend. Check and see if he has a cabin and try to find out if anyone saw him there over the weekend. Also, see what you can come up with about a mailman named Fred Hartley. One more, Sam. Check up on Mrs. Nelson's maid, a woman named Murphy who lives on Magnolia. I think she's all right, but I want to be sure."

"Is that all?"

"That's it for now, Sam."

"You're not being any easier on me today than you were yesterday, Cy. I'll see what I can find out. Talk to you in the morning."

+++

I emerged from my house and groaned as I saw Heloise Humphert and Twinkle Toes out for their morning walk. Suddenly, my bad side envisioned a different version of twist and shout. I saw myself twisting my neighbor's neck and shouting for joy. I quickly regained my senses and recalled that not only does God want me to love my neighbor as myself, but He wants me to love my enemies. Does that mean I have to love that woman twice as much, since she is both a neighbor and an enemy? I wondered if it would be all right with God if I despised myself like I despised my neighbor. I pondered that but couldn't recall any scripture that would allow that. I remembered that I had heard prison food isn't nearly as good as what the Blue Moon Diner serves. I decided to try to tolerate The Wicked Witch and her version of Toto.

As I contemplated my task, I looked up as my neighbor sashayed toward me. Then, I looked down and noticed that both the woman and her pet were adorned with the same color of nail polish. It was some shade of blue, and I was sure it glowed in the dark. I became thankful that I had not yet eaten.

"Good morning, Cyrus. Have we caught our murderer yet?"

"Oh, did someone kill us?"

"Oh, Cyrus, you know what I mean by 'our murderer.'"

"I wasn't aware that we were working on a case together."

"I wasn't, either, but I'm ready anytime you are."

I shuddered, then continued.

"The answer to your question is 'no.' We haven't caught *our* murderer yet, but we have *him* under surveillance. We think it's the man who moved into the house behind yours. Wherever he has lived, he has had a habit of sneaking over the back fence in the dead of night and killing all the women and dogs in the house behind his. You might want to move out of the neighborhood while you can."

"I feel very confident that you'll protect me, Cyrus," Heloise Humphert said as she paused for effect and gave herself a hug. "I have an idea. Why don't you come over to my house and keep watch through the window?"

"I'm sorry, Miss Humphert, but I can't. I haven't had my shots yet."

Miss Humphert laughed her grating laugh. She always took my comments as humor, rather than put-downs.

+++

Lou was waiting for me when I pulled up. I could tell from the smile on his face that God must have given him a good clue for that day. He lingered at the car door before he opened it, thus prolonging my agony.

"Just open the door and get in, or I'll leave without you."

Not sure whether I would do that or not, Lou opened the door and slid down onto the seat.

"Morning, Cy."

"I'll morning, Cy, you. Okay, out with it. What's today's clue?"

Lou ignored my question. "I'm thinking about trying a new author this week. Well, a new author to me. Not new to everyone else."

"I'll give you a new author to try. Heloise Humphert."

"I didn't realize she wrote books. What are they about? Your romantic interludes together?"

"You're the one who's about to have a romantic interlude with her."

"I thought she was your girl, Cy."

"I think she's using me to get to you, Lou."

"Remember, Cy. She bought the house next door to you. She didn't move into my building."

"Could she help it if there were no vacancies in your building? Besides, I don't believe your building allows pets."

"That's good. Remind me not to move."

"I think she should advertise. I can see her ad now. 'Let Heloise Humphert give you some comfort.'"

"Did she send you off with a kiss this morning, Cy?"

"Is my face broken out?"

The two of us laughed.

"You'd better tell me God's message, or I'll get her for you or someone who's her spitting image."

"You'd never be able to do that, Cy. No one can spit like Heloise."

"Back to the matter at hand, or I'll advertise on the Internet. 'Robust cop looking for a relationship with a woman who can disarm a mugger.'"

"Maybe you should make it 'robust dog-loving cop.' It will increase your chances of hearing from your neighbor."

"Okay, enough time wasted. Am I going to give Heloise your phone number or are you going to tell me today's clue?"

"Okay, Cy. You win. Today's message is 'Hogan's contact.'"

"Do what?"

"I said today's message is Hogan's contact."

"Hogan who?"

"Hogan who? You're the one with all the DVDs. My guess is we're talking *Hogan's Heroes* here."

"But who's Hogan's contact? Are we going to meet some blonde with a foreign accent?"

"With our luck, I'd say we're going to meet some overweight dumb sergeant."

"I've already met him."

"Watch yourself, Cy. Just remember any time you look at me it's just like you're looking in the mirror."

"Tell me, Lou. How come God gives you the clue each day instead of giving it to me? After all, I outrank you."

"I'll admit you are pretty rank when you forget to shower."

"Watch it. So how come He gives you the clue? He could at least rotate between us."

"Beats me. Could it be that you're not on speaking terms with Him?"

"No, I speak to Him every day."

"Yeah, but do you take time to listen to Him? Could be He's giving you clues, too, only you're too busy telling Him how to run things and forget to listen to Him."

I changed the subject.

+++

As I drove, Lou gave me his second book review. For his second selection, he chose one of his childhood favorites, *The Adventures of Huckleberry Finn*. The book inspired Lou. It made him want to go and do likewise Lou Murdock style. Considering how poorly he did in woodshop class, he figured anything he put together would sink before it sailed, and the Mississippi was a mighty deep river. He planned to choose safer waters.

Lou told me that he envisioned the two of us mounted upon inflatable rubber rafts as we made our way across the pool at the Holiday Inn. As he pictured the two of us on our excursion, he wondered how much weight those inflatable rafts would hold. Did they have a heavy-duty model?

As Lou recalled his daydream, he shared a secret. He planned to get me to mount my craft first. I weighed eleven pounds more than he did. If I made it, he figured he would be okay, too. But what if I wouldn't agree to be the guinea pig? The sergeant had a back-up plan. Any good sergeant does. He determined to get up early before anyone flocked to the kiddie pool so he could try out his vessel to see if it was seaworthy. If not, he wouldn't have far to sink. And what was a pair of wet swimming trunks, anyway?

19

Lou and I chatted about the case while I drove to our new home away from home, Hilltop Place. I shared with Lou all the information Sam had given me. I pulled the car into the driveway at the Nelson house, and both of us stepped out. It had been only three days since fear struck our faces as we contemplated our first trip to the summit.

"Lou. I'll wait here while you go check and see what's new."

"Why don't I wait here? You need to exercise more than I do."

We were getting nowhere fast, and we realized that the house wouldn't move any closer to us no matter how long we waited. Lou and I walked over to the steps, grabbed the railing for assistance. A few minutes later we had conquered the climb.

"You know, Cy, this climbing is turning into a piece of cake."

"I'm glad you're finding it easy. Maybe next time you can pull me up the hill. I'll be seated on a sled."

I reached into my pocket and removed the key to the Nelson house. I slid it into the lock, turned the key, and pushed on the door. The door opened easily. Apparently, no one had entered the house since we had left it the day before. Either that or whoever it was decided not to play games with us this time.

"Any ideas, Lou?"

"Well, most tunnels I know are underground. What say we try the basement."

My face broke into a wide grin.

"Did I say something funny, Cy?"

"No, but I think we have an answer to our clue of the day."

"We do."

"Maybe. Col. Hogan's contact was someone from the underground. He and his men also dug tunnels. Could be this is our lucky day, my friend?"

In our excitement, both of us tried to get through the doorway at the same time.

After our initial failure, Lou stepped back and let me go first.

"After you, your majesty."

"No, after you. God gave you the clue, not me."

We hustled through the kitchen and lunged for the basement door. We opened the door, turned on the light, and crept down the stairs. After a few minutes of looking through the basement with a proverbial magnifying glass, we wondered if there was another Hogan other than the one on the classic TV show.

I walked over and plopped down on the third step from the bottom. Then, I stood up and started to sing *Twist And Shout*. A few moments before a possible coronary, I sat back down on the third step from the bottom.

After a good laugh, the two of us trudged up the steps to think of Plan B.

A few minutes later Lou broke the silence.

"Where else can it be, Cy?"

"My guess is under the house. How about if we buy two shovels and dig in the back yard? I'd say in a few weeks we'll find it."

"Do you think we might get there sooner if we start in China?"

"I'll start here. You start in China, and I'll meet you in the tunnel."

"I can see it now. 'Two detectives die as tunnel caves in.' What about it, Lou? Any ideas?"

"I don't know, Cy. We can always try the passageway again. Maybe there's one we didn't find before."

Both of us stood up. We failed to display the exhilaration we exhibited when we headed to the basement. I walked over to the pantry, twisted the jar of olives. The wall slid away.

"Oh, what I would have given to have had a house like this to play hide-and-seek in when I was a boy."

"Can you imagine what it would have been like if you'd had a tunnel, too?"

"How sad that we grew up in abject poverty. Not only couldn't we afford a tunnel, but we also couldn't afford any hidden passageways. Imagine having had passageways and tunnels when we were sent to our rooms? We could have sneaked over to a friend's house; our parents would never have known. And what if I had given my first true love her first kiss in my very own tunnel of love. It's too depressing to think about. After you, Lou."

Lou removed his package of M&Ms to take another guzzle. After he chugged a few, he almost dropped them as he tried to put them back into his pocket. He stumbled, fell, and landed on the first step with a thud.

"Ppptthhtt," he said as he spit cobwebs in several directions.

I didn't know whether to laugh or cry. Lou tried to brace himself in order to lift his hefty body to a standing position. He placed his right hand on the bottom step, only it slipped and smashed his knuckles against the back of the step. The sergeant tried to sit up, so he wrapped his fingers around the back of the bottom step.

"Hey, Cy! Something's here!"

"Is it slithering around your hand?"

"No. It's quite still and it doesn't breathe."

"So this is where they hid the gold coins."

"I'm not kidding, Cy. There's some kind of control box with two buttons."

"Well, push one of them, Lou. If it's time for you to go, I want to go with you."

Lou leaned over the step. It was a tight squeeze, but he managed to push a button. Nothing happened.

"I pushed one, Cy. Nothing happened."

"I can see that nothing happened. Push it again, Lou."

Again nothing happened.

"Maybe it's one of those time-release explosive devices that give us time enough to get out of the house before it implodes into the tunnel below. Push the other button, Lou. I'd rather go now than face those steps again."

Lou pushed the second button. The wall I didn't realize I had been leaning against slid away and I discovered that stout men can fly under certain circumstances. I also realized that all the facts I'd been taught in school about the law of gravity were true, and while it seemed painful in school, it seemed much more painful in real life.

20

Before I had finished my downward trek, I experienced the human version of an eight-rail bank shot, although the word "cushion" was not a part of the experience. The side of my face, which included my left ear, hit and bounced off the first "rail" of rough concrete bouncing me just enough that my right shoulder took the brunt of the blow of the second "rail." All this time my upper, middle, and lower back registered the protrusion of the edge of each wooden step as if I were descending a rollercoaster track without a car. Finally, I ran out of real estate as my right shoulder thudded against a wall or a door and I came to an abrupt stop.

I lay there pondering how I might deal with paralysis. Then it dawned on me that everything hurt, so I couldn't be paralyzed. I groaned, but the groaning didn't ease the pain.

Above me, I heard a noise that sounded like a berserk sergeant trying to get to his feet. Then I saw a column of light, and I waited to see if an angel was about to say, "Fear not." When this didn't happen, I realized the light was coming from the flashlight of a sergeant who was trying to think of something intelligent to say.

"Are you all right, Cy?"

It was then that I knew that the sergeant had decided to speak before he could think of something intelligent to say.

I decided to answer him with a slightly more intelligent remark.

"Is that you, Jill?"

In the best falsetto voice he could muster, Lou replied, "Yes, Jack, but with the way women's rights are in today's society, I no longer have to come tumbling after you."

Listening to his voice I was sure that my friend made the right choice when he didn't consider an acting career.

"I'm very much grateful for that. While I'm lying here in much pain, it would hurt me, even more, to think of what it would be like if you came tumbling down on top of me."

"My guess is that if my rotundness landed on your rotundness I would bounce back to the top, but I have no inclination to find out if I'm right."

I continued to lie with my head much lower than my feet, and I continued to groan in pain. It was not a position of choice. After a few seconds of silence from both ends of the stairs, I declared my revelation.

"If this is heaven, Lou, it doesn't look anything like I expected."

"Maybe you didn't go to heaven, Cy. Remember, you went down, not up."

I didn't feel like forcing a grin. My friend wouldn't be able to see it if I had.

"It's not hot enough to be the other place."

Lou shined the light down the steps and gingerly walked down to where I was lying at the bottom.

"Are you okay, Cy?"

"I think you already asked that Lou, or is it that my throbbing head makes me think you did. I've had better days, but I don't think I broke anything. Good thing I ate all that bacon."

"Since you're not in any position to see anything, Cy, let me fill you in. All we've found is a bunch of steps that lead down to a wall at the bottom."

"Maybe the other button moves the wall out of the way, Lou. Why don't you give it a try, but before you do, help me to my feet. I'm going up there and I'm not leaning against anything until you get through pushing those buttons. I've already had one trip too many today."

Lou moved my feet to one side and plopped down on the steps just above my feet. He tried to find the easiest way to help me sit up. There was no easy way. What made it harder was that he'd have to do all the helping. Every part of my body ached. I wasn't in any position to get up by myself. My feet were well above my head. Lou tried two or three maneuvers that didn't work.

As the two of us struggled to help me to a sitting position, Laurel and Hardy couldn't have been more proud of us than if the classic comedy duo had planned this charade. Because nothing else worked, Lou stood up and made his way down the remaining steps. He hoped to move me somewhat. I'd already been moved too much. He struggled to get between me and the bottom wall and push me to a sitting position.

"I'm already in pain, Lou. You don't have to make it any worse."

"Sorry, Cy. Maybe you should grip one of the steps and pull yourself up."

"Maybe you should build and attach a handrail and I can get up that way. By the way, are we allowed to sue a dead person?"

"I'm not sure. I don't think Mrs. Nelson would contest it in court."

After nothing else worked, Lou braced himself against my back. He leaned over and maneuvered my legs so that eventually they would be against the other wall. He hoped it would help me to sit up. The pain of each slight movement assured me that I still wasn't paralyzed. After many trials and almost as many errors, the two of us managed to get me into a sitting position.

I sat there for a few minutes. Each pain caused me to dream of retirement. Then, I realized that I would be home more if I retired. This meant that I would be in much closer proximity to Heloise Humphert. That thought alone was enough to get me to my feet.

Lou and I slowly climbed to the top of the once hidden flight of stairs and stepped out into the kitchen where the light was sufficient for us to see. I climbed more gingerly than he, although both of us had taken a tumble.

Once there, we tried to rid ourselves of the invisible cobwebs, as well as those that covered our bodies. Each of us looked at the other, and we began to laugh.

"In what round did you get knocked out, Cy?"

"Well, you should look at yourself. Your hand is bleeding, you've got a scratch on your face, and I think that eye's going to be changing colors on you."

Both of us wanted to see which of us looked worse, but neither of us felt like walking to a mirror to find out. After we sat for a few minutes, I grimaced as I rose to my feet.

"I know that button isn't going anywhere, Lou, but what say you go press that other button and see what happens."

Lou went over, lowered his body to the bottom step. Carefully, he reached over and pushed the button on the left while I shined my flashlight down the steps.

"That did it, Lou! The wall slid away and there's a door behind it. Push it one more time and see what happens."

Lou pushed the button a second time and the wall slid back into place, once again covering the door. When I let him know what happened, Lou hit the button a third time. The sergeant stood up, gazed down the steps.

"As far as I can tell, there's a sliding bolt just like on the front door. Is that the way it looks to you, Cy?"

"Yeah, only to me it looks like at least two doors and two bolts."

"Well, Cy, are you up to going down and seeing what we can find, or should we call in someone else?"

"It's our discovery, Lou. What say you and I tackle it?"

"I'm game if you are. Carry on, my good friend."

I crept down the stairs at a much slower pace than the time before. There was no railing. I braced my left hand against the rock wall, held the flashlight in my right, and carefully walked down the steps. As if it mattered at that point, I tried my best to make sure I didn't scrape my hand against the harsh surface. The narrow stairway didn't permit two men to walk down the steps side-by-side. Especially, Lou and me. So, Lou lingered a couple of steps behind me.

The steps went almost all the way to the door. That meant that the door opened out since there wasn't enough room for it to open into the passageway. I noticed a sliding bolt, but it was unlocked. I reached for the doorknob with my left hand.

"Ready?" I asked my friend.

Lou nodded.

21

I slowly turned the doorknob, cautiously opened the door. As I did, my nose detected musty dampness, as well as the smell of dirt. I shined my flashlight through the opening and discovered another flight of steps that led down to a dirt floor. From what I could tell, we had finally reached the tunnel, the cavernous open spaces below Hilltop Place.

I nodded to Lou, eased down the first step. I'd gotten to the second step when I heard a loud and piercing scream. The scream so unnerved me that not only did I drop my flashlight, but I slid feet first down another flight of steps. Once again, my back scraped against the edge of each step, and I landed with a thud on the dirt floor. The only difference was this time I went down feet first. Flying dust caused me to sneeze, but that was the least of my problems. Because I landed in a sitting position instead of face down, I scrambled to my feet and tried to find the flashlight that went dark when I dropped it.

Another shriek interrupted my quest. I abandoned my search for the flashlight and climbed the steps as quickly as I could. I almost made it. I was most of the way up the steps when I felt the attacker lash out and grab my ankle. I screamed, then cried out frantically. "Something's got me, Lou!"

Lou came down a step or two and pulled on my arm. He struggled against the force that pulled me downward. I began to resemble salt-water taffy without any elasticity, or the center of a tug-of-war with much greater consequences for the object in the middle. The only source of light came from the kitchen one flight up or a missing flashlight somewhere most of a flight below. I couldn't tell whether my enemy was a man or a beast. The scream didn't resemble either.

Lou tried to wrap his arms around my chest. That didn't work, so he tried to pull me up by both arms. Even though it wasn't working, he held on with both hands in order to stay even with our enemy. Lou dared not risk letting go with one hand in order to remove his flashlight from his pocket. Frantically, I tried everything I could to dislodge myself from my attacker. I kicked and tried to free myself, but whoever or whatever it was had a mighty grip. Lou continued to pull. He knew the two of us might be fighting for our lives.

Finally, I fell forward and landed on Lou. At the same time, my assailant fell back down the steps clutching one of my shoes. My unexpected lunge knocked Lou back against the steps. He hollered in pain as his back hit against the sharp edge of the step. Lou tried to push me off him without pushing me back down the steps. We needed to stand up, pull our legs inside, so we could get up and shut the door. Lou finally succeeded in wiggling out from under me. The sergeant stood up and groped in the dark until he found the door. As he started to slam it, he heard something or someone rushing up the steps, just as I struggled to my feet.

"Quick, Cy, I'll hold the door."

I fumbled until I found the bolt. Just as I located it and tried to slide it, the door lunged open, and we braced ourselves to keep from tumbling down the steps, and landing on our assailant. If that had happened, I doubt if our adversary would've caused any more problems. Lou looked like he was about to lose his footing, so I forgot about the bolt and grabbed for my friend in order to keep him from falling. Luckily, I grasped my friend's belt and held on to him. The force of the opening door banged against our assailant and we heard someone or something tumble down the steps and land with a thud. Once again, we hurried to secure the door. This time we were both on our feet and our assailant was probably on its or his back. We had an advantage.

We locked the door, tested it, and breathed a sigh of relief. But it was a short sigh. A few seconds later we heard footsteps, huffing and puffing, and the rattling of the door. The big bad wolf had returned. I reached out, pulled the doorknob with all the strength I had left. Whoever or whatever was on the other side of the door didn't give up easily. The struggle for supremacy continued. I remember that sometimes there's strength in numbers.

"Quick, Lou. Run upstairs and call headquarters. Get us some back-up. I'll try to hold on here until you get back," I uttered, breathing heavily.

Lou wasted no time with a rebuttal.

I held on each time our assailant rattled the door. Each time I managed to get some leverage, my sock foot slid across the floor. In a couple of minutes, Lou returned.

"They're on their way. Is it still there?" Lou asked in a voice that showed he was as much out of breath as I was.

I turned to reply while I kept my hand on the doorknob.

"I'm not sure. There hasn't been anything for about a minute. Look and see if you can find a button that will open and shut the wall."

"There's not enough light. In all the excitement, I left my flashlight in the kitchen. Wait for a second while I get it."

"I'm not going anywhere. At least I hope I'm not going anywhere."

Lou climbed the steps, breathing laboriously. When he got to the top, he paused for a moment, put both hands on his thighs, and rested. He could rest only a moment because neither of us knew the identity of whoever or whatever hovered on the other side of the lower door. Would that man or beast beat or claw his or its way through the door before reinforcements arrived? Lou hurried to pick up his flashlight, sat down on the next-to-the-top step, turned around, and shined his light under the top step.

"Yeah, there are some buttons here, Cy."

"Okay, I'm going to chance it, Lou. Maybe whatever it is won't come up where there's light."

I trudged up the steps, sidestepped Lou, stepped through the open pantry wall, and fell into a chair in the kitchen. As I groaned, Lou leaned over and pushed the button that slid the lower wall back into place. Not taking any chances, he stepped through and closed the pantry wall, too. Both of us were exhausted. The two of us went to the living room, plopped down in well-padded chairs while we waited for reinforcements.

+++

A few minutes later Lou and I heard sirens.

"Here come the Marines."

Several men came running up the steps. One of those men was Lt. George Michaelson, a good friend and long-time member of the force.

"What happened to you two? Have a falling out?" George exclaimed as he walked into the room and wondered if he had happened upon the aftermath of the main event or the preliminary bout.

"You should see the other guy," I replied. Actually, I had no interest in any of us seeing the other guy.

"You mean you called in this many back-ups for just one other guy?"

"There's only one that we know of, but we're not sure if it's human or not."

"Could be both. Maybe you ran into a werewolf or a vampire."

"Could be."

"So where is our mysterious beast?" George asked.

"Under the house as far as we know."

"So the house fell on the wicked witch, huh?"

"More like a wicked warlock, I'd say," I answered.

"Well, do you want us to take over from here?"

"I guess we'd better lead. You don't know the way."

An incredulous look appeared on George's face.

"You mean we don't go down to get under the house?"

"We do, but in all the excitement we forgot to mark the path."

George looked down at my feet.

"What happened, Cy? Find a shoe?"

"No, but someone did."

George laughed and wondered what predicament we had gotten ourselves into.

Lou lifted himself from the chair, walked hesitantly to the pantry. The rest of us followed him. It was George's first trip to the house. He looked surprised when Lou turned the lid on the olives and the wall slid away.

"Whoa! This is some set-up you've got here, Cy. I see what you mean about not marking the path."

Lou bent over, reached under the step, and hit the button that opened the wall. I watched George as Lou pushed the button. Each new button impressed George a little more.

"Say, how much are you paying for this place, anyway. I might want to sublet."

"We've got one more for you before we get to the big surprise, George."

All doubt had left George's face. He was ready to believe anything we told him. Well, maybe not everything.

Lou pushed the other button and the panel at the bottom of the steps slid away, revealing the door. I noticed that no one pulled on the other side. Lou and I led the men down the stairs. We grimaced in pain with each step. With no railing to lean on to help us in our descent, both of us felt the brunt of the pain with each downward step. Also, with each step, we grew closer to another possible encounter with the man or beast on the other side of the door.

"Be ready. He or it might be just on the other side."

"Yeah, yeah, okay. Just open the door, Cy, and spare me the histrionics," George said, quickly forgetting that everything I'd told him to that point had turned out to be true.

Lou reached for the bolt, slid it until the door was unlocked. He waited a moment to see if anyone charged us. When no one opened the door, he pushed it slightly open.

"Here! Get out of the way! I'll lead the way," George said.

22

George opened the door the rest of the way, beamed his flashlight in front of him, cut through the darkness, and focused on the steps and the expansive area below.

"What kind of place do you have here, anyway? And where's your monster?" he asked as he turned to face me.

There was no sign of life below. Lou and I exchanged perplexed glances. Had we scared our assailant away?

George led the officers down the steps and almost tripped over the shoe the maniac ripped from my foot. George recognized it, turned and flipped it to me. I took a chance, sat down on the step, and slipped my shoe back on.

When George got to the bottom, he shined his flashlight from side to side. Nothing. Nothing but a dirt floor and concrete walls. There appeared to be no end to the expansive underground. I guessed the area to be thirty feet wide and who knows how long. The group spread out and each of us flashed our lights back and forth. Finally, one man called out.

"I've got something over here!"

Everyone hurried to the officer who had shouted. Our lights joined his as we focused on a man, kneeling and whimpering. His clothes were filthy. His hair was matted with dirt, and he had not shaved in some time.

"Is this your monster?" George turned and asked Lou and me. We didn't know, but we assumed he was.

George stood around six feet three inches tall. Although gray was beginning to mix with his flaxen-color hair, his muscular body still looked capable of landing a punch, and his granite-looking jaw looked like it could still take one. Especially if he knew one was coming. Before George could turn around, the kneeling man sprang toward him with the quickness of a cat. Unprepared, George fell back onto the dirt. By the time any of us could respond, the man who appeared to live underground rose up and took off running in the dark. As far as anyone could tell, the man had no weapon other than his hands. Everyone tried to keep him in sight. We shined our flashlights on the disappearing man as we took off in pursuit. Naturally, neither Lou nor I was in the lead.

After two hundred feet or so, a wall signaled the end of the straightaway, but the dirt roadway took a hard turn to the right. The man vanished around a corner, a bevy of bluecoats bore down from behind. The hounds stalked the fox with no tree in sight. As I arrived at the first turn, I prayed that our path was not circular. I envisioned lemmings following one another in an orderly fashion for days on end with no cliffs to jump off, no place to drown, and all the dirt looking the same as the dirt before it.

As the first of the uniformed officers arrived at the end of the underground passage and turned right, he caught a glimpse of the disheveled man disappearing around another bend. Several of Hilldale's finest scrambled after him but arrived at the second curve to find no one there.

"Where did he go?" one of the men asked, surprised that the man they thought they had contained had disappeared into the darkness. When the rest of us caught up, everyone gathered in a circle and faced outward. We shined our flashlights in every direction, but only flying dust penetrated our lighted path. We saw no sign of our fugitive.

George shouted instructions to the others.

"Be careful, men. He could be hiding anywhere."

Actually, there weren't too many places the man could hide. While the dirt floor was around thirty feet wide, the only place our fleeing trespasser could hide was underneath some steps, unless he gained entrance to one of the houses.

"Unless he can get inside one of these houses, we've got him trapped. Let's spread out. If you find him, holler. Check under the steps first. If we don't find him hiding under someone's steps, we'll start trying the doors. Okay, let's go! I don't think he's armed, but I don't want anyone trying to be a hero. Understand?"

Lou and I formed the rear guard. The uniformed officers examined the path before them and realized that the dirt road dead-ended after a few hundred feet. I guessed that it probably ran the length of the street. While there was a connector on the end we came from, there was nothing to connect the underground of the two sides at the head of the street. A couple of officers remained at the bottom of the U portion of the underground, as did Lou and I. We were prepared in case the man we were chasing tried to double back. The others crept forward until they had canvassed the entire area. George remained halfway between us and his advancing men. A thorough search revealed nothing.

"Okay, men. It's time to check some doors. Start at the far end of the street. If your door's locked, start working back this way."

After several efforts revealed only locked doors, a uniformed officer tiptoed up the underground steps of Stanley Silverman's house. He twisted the doorknob. It opened. I watched him turn and whisper to the nearest officer. As the officer opened the door, no one lunged toward him. The policeman stepped inside, flashed his light up the steps.

"Hold it right there," I heard him say. Then, the officer opened the door behind him and shouted, "I've found him." Other policemen ran to the aid of the officer who had shouted.

I heard someone run down the steps toward the officer, and then the sound stopped. Evidently, the man had lunged toward the officer, because in a couple of seconds the two men flew out the door. The officer clutched the man and managed to hold on. The two falling men knocked down two other officers, as men went flying in a domino effect.

More officers ran up to the foray. Finally, they subdued the assailant. One officer handcuffed the man's hands behind his back. The man's shriek echoed the outburst of an hour or so earlier. It took three officers to get the man to his feet. Once they had him standing, I tried to question him.

"Who are you?"

The man said nothing. Further questions proved futile. A search of his person revealed nothing. He carried no weapon. Nor did he have any identification.

George told a couple of the men to take the unidentified man away.

+++

I stood and looked up the underground steps to Stanley Silverman's residence. I couldn't believe that Silverman hadn't heard the man trying to force his way inside. Was Silverman afraid of this man? Or could it be that Silverman knew the police were pursuing this fugitive, and he,

Stanley Silverman, had something to hide from the police? Was the man we arrested the one who looked out through Miss Penrod's blinds? Is it possible he could be the man in the raincoat, provided there actually was such a person?

My thoughts returned to the matter which brought us to this dilemma. Someone murdered Mrs. Nelson. Was it the psychotic man we'd just caught? Silverman? Or someone else?

George put his arm around my shoulder as we walked back to where we found the underground psycho. George patted me a few times, then smiled at me. I knew George Michaelson well enough to know that he was about to make a wisecrack.

"You know, Cy. You look as if you could use a shower."

"Well, George, you don't look like you're ready for an inspection yourself."

Both of us pointed at each other, slapped each other on the back and bent over in laughter. I winced as George slapped me across the back and gritted my teeth when I attempted to stand up straight. Luckily, George didn't notice. After we took a moment to realize what had happened, we walked back through the dusty underground to where we apprehended the deranged man. Then we retraced our steps and walked across the bottom of the U until we came to the curve where we'd first encountered the man whom we'd taken into custody. We stood in the underground below Mrs. Overstreet's house trying to figure out who the deranged man was. Who was he, and how did he get here? Was he crazy, or was he putting on an act? And if he was suffering from mental problems, were his demons, like Jimmy Reynolds's problems, caused by the war?

Our group studied the area to see what we could learn about our captive. My guess was our "friend" had resided in the dungeon for several weeks.

A search of the immediate area turned up a flashlight with dead batteries, a few cans of food, and drink containers. Nothing else was found, including a weapon, but then Mrs. Nelson was poisoned, not shot.

"Well, let's check out this side and see if we can find out who this guy is and where he came from."

Lou, George, and I talked as we walked until our flashlights illuminated something that silenced us.

23

Stunned, but not totally surprised, we hurried toward the body of a woman who rested against the back of her wheelchair.

"Any idea who she is?" George asked.

"I have a pretty good idea," I answered. "A woman by the name of Mabel Jarvis lived here," I said as I pointed to the steps beside us. "Neighbors told us that she was confined to a wheelchair. When she repeatedly didn't answer the door, we forced our way into her house. When we got inside, we searched her house. In the basement, we found tracks in the dust that looked like they had been made by a wheelchair. We found footprints that looked like they belonged to the person who pushed the chair, but we couldn't find Mrs. Jarvis. We discovered a secret passageway in Mrs. Jarvis's house much like the one in Mrs. Nelson's house, but it ended in a dead-end. Obviously, she's dead. Let's go up and call Frank and the lab boys and see what we can find out about her death. Just to be on the safe side, we'd better go up through Mrs. Nelson's house. We don't want to disturb any evidence, even though I doubt there's any to find."

+++

I sat, wondering what would happen next. Was the man we found the person who pushed Mrs. Jarvis's wheelchair? If so, was he the one who murdered her, and did he murder Mrs. Nelson, too?

I sat in a chair in Mrs. Nelson's house and wondered what would happen next. Lou and George appeared to have the same look. George had dismissed the other officers, knowing that Frank would handle things when he arrived.

"Any reason I need to hang around, Cy?"

"I don't see any reason, George. Frank and the SOC team will be here in a few minutes. Anyway, I can call you if I need you."

"Well, good luck. I think I'll go home and get cleaned up. You'd better do the same the first chance you get."

"You may merely be cleaning up, but I think Lou and I need to get over our aches and pains. Thanks, George. See you later."

George walked out the door and down the steps. Halfway down he met Frank Harris on his way up. Frank noticed his friend's dirty, rumpled clothes and his hair full of dirt.

George looked at the medical examiner and answered his friend's unasked question.

"Hi, Frank. Cy will fill you in. He's in the living room."

Frank Harris continued up the steps, smiling and shaking his head. He walked into the house, saw Lou and me.

"What's with you guys, anyway? Does the department have you handling domestic violence cases now, or did you have to evict someone who didn't want to go? And what's with George? He looks like he's been mud wrestling, only someone forgot to fill the pit with water. I'm glad I come in after the killing's over. Your side of things looks too dangerous to suit me."

I motioned for Frank to take a seat and filled in my friend on the latest of the day's events.

"How many bodies are you going to have for me, Cy? I do have other work, you know."

"No one hopes this is the last one any more than I do, Frank."

"I understand this one's another elderly woman. Does someone have something against little old ladies collecting social security for a few years?"

"That's what we're trying to find out."

"Well, let's take a look."

Lou and I groaned as we got up out of our chairs and lumbered toward the stairs once again. While we eased down through the Nelson place, another team checked out Mabel Jarvis's house. The only new information gained from going through the Jarvis house was that the secret passageway that led to the underground cavern went through a side wall in the basement instead of through the pantry and down, as in Mrs. Nelson's house. They discovered no new prints.

+++

After a thorough examination of the body, Frank had the deceased removed. Before Frank left, he told me he would let me know what they found out. I saw no reason to hang around the Nelson house any longer. Lou and I locked up and left.

+++

I called in to see if the department had any information on the man we apprehended. Investigators were trying to match fingerprints or see if they could identify him through dental records. When I asked if they had been able to pry any information out of our attacker, I was told that most of what came out of the man's mouth were guttural sounds and occasional screams, but that he kept uttering one phrase repeatedly, only no one had any idea what it meant. The man kept hollering something about a raincoat.

+++

To ease my pain, I asked Lou for another book report. It was fitting that he enlightened me about his attempt to read *The Catcher in the Rye* on the same night our pains were so severe. Because he was a Christian who tried to follow the Bible's examples on how to live, Lou didn't care for Holden Caulfield's use of profanity. The profanity didn't go away after a few chapters, and Lou found nothing likable about Holden Caulfield, so he tossed the book aside and contemplated his next selection. The sergeant did not condemn Caulfield because he used profanity. The sergeant figured that if he himself had to live part of the time in New York City and spend the rest of the time in a boarding school for boys, he might have grown up swearing, too. It made Lou wonder which was worse, New York or boarding school. He figured boarding school was worse.

+++

I dropped Lou at his apartment, then headed home. All the way home I tried to make sense of the information we'd gained. Did the same person murder both women, and if so, was there a single murderer or were two people working together?

I thought back to Saturday. On Saturday, we knew of only one murder and no underground labyrinth. On Saturday, Mrs. Wilkins seemed to have an alibi for everyone. At least she kept her eyes on Angela Nelson from the time she arrived until the time Officer Davis arrived, and she cast her eyes upon Mr. Silverman and Mrs. Reynolds and Jimmy most of the time. If Mrs. Wilkins was a credible witness, and other witnesses corroborated most of her story and didn't contradict any of it, the murderer or murderers must either be Miss Penrod or someone who entered the Nelson house from below. But who could it have been? Was it possible that there was someone I had not yet learned about?

I headed for the kitchen table, picked up a legal pad, and tried to make sense of the situation. I listed evidence and suspects: Angela Nelson, the granddaughter; Mrs. Murphy, Mrs. Nelson's and Mrs. Jarvis's maid; Irene Penrod, the next-door neighbor; Stanley Silverman, the observant neighbor across the street; Mrs. Reynolds and her son Jimmy, neighbors two doors down the street; Bobby, the grocery boy; Harry Hornwell, Mrs. Nelson's attorney; Mr. Hartley, the mailman; and the mysterious man found in the cavern-like area under the house. Of course, there were Mrs. Wilkins, Mrs. Overstreet, and other neighbors across the street, but for some reason, I had never considered any of them. Did one of these people murder one or both women? Or was it a stranger or someone we were overlooking? I couldn't see any of these people as a murderer. Unlikable, yes. Lonely, most definitely. But a murderer, no. And yet, surely one of them killed Mrs. Nelson, and probably Mrs. Jarvis. Because he or she used poison, the murder was probably premeditated. Did the fact that Harry Hornwell bought a couple of houses on the street have anything to do with the murders? What about the Reynolds's tempers? I thought of Stanley Silverman inheriting all of his mother's money, and saw how that might have caused him to murder his own mother, but not two neighbor ladies. Unless they had found out that he arranged his mother's demise.

After seemingly getting nowhere, I tossed the pad in disgust, headed for the TV. I was about to consult one of the greatest minds in finding solutions for the seemingly unsolvable, Jethro Bodine, otherwise known as Jed Clampett's nephew. In addition to being the world's number one expert on ciphering, that boy can eat, and he eats my kind of stuff. But I don't eat all of his. The easiest way to describe someone that eats my kind of stuff is to ask the question, "Does the boy know the meaning of the word 'culinary?'" If he does, I doubt if he eats my kind of stuff.

Lou had given me two DVDs, each with five episodes of *The Beverly Hillbillies*. I watched the first two episodes on one DVD, then fast-forwarded to the last one, which turned out to be my favorite. The Clampetts had recently moved to Beverly Hills, and it was time for Jethro to enroll in school. Jed sets out with Jethro in tow, eager to enter his nephew in the fifth grade.

+++

Lou told me he had decided to put the case aside until the next day. He planned to do some solving, but his plans were to pick up where he had left off in his crossword puzzle book. It had been a few days since he'd worked on it, and he was anxious to get back to it. He told me that he had gone through the across clues once before going to bed the other night, but had left off before tackling the down column. He was in the middle of a three-star puzzle, which meant the puzzle wasn't particularly easy or difficult. I'd seen Lou work many a puzzle on one of our slow days, so I knew he was seasoned enough that he could usually fill in each box on a medium puzzle by at least the third trip through the clues. Because of the unpredictable nature of our schedules, Lou had no idea when he'd get another chance to work a crossword puzzle. He told me he planned to spend at least a couple of hours working his way through the book.

I took a break from watching *The Beverly Hillbillies*. I'd had my fill of the negative aspects of underground life, I needed a few laughs from a different type of underground lifestyle. It was time to watch *Hogan's Heroes*. Who knows? Maybe I would find a clue that would help me solve the case.

Four episodes later, I had mixed emotions. I still had no idea who committed the murders on Hilltop Place, but I laughed repeatedly as Col. Hogan bested Col. Klink and Sgt. Schultz. As I watched the first episode of *Hogan's Heroes* first season, I noted that the underground beneath Hilltop Place is much larger than the one under Stalag 13, but that the Stalag 13 underground included more of the comforts of home. I had no idea how I felt about this, but I felt inferior as it took Col. Hogan only one episode to discover the identity of his nemesis, and I hadn't solved my murders, even though I had been at my task for almost a week.

I suspected the next day would be another busy day, so I called it a night. I changed into my pajamas, took one more trip to the kitchen table to see where I'd tossed the legal pad, looked it over again, and hoped that I would solve the murders in my sleep.

24

I woke up Wednesday morning and made a mental note to check on the prices of hot tubs, just in case my aches and pains continued. I turned over gingerly and looked at the clock. It was late enough, so I called Frank Harris to see what he could tell me about Mrs. Jarvis's murder.

"Good morning, Frank. Do you have any information for me yet?"

"Oh, did you finally get up, Cy? I've already put in half a day's work."

"It's only 8:30, Frank. So, Mr. Time-And-A-Half, what do you have for me?"

"Mabel Jarvis was poisoned, codeine, just like Mrs. Nelson."

"Anything different from Mrs. Nelson?"

"Well, no one gave her a sedative first. But, as you know, we didn't find her until a few days after she died, so the best I can pinpoint the time of her death is to say that it was probably sometime Friday, Saturday, or Sunday. My best guess is Saturday, but it could have been Friday or Sunday."

"I think someone's trying to play games with us, Frank. They leave enough clues to keep us interested, but manage to stay a step ahead of us."

"Well, Cy, let's hope they stop to rest before we do."

"Let's hope so, Frank. Well, I'll let you go. I'm going to call Muriel and see what I can find out about that man we found."

+++

Dr. Muriel Davenport was a police psychiatrist. I'd worked with her a few times and knew her to be thorough and competent.

"Hello, Muriel. This is Cy Dekker. Do you have any information for me regarding the man who was brought in yesterday?"

"Oh, hi, Cy. Well, we now have an ID on our mysterious man. His name is Don Hampton. A couple of years ago Mr. Hampton unexpectedly lost his wife and his mother within two weeks of each other. Their deaths were more than he could handle. He gave up. He's been pretty much of a street person ever since."

"Anything unusual about their deaths?"

"No, his wife died in a car accident. There were witnesses and Mr. Hampton was not in the vehicle. Investigators ruled that no one tampered with the car. His mother died of a heart attack. Nothing suspicious about her death, either."

"Has he ever been in trouble with the law?"

"A couple of times. Once he got arrested for public intoxication. Another time he lashed out at a woman in a bar. Both times were after his wife and mother died."

"Muriel, do you think he was capable of administering poison to two little old ladies?"

"It's hard to say, Cy. I think he'd be more likely to push a little old lady down the steps. What profile I have doesn't characterize him as someone who would poison their drinks."

"What about his current frame of mind?"

"Let me see if the information I have is right. Was he found in a dark dungeon-like place? And had he been there for a few weeks?"

"The answer to the first question is 'yes,' and the answer to the second question is 'I think so, but I'm not sure.'"

"It's hard to tell in these cases, but my guess is that when he first got there he was distraught but coherent. I think when you add to his history spending a few days in the dark with no visible means of escape, it caused him to worsen until he arrived at his current state."

"I assume you don't think he's faking his condition."

"No, Cy, I don't. I have no idea how he came to be there, but I feel pretty certain that he's not faking."

"Do you think he might have witnessed either murder? We found one of the victims in the same cave-like area where we found him."

"I have no idea, Cy, and I have no idea if we'll ever know."

"Are you saying you don't think he'll recover?"

"It's hard to say. He could. He might not."

"If he does, will he remember what happened on Saturday?"

"That's hard to say, too."

"Thanks, Muriel. Let me know if you come up with anything else."

+++

161

It was time for me to check in with Sam Schumann. I dialed his number, and my friend, expecting the call, picked up on the first ring. It didn't take him long to tell me what he had found out. Supposedly, Harry Hornwell worked long hours, but then Harry Hornwell saw no reason to hurry home each night. Mrs. Hornwell was an invalid. She wasn't expected to die soon, but all she could do was lie in bed hour after hour. She spent her time talking on the phone and reading two or three books each week. Her husband remembered the woman she used to be. No one entertained quite like Catherine Hornwell, but then Catherine Hornwell could no longer entertain. As Sam relayed this information to me, I wondered if anyone entertained Harry Hornwell.

"Oh, I checked on Hornwell's whereabouts. His alibi checks out. I called his wife and she informed me that her husband left for the cabin Friday afternoon and didn't return until Sunday night. She said he phoned her just after he arrived on Friday afternoon and again Sunday afternoon before he returned. In addition, she called him once on Saturday. Then, I asked her where the cabin was located. She knew, even though she's never been there.

"I called the county boys up north and had them check up on the cabin for me. Somebody was definitely there over the weekend. They were sure because they had lots of rain on Thursday. There's mud everywhere. They had a lot more rain than we did. There were tire tracks at the cabin, and one set of a man's footprints leading to and from the cabin. Oh, the guy laughed when he called me back. He said, 'That cabin is bigger than my house.' Also, he checked the country store near the cabin. The guy knows Hornwell and he said Hornwell stopped in late Friday afternoon and again on Sunday afternoon. The first time he bought some snacks, and Sunday he bought some gas, a soft drink, and a candy bar. He was definitely there over the weekend."

"How far is this place from here, Sam?"

"It's a good two hours, Cy."

After Sam told me what he had learned about Hornwell, he moved on to Fred Hartley. According to sources, Hartley wasn't the contented mailman he pretended to be. It bothered Hartley that most of his customers had far more money than he did. Some even laughed at him when he bought a metal detector. Hartley didn't think they would laugh at him much longer. He planned to have the last laugh, no matter what it took to get it. Sam had no idea what that meant.

I asked, but Sam didn't have any information about Mrs. Nelson's will. He planned to check some more. I had hoped to find a motive for more of our suspects. While I did get some, it seemed like I was getting more alibis than anything.

+++

After I hung up from talking to Sam, I phoned Lou to fill him in on what I'd learned from my phone calls. I found out that Lou's revelation for the day was "Morton salt." Having no idea what that meant, I told the sergeant that I'd be by to pick him up after I showered and dressed. While I showered, I tried to figure out what "Morton salt" had to do with the case we were working on. Could we be going back down into the salt mines below Hilltop Place? Did God consider Sgt. Murdock and me to be the salt of the earth?

The soothing water of the shower made me think of another option. "Morton salt. When it rains it pours." Was it going to rain? Was I going to drown in the shower? I shuddered, stepped out of the shower quickly to eliminate the last option, got dressed, and left to pick up Lou. Later, I felt better, because I'd failed to realize how much water it would take to drown me.

+++

It was time for another book report, which would be the last because Lou had only so much time between murders. It turned out to be a partial report. Sometimes murders interrupt even the best that classic literature has to offer. This time Lou wanted to get as far away from profanity and New York as he could, so he decided on a change of pace for his fourth selection. He selected *Wuthering Heights*. I laughed when Lou told me he had begun to read it, but I agreed with his reasoning. After all, it was written by a woman who lived a long time ago, possibly even before cursing became commonplace. At least it was before women wanted to be just like men, and women did not spit out profanities in those days. Emily Brontë was British. Lou decided that she wouldn't write about New York City, so he made up his mind to give the book a try and see if he could recommend it to someone at church. Because it was written by a woman and he had committed to reading it, Lou hoped that it wouldn't have any romance. If so, he wouldn't want it to get back to anyone else on the force that he had read it. Lou knew some of my secrets. He knew I would keep his.

Before Lou could tell me more about the book, we arrived at our destination. The book might be a good one, but no book is good enough to keep me from what I needed to do. I would find out more about the book later. Besides, Lou hadn't even finished the book. He had read only a little when duty called.

+++

I had driven to Hilltop Place to see if we could learn anything new. I maneuvered the car into the driveway of the Nelson house, and we pulled ourselves from the car. The car's name is Lightning, but that description would never define the speed with which Lou and I emerged from the car that day.

I looked at the climb that had become much too familiar. It looked like someone had added a couple of new steps to 125 Hilltop Place while we were away. Why had God allowed someone to build these towers of Babel so high?

Lou and I trudged up the steps. Every few steps, we stopped to admire the view. Heavy breathing accompanied each stop. Double heavy breathing. I expected someday we would solve this case. When that happened, I planned to take a vacation somewhere where the land was flat. I wanted to go somewhere where a speed bump would be considered a "scenic overlook."

Lou and I arrived at the front door sometime before sunset. I removed the key and inserted it into the lock. I turned the key and pushed on the door. The door didn't budge. Someone had been there since we had and had secured the second lock. I pounded my fist into my open hand. While I often had thoughts of doing worse things, pounding my fist was usually as violent as I got. I was tired of someone playing games with us. After all, we were the police, so we should have been the ones to make the rules.

I thought of alternative action.

"Lou, let's forget about this place for a while. It's only a little over an hour until Mrs. Nelson's funeral. What say we go to her funeral and then we'll go back to your place and go over what we've learned so far. Then, let's take a break, rest awhile, and come back tonight and hope Captain Midnight the trickster is once again on the prowl."

25

Lou and I arrived at Mrs. Nelson's funeral. Most mourners came disguised as empty pews. The sparse crowd didn't surprise us. We didn't recognize anyone but the grieving granddaughter. No one who lived on Hilltop Place had come to the funeral. Angela Nelson said that her grandmother had no other relatives, so Lou and I figured that most of the mourners were friends of Angela Nelson, except for a handful of elderly women.

Nothing unusual happened at the funeral. The pastor delivered the usual message spoken at a funeral and added some personal thoughts. From the way he spoke, my guess is that he knew the victim personally and didn't have to make up any of the good things he said about her.

The funeral ended, and we left for my place. We got as comfortable as two hefty men can get at a dining room table and began to work. Lou sat at one end. I sat at the other. Our scattered papers covered most of the surface, but both of us knew what was where and we could find what we wanted. After looking over our notes to see the progress we'd made, we began to talk it out and see if we could make some sense out of what we had.

"Okay, Lou. Let's look at what we have so far. Let's start with Mrs. Nelson's murder. According to Frank, she died sometime Saturday morning. According to Mr. Silverman, at least three people visited the house Saturday morning; Miss Penrod, Mr. Hartley, and her granddaughter Angela.

"We checked with the cab company. A driver picked up a fare at 121 Hilltop Place at 10:14. That would be Miss Penrod leaving. Another driver dropped off a fare at 125 Hilltop Place at 10:20. That would be Miss Nelson arriving. Officer Davis arrived on the scene at 10:33. We checked with the airlines. Miss Nelson's plane landed at 9:17. The driver confirmed that the fare he dropped off at 10:20 was the one he picked up at the airport at 9:52. After dropping her off on Hilltop Place, the taxi driver used the key she gave him, delivered Miss Nelson's luggage to her home, and left her key on top of the luggage. See anything that stands out, Lou?"

"I'd say it's more like everything checks out. What time did we arrive?"

"We received a call a little after 11:00 and arrived on the scene around 11:20. Let's take a look at Mrs. Jarvis. From what we know, Mrs. Jarvis was murdered either Friday, Saturday, or Sunday, so she could have been murdered before or after Mrs. Nelson. That means that the murderer could have gained entrance to Mrs. Jarvis's house, murdered her, and moved underground to Mrs. Nelson's house. Or the murderer could have murdered Mrs. Nelson first, gone underground and come out through Mrs. Jarvis' house, where he or she murdered her in the process. The murderer was either admitted by the victim, meaning that the victim knew the murderer, the murderer could have gained access to the house with a key, which may or may not have been supplied by the victim, or the murderer could have been someone who lived on the street who didn't need a key because he or she could have entered either of the victims' houses by sneaking up through the secret passageway. Does anything strike you, Lou?"

"Only that we haven't ruled out the possibility of two murderers, each committing one murder."

"You're always trying to complicate my life, aren't you, Lou?"

"Sorry, don't ask next time."

"Sherlock Holmes always asked Dr. Watson, and I'll always ask you. Anyway, let's get back to our murders. Let's take our suspects one at a time and see what we know about them and whether or not we can come up with a motive for murder. Let's start with Miss Penrod. Miss Penrod could have murdered Mrs. Jarvis before going to Mrs. Nelson's house. Then, she could have waited until Mr. Hartley left, murdered Mrs. Nelson, and sneaked underground back to her own home. That could be why Mr. Silverman didn't see her leave. Then, she conveniently exited a few minutes later and took a taxi on a prearranged trip. The only problem is 'what's her motive?'"

"Well, there is one other problem, Cy."

"What's that, Lou?"

"She wouldn't have had time to drug Mrs. Nelson, wait long enough to murder her and leave when she did. Have we located Miss Penrod?"

"No, that's another thing, Lou. The taxi driver said he dropped off Miss Penrod at the bus station, but then Miss Penrod seems to have disappeared."

"Disappeared?"

"Few buses left Hilldale that morning, and no one matching Miss Penrod's description left on a bus bound for anywhere."

"Maybe Miss Penrod meant to disappear, Cy."

"Maybe she sneaked back home and is hiding inside her house."

"The only problem is, how did she get inside her house with no one seeing her? As far as we know, there are no connecting tunnels from adjacent streets, and someone was on the lookout on Hilltop Place all day."

"Strike one. Let's take a look at the rest of the suspects. Next, we have Hartley. Maybe Hartley lied to us and he actually left after Miss Penrod, or else he doubled back after Miss Penrod left. Maybe he used his key to Mrs. Jarvis's house, killed her, and sneaked underground to Mrs. Nelson's house, where he murdered her, as well. Again, we appear to have no motive, unless we consider Mr. Hartley's eagerness to become wealthy a motive for murder, but I'm not sure how he would have benefited from her death.

"Next on the scene, at least as far as we know, is Angela Nelson. While she has an alibi keeping her out of the house until Officer Davis entered the house with her and supposedly didn't have enough time to murder her grandmother, maybe Officer Davis was wrong in his time estimation and she did have enough time to sneak upstairs. Still, it's doubtful that Officer Davis could have mistaken fifteen or twenty minutes for a minute or two. On the other hand, while Miss Nelson told us she didn't expect to inherit her grandmother's estate, we must assume that she will inherit it until we hear differently. That would give her a motive for murder. Are you with me so far, Lou?"

"I'm with you, but I'm not ready to make an arrest."

"While either of the first two could've killed both women within a short period of time, if Miss Nelson is our murderer, she would've had to have sneaked back on the street sometime later because she didn't get here in time to murder Mrs. Jarvis first, and she left with Officer Davis afterward. Also, if Miss Nelson killed her grandmother, she would've had to have done it while Officer Davis was present, wouldn't have needed access to Mrs. Jarvis' house to kill her grandmother, and would have no reason to murder Mrs. Jarvis."

Lou interrupted me.

"Still, we have to remember that time is on Miss Nelson's side. She wasn't in the house and away from Officer Davis long enough to commit murder, even if she'd planned it."

"Her alibi sure does seem good, Lou. That is if we can believe Mr. Silverman and Mrs. Wilkins."

"I think we have to believe them, Cy."

"Why's that, Lou?"

"Remember, the second bolt was locked on the door. Officer Davis verified that."

"You've got a point, Lou, but maybe she had a magnet and knew how to use it. Still, she couldn't have done that unless Silverman and Mrs. Wilkins are lying. So, let's move on to Silverman. Maybe Silverman made up part of what he told us in order to give himself an alibi. Maybe he was so distraught from his own mother's death that he couldn't stand to see any other older woman alive. Knowing that both women were alone and defenseless, he sneaked underground and murdered both victims. He could've done that without Mrs. Wilkins knowing anything about it. Oh, by the way, I don't know whether or not I told you, but I looked up Mrs. Silverman's death in the newspaper. From what I can tell, she died a natural death and was buried in a private ceremony at the Hilltop Valley Cemetery. I looked up the cemetery, but I couldn't find a listing for it. When we have time, we need to check with Silverman about its location."

"You're forgetting Silverman's alibi, Cy."

"You mean that Mrs. Wilkins had her eye on him?"

"That's right."

I paused to take in some much-needed air before continuing. I was quickly running out of people without an alibi.

"From Silverman, we move on to Mrs. Reynolds and her son Jimmy. Either of them had access to both houses. Plus, we know that Jimmy has a temper because he cold-cocked some guy with a shovel. Also, we know that Mrs. Reynolds would do whatever was necessary to protect her son. That only leaves us Hartley, Bobby, the grocery boy, who was probably in the house on the morning of the murder, the maid, and Hornwell, who has no motive that we're aware of unless he did it to buy their houses."

"You're forgetting one thing, Cy."

"What's that. Lou?"

"They all have alibis. Bobby was delivering groceries, and the deliveries were timed, the maid was at church with several other women, and Hornwell was out of town when Mrs. Nelson was murdered. He was at his cabin, where there was only one set of tire tracks and footprints, and he stopped in a store on Friday and again on Sunday."

"Do you think it's too late to rule this a suicide?"

"Just a tad bit, Cy."

"So, Lou, what do you think about Bobby? Do you think he was really in the house?"

"I'd say so, Cy, but unless he was already in the house before Angela Nelson and Officer Davis got there, then he couldn't be our murderer. My guess is that he spotted the police car and sneaked in to see what was going on."

"That's not very smart."

"Regardless of when he entered the house, he's not very smart if he really was in the house. Speaking of entering the house, it seems like it had to be someone who lives on the street because I don't see how anyone else could have gotten inside Saturday morning with Mrs. Wilkins and Silverman keeping watch. From where Mrs. Wilkins was situated, I don't see how anyone could have gotten inside any of the houses without her seeing him or her. Remember, Mrs. Wilkins came out on her porch a little after 9:00, which was before Miss Penrod or Mr. Hartley visited Mrs. Nelson. According to both of them, Mrs. Nelson was alive and well when they visited her. According to Mrs. Wilkins, no one else entered the house by way of the front door until Angela Nelson and Officer Davis entered around 10:30 when they found Mrs. Nelson dead. At least that concurs with Frank's time of death, which was some time that morning, but it seems to give all of our suspects an alibi."

"That bothers me too, Lou, but we're running out of suspects. Pretty soon we're going to have to chalk it up to osmosis."

"I don't think osmosis works that way, Cy. Would you settle for a voodoo doll, instead?"

"Probably not. How about if I confess to one murder while you confess to the other?"

Lou gave me the dumb look I deserved.

"Let's try again. If we can believe Mrs. Wilkins, the murderer has to be either Miss Penrod and Mr. Hartley working together, since they were the last two in the house or someone who scampered over to Mrs. Nelson's house using the underground tunnel."

"Or someone working with Miss Penrod, who could have drugged Mrs. Nelson after Mr. Hartley arrived, and if that's true, my best guess would be Mr. Silverman. I would have added Mr. Hornwell to my list. Before Mrs. Wilkins came out on her porch he could have sneaked into one of those houses he bought. If he had planned the murder, he could have driven two hours to get back to Hilldale and sneaked into one of his houses before daylight. The only thing saving him is that he was up there on Friday and again on Sunday, and there was only one set of tire tracks and footprints leading to and from his cabin. He was only there once, and the smart money fixes that once as from Friday to Sunday."

"If only Mr. Hartley hadn't been there, then Miss Penrod could have already drugged Mrs. Nelson before Mrs. Wilkins came out on her porch, and then returned to give her the poison."

"But why did she bother with drugging the woman, and why not do the evil deed earlier, when no one knew she was in the house?"

"Okay, let's try something else. Give me a motive for anyone you can think of."

Lou leaned back in his chair, gathered his thoughts before speaking.

"Well, as you said, the granddaughter probably inherits a sizable fortune. At least, from what we've heard, Mrs. Nelson was well-heeled. Hartley could've been stealing checks that came in the mail and one of the old ladies might've caught him, confided in the other, and told him there was another witness and who that witness was. Hornwell could've been stealing from Mrs. Nelson. As you said, Silverman could've been devastated by the loss of his mother, and maybe even responsible for her death, and wanted to put an end to other older women. He does seem to be a strange bird who still worships his mother, even though she's dead. Maybe Miss Penrod was tired of taking care of these older women and felt that they were so bad off they were better off dead. Bobby might have been stealing from them when he made deliveries, and Jimmy's mother might be as crazy as he is. Then, there's the guy downtown who may or may not be crazy and may or may not have needed a motive. I'd say all of our suspects are still intact."

"Thanks a lot, Lou. You've made our job so much easier."

"No problem, oh captain, my captain."

"It's oh lieutenant to you."

"I'll remember that."

"There's just one thing that's bothering me."

"Only one?"

"Well, actually there are several, but one in particular. The time element. None of the suspects had enough time with Mrs. Nelson to drug her, wait for it to take effect, and then poison her. The medication was administered forty-five minutes to an hour before the poison. The poison took another fifteen to twenty minutes to take effect. I'm stumped. Unless whoever was hidden in the passageway and came back for the fatal dose of grape juice."

"Maybe the old lady wasn't murdered after all. Do you think maybe we'll appear in the Dumb Detectives segment of Candid Camera?"

Lou and I continued to decipher all the information we'd gained. We decided to take a break to see if it helped. While we were in the midst of our break, Sam Schumann phoned.

"Cy, I've got a copy of Mrs. Nelson's will."

"Read it to me."

"Okay, Cy, here goes. 'I, Ethel Marie Nelson, being of sound mind, do make this my last will and testament. I leave to my granddaughter Angela Nelson all of my photographs and any two keepsakes of her choice. At the request of my granddaughter Angela, the two keepsakes are not to exceed five thousand dollars in value, and the house and all of the rest of its belongings are to be sold at auction. To keep the reputation and ambiance of the street intact, the buyer of the house must agree to occupy the premises for a period of no less than ten years or until death, whichever comes first, and must adhere to all the amenities of the neighborhood. All proceeds from the sale are to be split between the American Cancer Society and the American Heart Association.'

"That's it except that the will is signed by the deceased and is dated. The will is witnessed and also signed by her attorney, Harry Hornwell, and a witness."

I sat there bewildered by what Sam had read.

"Cy, are you with me?"

"Yeah, Sam. I was just thinking of the ambiance of my street."

Sam chuckled.

"You mean the character of your street?"

"Well, the characters on my street are what give it ambiance."

"I'd like to chat all day, Cy, but I have other work to do. Anything else?"

"No, that's all, Sam. Thanks. I'll get back to you later if I think of anything else."

I turned and relayed the latest news to Lou who let out a brief whistle.

"Maybe our suspect list is dwindling, Cy."

"Maybe."

"Who knows, maybe we'll have a signed confession before the day's over."

"I wouldn't count on it, Lou, unless we catch a murderer when we go back tonight. Now, let me take you home so we can get some rest. We might be in for a long night."

26

I woke up and turned over to look at the clock. It was already dark outside, so I had to turn on a light to see the clock. That's what I get for having an old-fashioned alarm clock. It was 7:37. I had no idea what time the intruder visited Hilltop Place, but I suspected that he or she waited until after much of Hilltop Place had retired for the night. If Lou and I were too late, or if the intruder didn't come, we would try again the next night. Of course, we hoped to spot the intruder as soon as possible. I sat up, reached for the telephone, and dialed Lou's number.

"That you, Cy?" came the expected greeting from the other end of the line.

"Hello, Sleeping Beauty. I'm calling to tell you that your prince is coming."

"That's fine with me, as long as he doesn't try to kiss me," Lou answered.

"I shudder at the thought," I replied, then tried a different approach to male bonding. "Are you ready to get to work?"

"If I'm not, does that mean you'll go alone?"

"No, it means I'll send my next-door neighbor over to keep you company tonight."

"Does five minutes sound okay?"

+++

I picked up Lou. We put on our game faces and tried to prepare for the evening at hand. As we drove toward our nocturnal exercise, I suggested that we park the car on a cross street and sneak down Hilltop Place undetected. While there would be some walking ahead of us, both of us were thankful that there were no inclines in the sidewalk.

"How long do you think we'll have to wait?" Lou whispered to me as we started down Hilltop Place.

27

Just as we reached Mrs. Jarvis's house, I heard the front door open. I motioned to Lou and we flattened ourselves against the hill. At least, we flattened ourselves as much as possible. If the cloud remained over the moon, and if the person who opened the door was deaf and did not hear a couple of "umphs" when the ground didn't give way to our stomachs, maybe we would go undetected. In the dark, we appeared to be nothing more than a couple of beached whales or front yard landfills.

I looked up to see if I could identify the creature of the night. A raincoat-clad individual stepped out of the house and closed the door. The lack of moonlight or streetlights kept me from telling any more about the person, and I didn't have time to sneak over to Stanley Silverman's to borrow his night-vision binoculars. The two landfills inched over toward the railing. Inching was something we'd always done well. Scurry wasn't even in our vocabulary.

The cloud cover remained, but I noticed a pair of dark galoshes coming my way. I tried to time my move and reached out to grab a leg. For once, I moved too quickly. A rubber boot landed on my hand. If the trespasser hadn't had a hand on the railing, someone would have gone tumbling down the steps, and for a change, it wouldn't have been Lou or me. The surprised intruder stomped on my fingers for good measure, spun around, and scrambled back up the steps. I cried out in pain. Before Lou or I could struggle to our feet, the intruder had rushed back into the Jarvis house and slammed and locked the door.

"Quick, Lou! Here's the key to the Jarvis house. Go up and unlock the door and throw me the keys. Then, I'll go down to the Nelson house and try to head off whoever it is, just in case Mr., Mrs., or Miss Raincoat tries to exit that way."

Lou reached for the railing. The overstuffed detective needed as much assistance as he could get. By the time he got the door opened and flipped the keys back to me, the person in the yellow raincoat had a sizable head start.

I grabbed hold of the railing with my stomped on fingers and winced. I grasped it again, held on to it, and reached over and picked up the keys where they had landed a couple of feet above me in the yard. I grabbed them and pushed myself to a standing position. I turned toward the Nelson house, took a couple of steps, changed my mind, and headed the other way. I had another idea and hoped I wasn't making a mistake.

I labored with each step and made it back to my VW as quickly as I could. I grabbed the police radio, called in, and gave John, the dispatcher, the home phone numbers of all our suspects who didn't live on Hilltop Place. I wanted to see if I could trim our list of suspects. No one could answer his or her home phone while trying to elude Lou. I didn't bother with anyone who lived on Hilltop Place. I figured that any of them would have had time to get home via the underground. My only hope remained with the five suspects who would've had to have traveled some distance to get there.

While I waited for an answer, I drove the car and parked it in Mrs. Nelson's driveway. I toyed with whether to wait for a response or climb the steps of the Nelson house. I was already out of breath. I decided to give John a couple more minutes.

John returned my call, but the response I wanted wasn't the one I received. He reported that he'd received a recorded message when he dialed Hartley and Mrs. Murphy. A woman answered at Bobby's house and informed him that Bobby was out on a date. A woman who identified herself as Mrs. Hornwell said her husband was working late.

Only Angela Nelson had answered the call. John told me the young woman seemed a little out of breath. I made sure I had given John her home number and not her cell phone number. When he confirmed that I had, I figured maybe she had been exercising. Who knows? Maybe she has to work out to keep her body looking so good. At any rate, she couldn't be the person in the raincoat. Not only did she live too far away to make it home so soon, but I would've seen anyone leaving any house on the street.

It was a good try, but I only trimmed our suspect list slightly more than I trimmed my waistline. I stepped out of the car and rushed toward the steps of Mrs. Nelson's house.

By the time I navigated all the steps, I was breathing heavily. I paused for a moment and walked over and inserted the key in the lock. My twist-and-push was fruitless. Why didn't we take time to force our way in when we were there earlier? Or would it have done us any good? I paced back and forth on the front porch trying to decide what to do. As I retraced my steps, I stuck a fingernail in my mouth and bit down. In no time at all, I'd given myself a cheap manicure. I contemplated whether to remain on the porch in case the raincoat-clad intruder came out through the front door, or if I should head back to the car to get some implement to help me pry away the plywood that still covered the front window. I decided to tackle the window with my chubby little hands but had no success. I looked for more fingernails to chew, but God had given me only ten, and I'd mangled them so well that no white was visible. I thought about going to the car to pick up my burglary tools, but I wasn't sure if I'd live through another rigorous experience.

Instead, I looked around the street to see which houses had lights on. Of course, even that wouldn't mean anything unless I saw someone standing in the window, and even then a person in the window could be someone who had just returned home from the underground. After much time and no success, I toyed with the idea of looking for Lou and was about to return to the Jarvis house when I heard someone jiggling the knob on the front door. I stepped back to avoid being seen and waited for my adversary to open the door. In a moment, the door opened and someone stepped out. I lunged, and before I could stop myself, two detectives landed with a thud on the front porch.

Two groaning men remained on the porch, neither of us able to move. It was a few minutes before either of us could rise to a sitting position. Both of us were in a lot of pain. Finally, the two of us crawled to a different porch column, and we managed to struggle to our feet.

Lou was the first to speak.

"Thanks a lot, Cy."

"I'm sorry, Lou. I thought you were some guy in a raincoat."

"Does this look like a raincoat to you, Cy?" Lou asked, grabbing the edge of his trench coat.

"In a way it does. Anyway, it was dark, Lou."

"It's still dark, Cy. What was I supposed to do, holler out, 'Ready or not, here I come?'"

"Well, it might have saved us some embarrassment."

"Saved you some embarrassment, Cy, and saved me some pain. My back and right shoulder are killing me."

"Well, my ribs have had much better days, too, Lou. Lock the door and let's get out of here."

"You're the one with the key, Cy. You lock it."

"By the way, if it was locked, how did you get it open, anyway?"

"It was simple, Cy. I just slid a bolt and twisted a knob. I think even you could do it."

I struggled as I made my way over to lock the door. After I locked it, Lou and I walked over and stepped down onto the first step. The grimace on both of our faces gave evidence that the pain of landing on each step was more than we could endure.

"There's got to be an easier way to get down, Cy."

Not thinking clearly, I crawled under the railing and lay down on the hill. Then, I started rolling. With no brake system in place, I wasn't able to come to a stop until I was in the middle of the street below. By that time, I was able to add facial abrasions and lacerations to my list of injuries. The only good news was that, somehow, I had missed the stone marker with the house number on it.

Sometimes it pays to go second. Lou learned from my effort. The sergeant slid down the hill feet first. While this method was some better, the sergeant groaned when his back and shoulder landed on the sidewalk below, and then the street. I groaned as well when Lou planted two feet firmly in my ribs as he came to an abrupt stop.

"Lou."

"What, Cy?"

"Morton salt. I guess a yellow dress and an umbrella are pretty close to a yellow raincoat."

"I'm not in any position to argue with you now, Cy."

"By the way, Lou, if that guy in the yellow raincoat comes back, will you tell him we promise not to prosecute as long as he helps us back to the car?"

"I was wondering if it's too late to find someone to give us a wheelbarrow ride to the car."

"I'm not sure if I could stand it when my ribs hit against the metal wheelbarrow each time we hit another crack in the sidewalk. Besides, I moved the car. It's in the driveway."

"That's still too far to suit me. Do they make Nerf wheelbarrows, Cy?"

"Maybe, but they can't handle stout-waisted men."

Both of us laughed, but we tried to stop as soon as we could because each laugh caused more pain. As I refocused on the problem at hand, I spotted someone hiding behind a tree. Whoever it was wasn't wearing a yellow raincoat.

"Lou, is there someone behind that tree, or is it a mirage?"

"Why don't you call the mirage and see if it comes to us?"

When Jimmy Reynolds ran from one tree to the next, I realized the identity of my mirage.

"Jimmy, come here. That's an order!"

Slowly, Jimmy sauntered over to where the two of us lay in the street. I hoped that Jimmy wasn't our assailant in the yellow raincoat and that he wouldn't think it was strange for two men to be lying in the street in the middle of the night. For a brief moment, I was thankful that Jimmy had mental problems.

"We've been spying on the enemy, Jimmy. Quick, help us up. Our enemies have gone. We must follow them."

I hoped that no talk of what had happened got back to anyone we knew. I was sure George Michaelson or Frank

Harris could manage a month's worth of material from our misadventures.

Jimmy Reynolds wasn't sure what to make of the situation. He reached over and helped me to my feet. Luckily, Jimmy was a big, young man. I looked at Lou who heard my cries of pain. He knew he was next, but at least if he was standing he would be better equipped to leave the premises. Soon, both of us were standing. We dismissed Jimmy Reynolds to another mission, and two portly men were thankful that I'd moved the car. As we walked to the car, I turned to my partner.

"Hey, Lou, from the rear, the two of us must resemble a couple of hippos with tender feet."

"What do you mean 'feet?' Every part of me hurts thanks to The Flying Dekker."

We had to take only a few steps to get to the car, but there were enough steps that both of us knew that our next stop needed to be the hospital.

+++

A nurse helped me peel off my coat and shirt. A doctor arrived to examine us. After x-rays were taken, he assured us that we had bruises, but no broken bones. Lou had a bruised back and right shoulder. I had badly bruised ribs and lacerations and abrasions on my face.

We left the hospital and gingerly lowered ourselves into Lightning. I dropped Lou at his apartment and told him to get as much sleep as possible. If I woke up alive later that morning, I would phone him to see if he too was still among the living. Then, I would phone the department and tell them about our injuries. I promised to spare as many details as possible.

28

With each toss and turn in the middle of the night, I woke up, sure that someone had shot me. I wondered if I should invest in a hammock, an extra-sturdy hammock. I lay awake and envisioned the hammock supports ripping free of the wall as I fell to the floor and landed on my bruises. I thought that I might have been better off if I'd given in to the mysterious person in the yellow raincoat instead of encountering my friend. Why didn't he call out?

I would've gotten out of bed and taken something for the pain, but getting up was too painful. I wish I'd have been the one who chased the yellow raincoat. I would've called out before I came out, and then no one would've been hurt. Of course, it would've been just my luck that the person in the raincoat would've been waiting outside instead of Lou and I'd have been bopped on the head. No, the only safe way would've been to wait at the bottom of the steps with a pair of binoculars. After all, Stanley Silverman used his binoculars proficiently, and he didn't seem to be the worse for wear. I wonder what the department would say if I asked to solve the case from Silverman's front window. I imagine someone would've shown me the door instead of the window.

I groaned at the thought of facing the coming day. The thought of having to work with all my pain made me groan, again. I felt a chill, attempted to turn over and pull the covers around me. But each move brought on another pain.

After lying awake half the night, I woke up very tired on Thursday morning, but not so tired that I wasn't well aware of my condition before my first movement. Every part of my body ached, even those parts I didn't bruise the night before. I wondered if I should follow the path of other men in the department who were my age. Surely a desk job would be less painful. But no, there was no way Lou or I would be happy with a desk job. We were made to catch criminals, not to push papers. Besides, these days desk jobs include computers. I don't own a computer, and I have no idea how to use one.

After much deliberation and effort, I managed to crawl out of my bed and kneel beside it. My initial intent was to find some way to lift myself to a standing position, but the pain I continued to endure and the position in which I found myself caused me to pray first. Prayer was not new to me. I always pray when I remember to do it, and I attend church on those Sundays when Lou and I aren't in the middle of a murder case.

After I finished my prayer, I inched over to a nearby chair and tried to lift myself to a standing position. Each movement caused more pain. The nurse had told me that I'd be very sore for several days, and by experimenting, I'd find the best way to move with the least amount of pain. I hoped I soon made that discovery.

With the help of a chair, a dresser, and a chest, I slowly stood up and gingerly walked to the bathroom. On the way to the bathroom, I wondered if a shower would help or hurt. I walked into the bathroom and temporarily forgot all about the shower. As I looked at myself in the mirror, I tried to remember in what round I was knocked out. I had a black eye and scratches on my nose and forehead. There was a little swelling around my jaw and more scratches. Only Lou had any idea what I looked like at that moment, and I figured I probably looked some better the last time Lou saw me. Besides, Lou was also in pain, and it was dark when the fiasco happened. I wondered how I was going to keep away from everyone else until I healed. My thoughts about healing and years of reading the Bible made me wonder if I should wait until the waters stirred before I got into the shower.

The shower wasn't as painful as I expected, but getting dressed was both more painful and difficult to do. After surviving this struggle, I walked gingerly to the telephone to make the call I didn't want to make. Like most things I own, my telephone is old and heavy, and the receiver is separate from the dialing mechanism. I laid down the receiver, dialed the number I knew from heart, and then attempted to pick up the receiver again. I dropped the receiver as I tried to lift it to my ear. As I reached to retrieve it, I heard someone on the other end of the line. I forced the phone to my ear and began to talk.

"Sorry about that. I dropped the phone. This is Lt. Dekker. I'd like to report an altercation that happened last night. Sgt. Murdock and I were chasing an elusive burglar and both of us ended up having to go to the hospital for treatment."

The voice on the other end interrupted me.

"If the burglar was elusive, how in the world were you and Sgt. Murdock hurt?"

The voice on the other end of the phone sounded somewhat familiar, but I assumed it was because all voices at the department sound vaguely familiar, and I wasn't thinking too clearly.

"You weren't shot were you, Lieutenant?" asked the voice on the other end of the phone.

"No, but it feels like it."

"Any other weapons used?"

"No."

"Well, I need to get some information, Lieutenant. Do you feel up to answering a few questions?"

"If I say 'no,' does that mean I don't have to answer them?"

"We'll need to do this sometime, Lieutenant. Would it be better if I sent someone by?"

There was no way I wanted anyone to see me, so I thought quickly and then answered.

"No, I think the phone's much better. Go ahead if you must."

"How many attackers were there, Lieutenant?"

"I think just one, but it seemed like more."

"But only one that you know of?"

"That's right."

"And that one person attacked both yourself and Sgt. Murdock?"

"That's right."

"I assume he used the element of surprise."

"Oh, you wouldn't believe how surprised we both were."

"Did you or Sgt. Murdock know who your attacker was?"

"Neither of us knew who or what hit us."

"So, tell me, Lt. Dekker, what happened?"

"Well, uh, I was standing on a front porch, and Sgt. Murdock was coming out the door. Someone lunged for Sgt. Murdock and before we knew it, we were both lying on the porch. We tried to get up, but fell down the hill and landed in the street."

"I'm not sure I'm getting this, Lieutenant. Are you saying that someone pushed Sgt. Murdock out the door, and that Sgt. Murdock fell into you, and you both crashed to the porch?"

"Well, Sgt. Murdock was attacked, but I think it was more I fell into him."

"I don't understand, Lieutenant."

"Neither did we."

"Okay, let's try to get this finished, Lieutenant. Tell me again how you got from the porch to the street. Did your attacker throw you into the street, or did a big burst of wind come along and deposit you there?"

I thought of hanging up, but I knew I had to finish with as little embarrassment as possible.

"No, it was more like we tried to get up, winced from the pain, and the next thing we knew we were lying in the street."

"Lieutenant, I need to ask you this. Were either you or Sgt. Murdock drinking last night?"

"We were working on a case."

"It sounds like it. So, did you finish off the whole case?"

"I'm talking about a murder case. We were on Hilltop Place, see. Those houses are high above the street. A person could fall out of his or her yard mowing the lawn."

"Okay, Lieutenant. By the way, what happened to your attacker?"

"You mean the burglar?"

"I don't know, Lieutenant. It's your story, not mine, and it sounds like a whale of a story."

"Our burglar, who may or may not be a murderer, just disappeared, and neither Sgt. Murdock nor I felt like looking for him or her."

"You say this person may or may not be a murderer. Should we be looking for bodies on other porches? And you say that this person may or may not have been a woman. Are you saying that it is possible that a little, bitty woman may have overcome both you and Sgt. Murdock all by herself? Are you sure we're not talking about a little girl with black patent leather shoes who carried a dolly? We've got one who answers that description on the 'most-wanted list.'"

"Just put down that we were tackled by a football team. All of them were carrying Uzis."

"That sounds more feasible. At least I don't have to ask who the tackling dummies were."

After having been insulted repeatedly, I slammed down the phone, which caused me to wince in pain. While I contemplated what to do next, the phone rang. I picked it up and huffed out a "hello."

"I just need to ask you one more question, Lieutenant," said the familiar voice I'd hung up on. "Did you or Sgt. Murdock suffer any brain damage as a result of your altercation?"

Before I could hang up or come up with an answer, the person on the other end began to laugh.

"Cy, I love your story. I'll make sure everyone else gets to enjoy it, too," said the voice on the other end, who changed in mid-sentence from the voice who had abused me to the voice of my good friend George Michaelson.

"How long have you been on the phone?"

"It was me all along, Cy. I just happened by the desk when the phone rang, and no one was here to answer it. When you identified yourself, I decided to have some fun with you."

"I'm not amused, George, but now that I've got you on the phone, I need some help. I've got bruised ribs, and Lou's got a bruised back and shoulder. In other words, neither of us is getting around very well. Grab Frank Harris, the SOC team, and some uniformed officers. I want us to go over the Nelson and Jarvis houses and the underground area below them and see what we can find. Could be our guy in the yellow raincoat or our murderer, which could be one and the same, may have left some clues for us. After all, it was the person in the raincoat who we were chasing last night."

"Why do you want Frank?"

"Well, every time someone runs through the house we find another body. I want to be prepared."

"I'll see what I can do, Cy. How long will it take the two of you to limp over there?"

"We should be there by 11:00."

29

I phoned Sam Schumann. I didn't expect him to shed any new light on the case, but I had more questions that needed answers.

"Cy, I was waiting for your call. I've got some more information for you."

"Really, what've you got?"

"You know Bobby Cooper, the grocery boy? Well, one of the customers he delivered to called in. She caught him taking something of hers. Since it was something small, at first she didn't plan to report it, but then she remembered small crimes sometimes lead to bigger ones. Anyway, we got a search warrant. It turns out the boy has a dresser drawer full of stuff he's taken from customers. He admitted that one of them came from the dead woman, Mrs. Nelson."

"Did he by any chance admit to being in the house on the morning of the murder?"

"Not that I know of, Cy. I'll check and see. Of course, whether he was in the house or not, I doubt if he'd admit it."

"Listen, Sam, I've got someone else I want you to check on. Irene Penrod, the next-door neighbor. See what you can find out about her and where she might've gone. She left home in a taxi on Saturday morning. The driver dropped her off at the bus station, but she seems to have disappeared from there."

"I can already tell you one thing, Cy."

"What's that, Sam?"

"One of the neighbors overheard her saying that she wouldn't have to take care of Mrs. Jarvis much longer."

"Really? Anything else?"

"I just found out that an anonymous donor has paid for Mrs. Jarvis's funeral expenses."

"Really? Carte blanche?"

"No, the funeral home received ten thousand dollars in cash. That won't pay for a high-priced casket, but it's enough to pay for a decent burial."

"And you don't have any clues as to who sent it?"

"None yet, Cy, and if we don't find any fingerprints, I doubt if we'll ever find out. I'll keep checking, though."

"That all you have, Sam?"

"It is for now, but I'll see what else I can have for you tomorrow."

"Talk to you then, Sam."

+++

I struggled to close my front door.

"Good morning, Cyrus," said the screeching voice of my next-door neighbor.

I wondered if Heloise Humphert ever slept, or if she camped out in her front yard with her watchdog on duty. I slowly turned to face her.

"Oh, Cyrus. What happened? Did you fall down and hurt your little body?"

"No, I had a nightmare about you and fell out of bed."

Heloise Humphert chuckled at my put-down.

"Well, Cyrus, I could give you a massage to help you feel better."

I thought of my neighbor giving me a massage. Suddenly, the tumble down the hill didn't seem so bad.

"That's okay. I have some poison ivy that will give me the same result."

"Oh, Cyrus. You're so funny. Would you like me to fix you some chicken soup?"

I shook my head until I realized how much it hurt to do it, then made my way to the car as quickly as my aching body allowed.

+++

I watched Lou walk down the sidewalk toward Lightning. I was sure the sergeant wished Lightning could roll toward him. Not that the sergeant wanted to be struck by Lightning, but I knew the sergeant wanted to take as few steps as possible. At least, he was walking better. Lou arrived at the car and opened the door slightly.

"Cy, it's me. Lou. You know, the guy who never wears a yellow raincoat. I just want to make sure that your seatbelt is strapped on good and tight, because I'm getting in now, and I wouldn't want you to lunge at me."

First George and then Lou. Could Frank be far behind? Surely, many years ago there must have been a comedian strike at the same time there was a shortage of policemen. Lou bent over to get in, grimaced as he did.

"You looked fine coming out of your apartment, Lou. Is this flash of pain for my benefit?"

"I wish it was, Cy. I'm doing okay walking. It's those up and down movements and twisting and turning in the bed that causes me so much pain."

"Want to trade injuries? Mine hurts only if I move or don't move."

"Yours should be worse, Cy. After all, you're the one who caused all of this."

"That reminds me, Lou. I need a favor from you. I called and reported last night's fiasco. I told George that you and I were attacked last night. Play along with me on this."

"In other words, it was our mysterious person in the raincoat that caused all my injuries?"

"Well, in a way it was."

"How much is it worth to you, Cy?"

+++

My pain escalated with each turn of the steering wheel. In a few minutes, I managed to stop the car in front of the Blue Moon Diner, and the walking wounded exited the car and headed for nourishment.

"Well, what happened to you?" Rosie asked, seeing my decorated face. She knew me well enough to know that whatever answer I gave her would not be the truth.

"A cat got stuck in a tree," I answered.

"I thought that was the fire department's job."

"They were all putting out fires at the time."

"Why didn't you send him up to get the cat?" Rosie asked as she pointed toward Lou.

"It was his job to catch the cat when I flushed him out of the tree."

"So, did you catch the cat yet?"

"Not yet. Remember they have nine lives."

"Hopefully, you do, too. It looks like you've used up one of yours."

"It feels like more than one, but let's cut the chitchat. We're famished."

At 10:30, Lou and I waddled and limped from the Blue Moon like two ducks which had tried to cross the road while walking too close to a possum. We were not a pretty sight, and two snails passed us as we made our way to the car. I remembered how painful the short drive had been and offered Lou a turn at the wheel.

"Say, Cy, your roll down the hill didn't cause you any memory loss, did it?"

"What do you mean, Lou?"

"Well, we've been together over an hour now, and you haven't asked me about my message for the day."

"He didn't by any chance tell you that Job and Jonah had it worse, did He?"

"No, but from what I've read, they did have it worse."

"Well, Jonah deserved it. Anyway, what tidbit did God give you this morning?"

"Can you dig it."

"Can you dig it? What are we, beatniks? I can see it now. Today we have Cy Dekker on the bongos as he accompanies Cool Lou, the poetry machine. Cool, huh, man?"

Even though Lou had spent years around me, I never ceased to amaze him.

"Tell me, Cy, how fast were you going when your head hit the concrete?"

30

On the way to Hilltop Place, Lou and I discussed the person in the raincoat.

"Any idea who it was, Lou?"

"No, I never saw anyone after I entered the house. At least not until I looked up and saw you lying on me."

Eager to change the subject, I offered a guess.

"Whoever it was either lives on Hilltop Place or he or she was still in one of the houses until after we left. Did you look through Mrs. Jarvis's house?"

"No, I figured whoever it was headed for the underground. However, I did check out Mrs. Nelson's house before you jumped me."

I winced as I slowly maneuvered the car around the corner onto Hilltop Place and noticed that he and I were the first to arrive.

"No one's here yet. Just pull down in front of Mrs. Nelson's house. If the door is double-bolted, we can use George as a battering ram. With his head, it shouldn't take us more than a couple of tries to get in."

Lou and I talked while we waited. We were interrupted by a call from the dispatcher.

"Lieutenant, do you know a Mrs. Wilkins?"

"I sure do."

"Well, she called in this morning. She wanted to talk to you about what she called 'The Hilltop Murder Mystery.' Sgt. Collins talked to her and told her you weren't in. At first, she was reluctant to leave a message, but finally, when she decided she could trust Sgt. Collins, she told him that last night she saw Mr. Hartley coming out of the house next door to hers. Does that mean anything to you, Lieutenant?"

"Yes, thanks. I'll check on it."

Lou and I discussed this new bit of evidence until I looked in the side-view mirror and noticed Frank Harris's wagon pull up behind us. Frank got out of his car and approached the sitting wounded. The medical examiner bent over and looked in the car and was barely able to suppress a laugh.

"So, this time they brought the bodies out to me."

"I would laugh, Frank, but it hurts too much."

"It looks like I lost a bet, Cy."

I knew it was coming.

"Go ahead. I'll bite."

"Well, I told George that I didn't think you could look any worse than you did before. Looks like I was wrong."

"I love you, too, Frank."

"So, Cy, how many new bodies do you have lined up for me this morning?"

"I don't know. Do the two of us count?"

"Funny you should mention it. Some of the guys in the department have been wondering if the two of you can count."

"Very funny. Today, I'm counting on you, Frank. Somebody has to keep you busy. I know even you'd feel guilty drawing a paycheck without doing any work."

"That reminds me. It's good to see that you and Lou are finally doing something to earn your pay."

Frank and I continued our repartee while Lou sat and enjoyed it. A couple of minutes later, George pulled up behind Frank, followed by a couple of squad cars and a couple of the men from the police lab. When they got out of their cars, I noticed that one of the uniformed officers was Officer Davis.

Lou and I tried not to advertise our injuries as we pushed our way out of the car. From the smirk on George's face, I could tell that he had a few put-downs lined up, but he wouldn't put me down in front of the younger men.

"Hello, Cy. So nice of you to get all of us together on this wonderful morning," George said as he got out of his car.

"It's so good to see your beautiful face this morning, George."

"Sorry I can't say the same about your face, Cy," George whispered as he caught up with me. "So, Cy, after you," he said as he motioned for me to go first.

I wanted to bring up the rear, but George had forced my hand. I walked gingerly over to the railing, hoping to use it to hoist myself to the top. I made idle conversation to take George's thoughts off the slowness of our journey.

"What'd you do last night, George?"

"Just turned on the TV and watched a little Texas Hold 'em."

"I've never been much on wrestling. It's all fake," I replied.

George gave me a look. I assume the fact I don't like wrestling offended him. He remained quiet until we got to the porch.

"Nothing like a leisurely stroll to the top of a mountain, I always say," George said, as I finally managed to navigate the last step and arrived at the porch.

"I always take it slow when I notice I have some old people on the tour," I replied.

I grimaced as I made my way to the front door. I eased my hand into my pocket, pulled out the key, and inserted it into the lock. I turned and pushed, but to no avail. It seemed like someone had spent more time at the Nelson house than I did. Did our friend in the raincoat linger around the house or return after Lou and I left with our injuries?

"I'll let you have the honors, George," I said, as I motioned for him to lead the way.

"The door seems to be stuck," he said after he gave it a try.

"It's not stuck, George. It seems our friend is playing games again. Officer Davis, you've done this before. Why don't you go to your car and get something to force the plywood away from the window. And if you have any duct tape, please bring it, too."

Officer Davis jogged down the steps to his cruiser. His return trip took much longer, although he did his best to make a good impression. He handed me the tape and used a crowbar to work on the window. He pried the plywood far enough away from the window so that he could reach in, unlock the window, and climb into the house. Then, he hurried over to the door and slid open the second bolt and the rest of us strolled inside. Just after we entered the house, two more officers pulled up. We were accumulating quite a crew. It was getting to be a habit.

I removed my pocketknife from my pocket and cut a piece of duct tape. I took a chance that my actions would not lead to curiosity seekers. Besides, the scene of the crime had already been trampled on more than once. I secured the bolt that kept us from entering the house each day. After a few minutes, I'd used enough tape to severely hinder our opponent's shenanigans. We wouldn't have any trouble entering the house next time.

"Frank, it's your party. We'll just take a seat until you can see what you can find out," I said as I eased my body into a chair.

"Well, I'm not used to going out without knowing there's a body, but the way this case is going, chances are we'll find another body today."

An hour or so later, the lab crew, assisted by the medical examiner, reported their findings to me.

"There's definitely been some traffic, but nothing significant to lead us anywhere."

"Well, then, gentlemen. I'll lead us somewhere. Let us head to the dungeon."

I lifted myself from the chair, ambled to the pantry as the others followed. I twisted the lid on the jar of olives. It was not all I twisted. I winced but hoped no one else noticed.

"Officer Davis, if you would help us out, there's a couple of buttons at the back of that bottom step. Would you be so kind as to bend over and push both of them for us."

Officer Davis bent over, and, after a few seconds of searching, located the buttons. He pushed both of them and the wall slid away.

I stood at the top of the stairs and looked down at the door below. I winced again as I thought back to a short time before. Police work was getting dangerous.

I led the way, slowly making my way down the steps. When I arrived at the bottom, I turned to face the others.

"Men, we don't know what's on the other side of this door. Let's all turn off our flashlights and remain silent until we find out."

The men followed orders and grew quiet. I left my flashlight on until I found the sliding bolt that held the door locked. Then, I extinguished my flashlight and slowly opened the door. Everyone stood in silence as we heard the sound below. Someone was digging.

31

I opened the door the rest of the way and eased down the steps. I clutched my flashlight in one hand while I wrapped my other hand around the handrail, something nonexistent anywhere inside the house. The only light shined in the distance. We couldn't see the source of the light. It came from slightly around the bend. Otherwise, there was only darkness. Each of us descended the steps slowly, carefully. Even the slightest squeak of a step might alert whoever was digging. After everyone had made it to the dirt floor, I motioned for the men to spread out. On my orders, each man slowly made his way toward the digging sound. As we drew closer, the dim light revealed a lone figured bending over a shovel.

"Hold it right there," I shouted, as I turned my light on and spotlighted the digger. The other policemen followed suit and illuminated the underground area.

Not suspecting she had company, and unnerved by the sudden light and command, the digger dropped her shovel.

"Just leave it right there," I hollered, as she started to bend over to pick up her shovel. "And just what are you doing down here, Mrs. Reynolds?"

"Raisin' a garden, if it's any of your business," the older woman replied. "From the number of flashlights, I assume you've brought more riffraff with you this time."

I ignored her comment, picked up where I'd left off.

"Oh, I love gardens. Let's see what you've planted."

"Didn't plant nothin'. My guess is you planted it, Lieutenant, and waited in the dark until I found it," Mrs. Reynolds answered.

She recognized the voice of her caller, even though the blinding light kept her from seeing me, even when she raised her arm to shield her eyes.

"You just happened to come down here and find it. Is that right, Mrs. Reynolds?" I replied as we continued to walk toward her. "Oh, lucky us. It looks like we got here just in time for the harvest. Officer Davis, why don't you do the honors? Let's see how Mrs. Reynolds's garden has done this year."

Officer Davis moved over to the shovel, picked it up, and started to dig. The older woman stumbled backward. When she regained her position, she answered my accusation.

"I told you, Lieutenant. I didn't plant nothin'."

"Sure you didn't. Then it looks like *all* of us will be surprised. Doesn't it, Mrs. Reynolds?"

Mrs. Reynolds jumped each time the shovel hit the ground and eased a little closer to the wooden steps that led to her house. In a few minutes, Officer Davis had uncovered the buried treasure.

"Well, Mrs. Reynolds. Look what we have here. A yellow raincoat, galoshes, and a ski mask. Why don't you try them on to see if they fit?" Mrs. Reynolds turned and ran up the steps. None of us were close enough to stop her. She managed to lock the door before the nearest officer could detain her. I kicked the dust. I didn't expect Mrs. Reynolds to be so spry. We decided to deal with her later. For the time being, we wanted to study what we'd found and see what else we could turn up.

"Well, it looks like we've found the mysterious yellow raincoat. Let's bag it and spread out and see what else we can find. We'll begin on this side of the underground area. Let's start at the head of the street past Mrs. Jarvis's house and work our way back down to where we are now. Then, we'll go over and check out the other side."

Each man had been told to bring a Maglite so he could do a thorough search of the underground area. As we spread out and started up the cave-like stretch in front of us, George eased over to me with a smile already in place. I braced myself.

"So, Cy, was that your attacker? Was she the one who overpowered you and Lou last night? Tell me again how she gave you the black eye. She must have used the shovel. Or could it have been Miss Peacock in the conservatory with the lead pipe?"

Before I could choose whether to respond or ignore my friend, one of the men hollered that he had found something else. Frank was nearby. He donned some surgical gloves, bent over and picked up the envelope the officer had found.

As I caught up with him, the medical examiner filled me in.

"Looks like we've found a letter, Cy. It's addressed to Irene Penrod. She's the lady who's gone away, isn't she?"

"That's right, Frank. Who's it from?"

"There's no return address, and the postmark is smudged.

"Has it been opened?"

"Yes. You want me to take it out and read it?"

"Might as well. Read it, then bag it, although I doubt if we find any prints on it. But maybe it can tell us something."

"Dear Irene," Frank read. "I'm so happy you'll be coming to spend a few days with us. Herbert and I are looking forward to your visit. I wanted to let you know that Donald might be able to bring you. He's on his way home, and he might come through Hilldale Saturday morning. If he gets there before your bus leaves, he can bring you, and you'll get here quicker. Just go to the bus station as planned, and wait until the last minute to buy your ticket. If Donald makes it through there Saturday, he can meet you there and bring you to us. Love, Martha."

"What do you think, Lou?" I asked.

"It could be anything. Maybe it's genuine. Maybe it's phony."

There were a few murmurs as Lou paused.

"Maybe Hartley murdered the old ladies and dropped this letter as he sneaked from one house to the other without being detected. Or possibly the letter was delivered and someone entered Miss Penrod's house and took the letter in order to draw suspicion to her or Hartley. And then there's even a chance that Miss Penrod wrote this herself to give herself time to get away after the murders, knowing that we'll be told that she has gone away for a few days. She could be out of the country by now."

There were too many possibilities to suit me. I realized that the further we delved into the case, the more we were coming up with more questions than answers. Did Mrs. Reynolds get caught with her hand in the cookie jar, or was the disguise buried there by someone else, as Mrs. Reynolds claimed? Was Irene Penrod's letter a clue that would be vital in solving the murders, or did someone plant it to muddy the waters?

I had no idea. I knew only that my pains were increasing more than my results. I felt there were more clues to be found, so I instructed each man to return to work. No one found anything else until we got to the dead-end portion of the underground.

"Hey, Lieutenant! We've found another shovel here!"

Everyone hurried to the officer who located the shovel. The sum of each man's light flooded the tunnel. Not only did we find a shovel, but someone had been digging. Careful examination revealed something hidden under a tarpaulin. One officer worked feverishly to untie the knots and toss away the rope. Whoever had been digging had some help of a sort. Under the tarp, we found a device used to locate buried treasure. I looked up at the house beside us. It was the second house on the street. I remembered Mrs. Wilkins told me someone had rented this house. Was this device the reason someone rented it? Or did someone put this apparatus here because he or she knew the house was empty? And was this the house Mrs. Wilkins said she saw Hartley come out of last night? I rounded up the print crew, told them to see if they found anything. Then, we planned to recover the device and retie the rope. I was not yet ready to alert the digger that we were on to him or her, but I did want to look inside the house and see if I found anything when time permitted. First, I needed to follow proper procedure and get a search warrant.

"Okay, men, we're halfway done, so to speak. Let's backtrack and do a thorough search of the underground on the other side of the street."

Each of us paused as we returned to the steps leading from the Reynolds house. I sent a man up to check the door, but it was still locked. Mrs. Reynolds didn't want to be followed. A second search revealed nothing more, so we continued around the curve to the steps behind the houses on the other side of the street.

32

I labored as I walked. It had been some time since a case had been this tough on me physically. I looked around and noticed that Frank hovered over me like a vulture waiting for an opportunity, or at least a medical examiner who knew where his next victim was coming from.

"It's okay, Frank. I've got a few more good days in me," I said, as he walked abreast of me. I think I was trying to convince myself as much as I was my friend. I looked at Frank, who was of medium build and height, wore rimless glasses, and had sandy brown hair. He looked like he had more days left than I did.

"Cy, as far as your body is concerned, I think your best days are well behind you. It's that gristle between your ears that keeps you going."

"As you know, Frank, there are times when we must forge ahead on autopilot."

Turning serious, Frank asked, "Cy, do you know what you're looking for down here, or have you already found it?"

"Frank, I'm not sure what we're looking for anywhere, other than the fact that I'm trying to come up with who murdered these two women and why they did it. I'm running into more dead ends than I'm finding in this underground tunnel. I'm finding all kinds of accessibility, but very little motive. Even the granddaughter is not eager to inherit her grandmother's estate, and I've checked into the financial records of everyone concerned. Everyone's sitting pretty except the grocery boy, but he's the only one we know has done something wrong. The mailman doesn't have nearly as much money as the rest of the suspects, but he's doing okay."

"If it wasn't for the fact that both women were poisoned, Cy, I'd be inclined to think they were random murders, but random and poison seldom walk hand in hand."

"Lieutenant, it looks like we might have something else," one of the men in front of the pack exclaimed, putting an end to the conversation between Frank and me.

I hurried toward the officer as quickly as my aching body allowed.

"What have you found, Son?"

"It may not be anything, Lieutenant, but it looks like someone's been digging here, too, only I'd say this dirt's been back in place a lot longer than what we just found."

I looked down at the dirt. It took a lot of light and a careful eye to see where dirt had been removed and replaced, which was why we didn't find it on our previous visit. I tried to get my bearings. After I did so, I realized that this archaeological dig was very near Stanley Silverman's steps.

"Son, go up there and try the door and see if it opens."

The instructed officer climbed the steps, found the door secured. I remembered that on our previous visit when we apprehended the incoherent man, the door to Silverman's house was quite accessible. That meant that Silverman had descended the steps to the underground, or at least someone had walked down his steps.

"Officer Davis," I called.

"Yes sir, Lieutenant."

"Officer Davis, I believe I've got some more digging for you to do. Can you locate Mrs. Reynolds's shovel? I would ask her if we can borrow it, but I'm sure she wouldn't mind."

Officer Davis ran to the place where he'd left the shovel.

"What are you expecting this time, Cy? More raincoats?" George asked.

"As my dear partner tells me from time to time, we need to be patient. We'll soon know."

Officer Davis located the shovel, returned to the group gathered around the excavation project. He sank the shovel into the dirt and tossed the dirt to one side. A second and third shovelful produced nothing but more dirt.

"What do you think, Lieutenant? Do you want me to go down or wide?"

"Just keep digging deeper and see what you find. We've got nothing but time, and I'm convinced that someone has been doing something more than moving some dirt around."

Another five minutes of digging produced nothing but more dirt. Idle conversation had started. No one was doing any work other than Officer Davis.

"Are you tired yet, Officer Davis? Do you want me to have someone relieve you?"

"No, I'm fine, Lieutenant."

"Okay, listen up, men. While Officer Davis continues to dig, why don't the rest of you carry on with your search and see if you can find anything else."

The group separated and the search continued. With each new shovelful, I began to anticipate what we might find. Lou and Frank sensed what I was thinking. Officer Davis might have too because he dug with more fervor.

After a few more minutes, and after a few feet of dirt had been unearthed, I heard the sound I'd expected. Officer Davis had struck something other than dirt.

"Okay, Officer Davis, I think we've gotten the depth that we want. Now, try to get me a little more width. Let's see what we've found."

"Lieutenant Dekker," one of the returning men called out. "We're through. We didn't find anything else, but I did find another shovel. Do you want me to get it and help Officer Davis?"

"If we've got as big of an area to clear as I think we have, Officer Davis will need all the help he can get."

The officer rushed off and hurried back with the second shovel. I instructed him to start digging in an area about four feet from where Officer Davis was digging.

While they were digging the SOC team returned with news that they had found two partial fingerprints. Maybe our luck was changing.

The two men continued to dig and several minutes later they had completely uncovered the top of a metallic blue coffin.

"Do you think it's Mrs. Silverman?"

"I'm more inclined to think it's a passel of raincoats," I replied.

"Are we going to exhume the body, Lieutenant?"

"I assume so, but that comes under the jurisdiction of our esteemed colleague," I replied, motioning toward the medical examiner, Frank Harris. "If we do so, and find out that Mrs. Silverman was poisoned with the same poison as our two latest victims, then we can presume we have a murderer on our hands."

"I thought the first two murders were enough to presume that we have a murderer on our hands," George whispered in my ear.

"I mean we'll have a pretty good idea as to the identity of that murderer," I whispered back, a little louder than I intended.

"I assume you mean Mr. Silverman," replied Officer Davis. "You don't think he's responsible for murdering three women, do you? Especially since one of them was his own mother."

"Evidently, you didn't see *Psycho*."

"Yeah, but that was only a movie, and Mr. Silverman isn't pretending to be his mother half of the time."

"At least not the half we've seen him. Remember, truth is stranger than fiction. Anyway, I don't think anything at this point, but I do know that men have been murdering their mothers for years. Come on, Lou. It's time for us to call on Stanley Silverman."

+++

As quickly as our pains allowed, Lou and I plodded across the cavern's dirt floor and up the steps through Mrs. Nelson's house. All of a sudden, all of our pain wasn't of a physical nature. Now, we were to confront a suspect who might have murdered his own mother and two other elderly women. The thought that someone would commit such a heinous crime repulsed us, yet our years on the force reminded us that such crimes occur much more frequently than most people think they do. Even by people who look as incapable of committing murder as Stanley Silverman.

To ease the pain of walking down the steps from Mrs. Nelson's front porch to the street and mounting an equally large number of steps to Silverman's house, the two of us took some weight off our feet and put it on our hands. We grasped the railing and quickly found out this move

213

increased our pain. I decided to reposition some of my weight. I removed a candy bar from my pocket, unwrapped it, and took a nibble. My smile caused Lou to guzzle a few M&Ms before we encountered our suspect. We trudged up the steps to Silverman's house. As we neared the front door, I hoped that Silverman didn't physically confront us. Even though there were two of us, neither of us was in any position to jostle with him, even though he was slight in stature. I climbed the last of the steps and glanced over at the front window where Silverman often sat spying on his neighbors, but Silverman and his binoculars were nowhere to be seen.

Finally, out of breath and in much pain, Lou and I reached the front porch. I walked over, rang the doorbell, and waited to confront Silverman. When Silverman didn't answer the door, I rang again. Again, no one responded. This time I reached up, pulled on the brass knocker, and let it drop. I repeated this several times. Still, our call went unanswered.

Did Silverman realize the nature of our call? Was he upstairs visiting his mother's shrine? Was he in hiding? Had he left the house? Or had something happened to him?

33

I realized that Silverman was not going to answer the door. I shuddered as I contemplated walking back down the Silverman steps, across the street, up the Nelson steps, through the Nelson house, down some more steps, and then through the underground to let the others know that our call had gone unanswered.

As we turned to leave, I felt relieved to see that Frank, George, and two uniformed officers watched us from the porch of the Nelson house. Their presence caused me to celebrate with another small chocolate and almond delight. As Lou and I made our way down one set of steps, our compatriots made their way down another set of steps. I paused halfway down in order to lick my fingers clean. My abrupt halt surprised Lou, and both of us almost went tumbling down the remaining steps. I grasped the railing to stop my fall and encountered a new pain. Lou bumped against me and coughed. I felt a saliva-covered M&M slide down the back of my shirt. I had no idea what color it was. All M&Ms feel the same to a Hershey Almond connoisseur.

A few seconds later we met the others in the street.

"Well, Frank, what's next?"

"I'll have to make a phone call to check, but I believe the way the city ordinance reads, the coffin is not considered to be on anyone's property. Since we don't know for sure who or what's in the coffin, it'll probably be okay for us to exhume it and take it to the morgue and check it out. If there's a body inside, we should be able to find out if it really is Mrs. Silverman, and, if so, whether or not she died of natural causes."

"So, the property below doesn't belong to the street's residents?"

"That's one of the things I'll have to check. I doubt if there's any record of the underground area. Since we're not dealing with a marked grave, a deeded area, or an identified body, my guess is that we won't need a court order to exhume the body. At least if we do need one, it'll be easier to get."

"What do we do now, Cy?" Lou asked. "It looks like Silverman has gone on the same trip that Miss Penrod took."

"I'm not sure."

Turning to the medical examiner, I asked, "What about you, Frank? What are your immediate plans?"

"Well, I plan to make the necessary calls. Then, I'd say that sometime today or tomorrow, we'll get an okay to remove the coffin and see what's inside."

"Do you plan to post anyone with the coffin?"

"Someone will stay with it until we get an okay, but from the looks of you two, I'd say you'd better get some rest, and call it a day. Of course, I did have you down as two of the pallbearers when the time comes to carry the body up and cart it away."

"But you'll have already carted it away before you know whether or not there's a body inside. What do you plan to do? If you find a body do you plan to bring it back here for Lou and I to hoist it back up?"

"Of course. You wouldn't mind, would you, Cy?"

"Lou and I'd would've been hurt if you hadn't asked, Frank. Of course, we'd be glad to. You are going to ask Mrs. Reynolds, too, aren't you?"

The medical examiner smiled at my comment, then, once again I turned serious.

I turned and called Officer Davis.

"Officer Davis, I'd like for you to stay on the street until your shift ends. If you need to leave for any reason, call for someone to replace you. I want to know if you see Mr. Silverman or anyone else you think I might want to know about.

"And Frank, just in case Silverman is hiding in his house, I'd like someone posted underground, even after the body is removed, just in case Silverman decides to pay a visit to the dearly departed, provided there is a dearly departed inside."

"Consider it done."

Lou and I were getting ready to leave when one of the SOC team came running out of Mrs. Nelson's house. He seemed excited.

"Something wrong?" George asked as the man made his way down the steps as quickly as he could without falling.

"We found a couple of things in the pocket of the raincoat. One could be poison. The other is a large magnet."

"Okay, you go back underground, leave one man to stay with the coffin and have the rest of the men down there see that the Reynoldses do not escape by using the tunnel to get to someone else's house. Those of us up here will call on Mrs. Reynolds."

Several of us climbed the steps to the Reynolds house as quickly as we could. I rang the bell. No one answered, so I pounded on the door. Again, no one answered the door.

It seemed to be harder and harder to find anyone at home on Hilltop Place.

"George, do you mind going downtown and getting us a search warrant? It seems that Mrs. Reynolds is not inclined to answer her door. And would you get one for 101 and 105 Hilltop Place? Tell the judge that neither is occupied but both are owned by and one is rented by a couple of our murder suspects. If you need to, explain that we found some evidence outside of one of the houses."

"Glad to oblige, Cy."

+++

George returned an hour later with search warrants. We forced our way into the Reynolds house, spread out to find Mrs. Reynolds and her son Jimmy. We searched each room, closet, and passageway. Then, I sent an officer down to the tunnel below, and he called out to the men guarding that exit. Mrs. Reynolds and Jimmy had disappeared. Hilltop Place was becoming a ghost street.

I felt like kicking myself, but I had enough bruises already. Still, I had no idea that Mrs. Reynolds would take her son and leave Hilltop Place. Instead, I rather suspected that she would install more dead-bolt locks and brace a chair against each door in order to keep us from entering her house. Did she flee because she was guilty? Or did someone plant the raincoat and make Mrs. Reynolds believe she or her son would be arrested for a crime someone else committed?

We reported the missing mother and son and George agreed to follow up on their disappearance after we searched the two empty houses. We left the Reynolds house and made our way through the underground tunnel to get to the other two houses. The fewer people who knew where we were going, the better. Lou and I were going to have to do another up-and-down at Mrs. Nelson's house, anyway. Who needed a Stairmaster? We had Hilltop Place.

I dreaded the up-and-down-and-up walk, but there was no one to beam us into the houses. A few days later, when Lt. and Sgt. Huff-And-Puff arrived at and searched the two vacant houses, both houses revealed that someone had been inside recently. Each house had a mattress lying on the floor, both mattresses looked as if they had been slept on, and from the looks of things, someone had eaten in each house. There were crumbs on the floor and a small amount of trash. Could the man we found in the tunnel have stayed in either of these houses before he wandered into the tunnel and became incoherent? And if he stayed in either or both houses, did anyone know he was there?

The SOC team lingered to search for prints. The rest of us continued our search as we moved upward one floor at a time. We found nothing else in the first house but were startled by what we found in the attic of the rental house. In an attic closet, under a couple of loose floorboards, we found a large, waterproof pouch. I donned a pair of gloves, unzipped the pouch. I let out a whistle. Inside the pouch, we found a large sum of money. George and I counted it. Eighteen thousand dollars. But whose eighteen thousand dollars, and did the money have anything to do with either murder?

We pondered what to do with the money. Should we return it and take a chance that someone might get away with stolen money? Or should we take it and possibly alert someone that we were on to him or her? Someone could have earned the money, but I had my doubts.

After careful deliberation, we called headquarters and got an okay to replace the money with marked bills of the same denominations. Hopefully, if someone had stolen the money, he or she wouldn't realize that the bills had been switched. Because Lou and I were in much pain, George offered to go to headquarters and pick up the money. The rest of us remained behind. I contemplated walking down the stairs and reclining on the mattress until he returned, but opted to sit on the floor like everyone else.

When George came back, the switch was made. George recommended Lou and I call it a day, and we agreed. Both of us were sore, tired, and hungry.

34

"What do you think, Cy?"

"About what?"

"About what's in the coffin."

"Well, the way things have been going for us, my guess is that it is either full of yellow raincoats or Mrs. Silverman's inside and we find out that she died of natural causes."

"What if her son's in the coffin?"

"Then, I'd say we have one fewer suspect."

+++

On the way to his place, Lou talked about what he planned to do when he got home. He said he was glad he hadn't taken up horseshoe pitching or volleyball. The way he felt, the only activity that he wanted to do was one he could do sitting still. He wasn't sure what hurt the most; bones, muscles, or bruises. He eagerly awaited the time when his bruises went away so he could reduce his choices to two. I agreed with him.

Lou didn't normally consider crossword or jigsaw puzzles a physical activity, but both of them were slightly more strenuous than reading. Plus, it was easier to recline and read than to recline and do either of the other two.

I laughed as Lou pictured himself lying on a chaise lounge, holding a grape in one hand, and a piece of a puzzle in the other, while someone stood over him fanning him. I let him know that I wouldn't be the person fanning him. He laughed and said he figured that he was seeing visions like that because of his strenuous work activity and the ailments he suffered. I agreed that that was possible.

Just before we got to Lou's place, he made up his mind to read. He told me that he was one hundred or so pages into *Wuthering Heights*. Lou asked me if I was familiar with it. He must have been tired. We'd already talked about it. I didn't tell him the first time we talked that I'd already read it a long time ago, and I wasn't about to tell him then. When he asked, I merely nodded my head.

I couldn't believe we sat in front of Lou's apartment for five minutes discussing that book. Lou asked me if I knew how the author came up with the title. I didn't know, and I didn't care. I just wanted to get home as quickly as possible. But he was my friend, so I let him share his thoughts about the book. Lou had read far enough that he knew that the book was named for a residence in the book, but he wondered why anyone would choose a name like that. I didn't reply. I figured if only one of us talked, I'd get home sooner. Lou went on and said he thought wuthering sounded even worse than withering, and withering sounded like someone on the verge of death. If that was true, I think I had been one of those words for a couple of days or so.

Lou changed from wuthering and talked about cursing. Lou had already read enough to know that people cursed back then, just not as much as Holden Caulfield did. At least unlikable people used profanity, and most of the characters in *Wuthering Heights* weren't the kind of people Lou wanted to hang out with. He toyed with whether or not he would tell anyone other than me that he was reading that book. After all, he guessed you could say it had romance, but it was not the mushy kind. At least not in the first one hundred pages. Finally, I suggested that Lou get out and go in and read his book. He must have said his piece because he told me good night and went in.

I left Lou's apartment and drove home. I'd already made up my mind about what I was going to do next, and it wasn't read *Wuthering Heights*. I planned to put the phone next to the bathtub in case anyone called with information pertinent to the case, and then I aimed to soak in a tub of hot water until I turned into a prune, even if I wasn't Danish.

I went home, prepared my bath, dropped into the tub, and lingered there with a smile on my face. Once I felt satisfied that I had more wrinkles than an octogenarian, I decided that I'd remained in the bathtub long enough. It was then time for me to enjoy my favorite form of exercise. I pulled the bathtub plug and fought the current.

Since the warm water had soothed my body aches just a trifle, I began the twelve-step process needed to remove myself from the bathtub. It was on nights like this that I wished that all I had to do was push a button and rise up out of the tub. Instead, my routine was more jerky than fluid and included lots of gasps along the way.

I noticed the progress I'd made in just the previous few hours. Only that morning I'd chosen a shower rather than a bath because I felt that if I lowered my body into the tub someone would remove the bathtub ring before they could extract me.

Once I'd scaled the side of the tub, stumbled out onto the tile floor and donned my lounging clothes, I was ready to enjoy something from my video collection. I would sharpen my sleuthing skills by watching the greatest crime-fighter of all time. In my mind, no one fought crime and used his deductive reasoning quite like Barney Fife. I selected an episode of *The Andy Griffith Show* in which Andy went on vacation and left Barney and Gomer in charge.

After I watched, I let my mind wander. I imagined Barney Fife on our current case. I pictured Barney trying to scale the front steps of Mrs. Nelson's house and either shooting himself with his one bullet as he climbed the steps or arresting Officer Davis once he had survived the climb and regained consciousness. I watched four episodes, not counting the ones I slept through, and then went to bed.

As I headed to bed, the phone rang. Officer Davis called to let me know that he saw someone sneak away from one of the empty houses on Hilltop Place. Officer Davis could tell that it was a man, and the man wasn't wearing a raincoat, but he could tell nothing else. Had someone returned to count or retrieve his or her money?

35

I had planned to sleep Friday morning until something woke me. That something was the telephone, and the someone on the other end of the phone was Officer Davis. He called to inform me that neither he nor the officer who relieved him had seen any new activity on Hilltop Place. No one other than the mysterious man he had reported had entered or left any house on the street. I asked Officer Davis to remain on duty through the weekend and report to me if anything warranted my interest. Officer Davis arranged for another officer to relieve him when needed, but he planned to do the bulk of the watch.

A few minutes after I hung up from talking to Officer Davis, the telephone rang again. It was Frank. He informed me that the coffin had been removed and, when the inspection revealed that a body was inside the coffin, the body was brought in for an autopsy. Frank told me that it was a woman's body, and he should be able to give me an identification of the body and cause of death no later than Monday morning. Frank also told me that George had not been able to locate Mrs. Reynolds or her son.

I hung up the phone and lay in bed pondering my next move. I called Dr. Muriel Davenport and found out that there was no difference in Don Hampton's condition. The homeless man was not yet capable of answering questions.

My fourth phone call was one I made to Sam Schumann.

"Glad you called, Cy."

"I just called to see what you found out about Irene Penrod."

"She's a blueblood, Cy. The Penrod name comes with lots of money and connections. Either because of it or in spite of it, our girl Irene got in lots of scrapes growing up. Having money and connections got her out of most of them. Also, she usually comes across as a calm person, but she has quite a temper when cornered. I'm not sure what, but she did something in college that was against the rules. Another co-ed found out about it and told on her. When Irene found out, she promised to get even with that girl. From what I can gather, she made good on her promise. I'm still checking, but rumors are Irene must've squandered some of her money. She doesn't appear to be as wealthy today, and her family is in no hurry to bail her out this time.

"One of Irene's neighbors tells me she's quite a liar. She said one time when Irene talked about visiting friends in The Hamptons, she, the neighbor, spotted Irene filling her gas tank near a Hampton Inn only twenty miles from her home. The curious neighbor followed Irene to a ramshackle motor lodge that seldom has guests return for a second stay."

News of Irene Penrod made me wonder where she had disappeared to. Did she murder her next-door neighbors and then vanish, or was her disappearance merely a coincidence?

"Anything else you have for me, Sam?"

"Just one thing, Cy. Mr. Hartley, the mailman, is the one who rented that house on Hilltop, and it's his finger-prints on that equipment you found under that house."

"The mailman? So that's why he's been sneaking around on Hilltop Place in the middle of the night. But why would he rent it? He's not living in it, is he?"

"No, he's still living with his wife. No one knows for sure why he rented the place, but there's that rumor about treasure being buried somewhere under Hilltop Place. Remember, he said he would have the last laugh on those people."

"Thanks, Sam, for making my job easier and more difficult at the same time."

Sam laughed, and we hung up.

I checked off another item from my list and dialed Lou's number.

"Murdock here."

"Be right there, and oh, by the way, have you been up long enough that God told you His word for the day?"

"Funny you should phrase it that way. Today's message is just one word. Patience."

"Patience. Is that with a 'ts' or a 'ce?'"

"My messages are not written down, nor are they spelled out. All I know is today's message is patience. You figure it out."

"See you in a few minutes."

+++

Although it meant I had to walk a greater distance to get to my smiley-faced Lightning, I had parked behind the house when I got home on Thursday night. It was my latest attempt to get away from my overbearing neighbor without being spotted.

I closed the back door of the house as quietly as possible and tiptoed down the back steps. Eventually, I reached the car without catching sight of or hearing the grating voice of my next-door neighbor. I unlocked the door and slid onto the seat as quickly as my pains allowed.

I started the car and turned on the radio, something I seldom did because it kept me from hearing any calls I might receive from the dispatcher. But for the next few seconds, I hoped it would keep me from hearing my next-door neighbor's irritating voice. Once I'd put some distance between myself and my next-door neighbor, I would turn the radio off.

I backed the car toward the street. As I neared the street I noticed my neighbor with the built-in radar approaching my car. I smiled and continued backing into the street. As I pulled away to pick Lou up, I continued to smile. I looked in the rear-view mirror and watched the diminishing figure of my next-door neighbor. Then, I adjusted the mirror for a moment, looked at myself, and noticed I was smiling. I couldn't remember ever smiling when I saw my next-door neighbor, but then there was something about her figure growing smaller while the distance between us grew larger that was enough to put a smile on my face.

36

Our first item of business was to search for Hartley. We drove down Hilltop Place. Hartley had already delivered the mail.

"Boy, he sure gets an early start. Do you reckon he does without breakfast?"

"That could be why he's so anemic looking, but I bet he has one of those breakfast shakes or some yogurt."

"Yeah, but he'd still need to eat breakfast, wouldn't he?"

I turned the car around and drove down Elm Street. Elm Street crossed most of the other streets in the area and gave us a better chance of finding Hartley. As we crossed each street, I looked left while Lou looked right. We'd gone only two or three streets before we spotted a mail truck. I turned the car onto the street and pulled in front of the mail truck. Two eagle-eyed detectives spotted the blur of a man delivering mail and soon found out that our blur was Hartley.

Upon seeing us waiting for him, Hartley called out.

"Oh, hello, detectives. Have you Mounties found your man yet?"

"Sergeant Preston and Yukon King are on the trail."

"Which one of you is Yukon King?"

Lou answered before I had a chance.

"Well, since I'm the sergeant, he must be King."

"I'm not yet a king, but give me time," I interjected.

Hartley drew close enough to see our battle scars.

"Boy, it looks like the two of you caught something. You haven't been working out with the Green Bay Packers without a helmet, have you?"

I looked Hartley in the eye. I wondered if he was responsible for our injuries.

"It was supposed to be a secret. How did you find out?"

The mailman laughed, then continued.

"Well, I hope this is as a result of making progress on the case."

"We're continuing to make progress, Mr. Hartley. Tell me, have you seen anyone on Hilltop Place in the last couple of days?"

"Now that you mention it, I haven't. Do you believe everyone's left town or fallen over dead?"

"I don't know, Mr. Hartley. Has anyone stopped their mail?"

"I don't believe I've ever had anyone stop their mail before they died, although Mrs. Nelson stopped hers while she was in the hospital."

"What about leaving town? Did Miss Penrod stop her mail?"

"You know, now that you mention it, she didn't."

"Did you notice any mail in her box?"

"I really haven't paid attention, what with my mind being on Mrs. Nelson and Mrs. Jarvis."

"What about Mr. Silverman? Have you seen him, or did he stop his mail?"

"No to both questions."

"Do you remember putting anything in his box this morning?"

"I believe I did, but I'm not sure."

"Mr. Hartley, have you by any chance been on Hilltop Place at night any time in the last few days."

"Why do you ask?"

"Just curious."

"Now, why would I be over there at night? You know I carry the mail only in the daytime."

"Why don't you tell us why you've been over there?"

"Did someone say I was on Hilltop Place at night?"

"Let's just cut the chitchat, Mr. Hartley. Why didn't you tell us that you rented a house from Mr. Hornwell?"

Hartley almost dropped his mail.

"How did you find that out?"

"One of our men spotted you on the street the other night. What were you doing on Hilltop Place after dark?"

"Just checking on my house."

"And checking on your digging equipment?"

Hartley appeared stunned and took a moment to answer.

"I haven't done anything wrong. The area below those houses doesn't belong to anyone. I checked before I rented the house."

"Maybe you haven't done anything wrong. Just see that you don't. We'll keep in touch."

Hartley didn't respond. He stood there sweating. I was sure that he was wondering how much the police department knew about his activities. I could tell that up to a few seconds ago he thought his movements had gone unnoticed. I wondered if the money we had found was his.

Lou and I left Hartley and went back to Hilltop Place. We saw Officer Davis parked in front of Mrs. Nelson's house and pulled up to talk to him.

"Good morning, Officer Davis. Any activity on the street this morning?"

231

"Nothing but the mailman."

"And have you seen anyone open his or her door and collect the mail?"

"Not anyone at this end of the street. I assume those are the ones you're interested in."

I walked over and looked up at the Reynolds house. There was mail in the mailbox. Then I walked around and saw mail in Silverman's box, but saw no one sitting in the window holding a pair of binoculars. I returned to Lou and Officer Davis.

"Officer Davis, am I correct when I say that you haven't seen anyone at the Jarvis, Penrod, Nelson, Reynolds, or Silverman houses since you've been on detail here?"

Before he responded, Officer Davis took a minute to think about the five houses I had mentioned.

"That's right, Lieutenant. No one. Do you want me to continue to stay here?"

"Yes. At least through the weekend. I want you on the job as much as possible, and make sure you find someone to relieve you anytime you need to leave. I want to know if anyone enters or leaves any of these houses, at least until we get some new evidence or an autopsy report."

"No problem, Lieutenant."

"A couple of other things. Now that you've had time to think about it, do you think you can identify the person who was in Mrs. Nelson's house when you and Angela Nelson were upstairs?"

"Sorry, Lieutenant. I didn't see whoever it was."

"Think for a minute. From the sound of the footsteps, do you think they were made by a man or a woman?"

"My guess is a man, but I can't say for sure. At least it wasn't someone wearing high heels."

"Also, is there any way that Angela Nelson could have gotten up those steps and poisoned her grandmother while the two of you were in the house."

"How long did it take her to die, Lieutenant?"

"Approximately fifteen to twenty minutes."

"Then there's no way, Lieutenant. Miss Nelson never went up those steps until about a minute or so before we found her grandmother dead. I'm sure of that. We hadn't even been in the house anywhere near fifteen minutes. I'd say we'd been there less than five minutes."

"Officer Davis, think carefully. Did you hear anyone in the house prior to the two of you entering the house, or did you hear any noises in the house prior to hearing someone running from the house?"

"Sorry, Lieutenant. I didn't hear anything."

"Then we don't know if the intruder followed you or was already hiding in the house when the two of you entered," I said, as I turned away.

I thought of something else and turned back to Officer Davis.

"One other thing, the man you phoned me about the other night, the one you saw on the street after dark, do you have any idea if it was the same person you saw running from the Nelson house the morning of the murder?"

"Since I didn't see the first person, I really can't say."

"I didn't think you could, but I thought I'd ask. Could it have been Mr. Hartley?"

"I guess so."

"Thanks for everything, Officer Davis. I'll be in touch."

"Well, Lou, I think I've discovered something."

"What's that, Cy?"

"Something none of us likes to discover. I think our word for today is patience with a 'ce.'"

"Does that mean that we're to lie low until someone confesses?"

"I don't think that's going to happen, but it might mean that we're supposed to cool our heels until the next clue presents itself."

"Where do you think we are, anyway, Cy?"

"I'm not sure, Lou. From what we have on the table it looks like our murderer would have to be either Hartley, the postman, or Miss Penrod, the next-door neighbor. That is unless it was our mysterious intruder, who could be Hartley, but not Miss Penrod, or someone who came up through the underground, which could have been the person Silverman saw in Miss Penrod's house, provided there was such a person. And if it was someone from the underground, he or she would have had to have timed his or her murder sometime between when Miss Penrod and Hartley left and before Officer Davis and Miss Nelson arrived on the scene. Although if this person was acting alone, I doubt if he or she knew that Mrs. Nelson would have company so soon. Oh, well! Something tells me that things will begin to clear up soon."

"Yeah, maybe as soon as we locate the Reynoldses. At least, I hope so."

"Does that mean that we won't have to navigate all those steps again?"

37

I drove toward McAdams department store to call on Angela Nelson. I hoped that calmer surroundings and a few days distance from her traumatic experience might enable her to think of something she had forgotten the day she found her grandmother. I parked the car. Lou and I entered the store and asked a clerk where we might find Miss Nelson. She directed us to the proper department.

"Well, good morning, Lieutenant. What brings you here today?" Angela Nelson asked, surprised to see us. "And what happened to the two of you? You look like you've been in a fight."

"The rigors of being a police detective, Miss Nelson."

"You haven't found out more about my grandmother's death, have you?"

"Nothing that I'm ready to reveal at this time. I just had something I wanted to ask you. Other than Officer Davis, did you see anyone near your grandmother's house prior to your finding your grandmother?"

"Well, I think I might have seen Mr. Silverman in his window. But I think I already mentioned that to you."

"Did you see anyone else or did you see any activity as the cab driver drove down the street?"

"No. Why, do you think I might have just missed whoever murdered my grandmother?"

"There's a good possibility of that, Miss Nelson. You didn't by any chance see whoever else was in the house, did you?"

"No. Sorry, Lieutenant."

"What about when they were running out the door? Did you catch a glimpse of anyone?"

"I'm afraid not. Officer Davis and I were just beginning to come down the stairs when we heard whoever it was. Then, we ended up tumbling down the steps."

The thought of tumbling down the steps stopped me for a moment.

"You didn't happen to look out the window after Officer Davis ran out to his cruiser, did you?"

"No. Sorry, Lieutenant. I guess I'm no help."

"What did you do while Officer Davis was outside reporting your grandmother's death?"

"I'm not sure. I was so upset. I guess I sat on the couch, but I couldn't say for sure."

"You didn't by any chance go back up to see your grandmother, did you?"

"I might have. I don't remember. Like I said, I was so upset to find out my grandmother was dead."

"I don't guess you have any idea what Officer Davis did when he left the house."

"You mean to report my grandmother's death, or afterward? In either case, I don't know."

"You haven't by any chance been back to the house since your grandmother's death, have you?"

"I thought about it. I thought spending an hour or so reliving some of the memories my grandmother and I had might help bring closure, but then I realized that I wouldn't be able to get in. Besides, I wasn't sure if I was allowed, or if you're still treating it like a crime scene."

"Well, it would be best if you stayed away a few more days. I'll let you know when it's okay to go back."

"Thanks, Lieutenant. I appreciate everything you're doing."

"You're welcome, Miss Nelson. I'll let you know if anything comes up. Oh, one other thing. Do you know who owns the two empty houses up the street?"

"I've never really thought about it, Lieutenant. I'm sure there's someplace where you can check. I have no idea if they're owned by the estates of the people who used to live there, or not. Sorry, I can't help you."

"That's okay, Miss Nelson. I'll check back with you when I find out something else."

Lou and I had just left Angela Nelson when we received a phone call that a ladder had been found just outside the back wall at the Silverman's house. Had Silverman escaped, too? Or had he returned? I didn't figure I could get a search warrant until we got the results as to the cause of Mrs. Silverman's death. Until then, there was no way I could get into the Silverman house unless Silverman admitted me. I would ask if anyone had seen Silverman, but who was there to ask? Everyone was gone, or dead and gone.

After we left, I came up with an idea to check on our suspects. I called in, received approval, and called the telephone company in order to look over a copy of the phone and cell phone records of everyone who interested us. If anyone started answering the telephone in either the Silverman or Reynolds households, I'd know that one suspect had returned and another had never left. Also, sometimes cell phone records reveal the whereabouts of a person making or receiving a call. I was told I could pick up the records on Monday.

Lou and I had been working hard on the case, so unless a new clue turned up, we would rest until Monday.

38

I drove home. Lightning seemed eager to get home, and so did I. I wanted to mull over the evidence we'd uncovered, and then enjoy a relaxing evening at home. Everything proceeded reasonably well until I noticed the figure who only that morning had gotten progressively smaller in the rear-view mirror of my car was now growing frighteningly larger as I approached my house. Not only did my next-door neighbor seem to be on the lookout for me, but her "fluffy, furball" stood protectively by her side.

I pretended not to see Heloise Humphert as I turned into the driveway. I hoped that my failure to acknowledge her would send her scurrying back to her house. I hoped wrong.

"Well, Cyrus, you're home early today. We must celebrate," Heloise Humphert hollered as she hurried down my driveway uninvited. "Oh, poor Cyrus. You still have your boo-boos. Is there anything I can do?"

"How do you feel about becoming the first person to sail around the world on a raft? I understand you might win the Mark Twain award."

"Cyrus. I don't know anyone as funny as you."

"Maybe it's time for you to get out and meet some people. Have you tried the New York City subway after dark?"

"Oh, Cyrus. Are you trying to tell me that we're going to take a trip together?"

"If you like. Let's go out into the middle of the street, and I'll trip you first."

"Let's be serious for a minute, Cyrus. Are you ready for us to celebrate your coming home early?"

Quick on my feet, I replied, "I think experiment might be the better choice."

"Oh, Cyrus, you devil you. You must have heard about my collection of flavored lipsticks. I bet you want me to try on some of them while you close your eyes and kiss me."

"If I had to kiss you that would be the way I would want to do it. Of course, I'd have to get plastered first. But that was not the type of experiment I had in mind."

Heloise blushed and decided to satisfy her curiosity.

"Well, tell me, Cyrus. What did you have in mind?"

I decided to lie and ask for God's forgiveness later.

"I just came from the doctor. He said what I have is contagious, and while it probably will not prove fatal to me, it could very well prove fatal to anyone who comes in contact with me. He said my condition is particularly dangerous to small animals."

"Oh, Cyrus, you're kidding me." When I didn't respond, she continued. "You are kidding, aren't you, Cyrus?"

"Who knows? We know that doctors sometimes exaggerate a condition to scare people into changing their lifestyles. There's probably nothing to it. You hurry home and get your lipstick collection, and hurry back with Muffy. We'll keep an eye on her between kisses and if we see her keel over we'll know that it might be a good idea for you to go home. That is unless you want to go where Muffy goes."

My neighbor grew apprehensive.

"I'm not sure, Cyrus. Twinkle Toes is just getting over a cold. I think maybe it might be best if we wait until another time to test my lipstick collection."

With that, Heloise Humphert spun around so fast she almost tripped on Twinkle Toe's leash. After unwrapping the leash from the lower half of her body, she hurried to her own house. She muttered something about dialing the veterinarian to see if she could bring in Twinkle Toes. She wanted to know if the dog had been exposed to a deadly disease.

I rushed up the back steps of my house, opened the door quickly, and hurried inside. I found a quarantined sign I'd once used as a gag and hung it on the front door in case my neighbor returned. Then I relocked the door, smiled at myself in the mirror, and pictured one of my heroes, Wile E. Coyote.

+++

I leaned back in my recliner, mulled over our case. An hour later I was no closer to solving the case than when I began, so I forgot about it for a while. I hated to take time off before a murder case was solved, but I was trying to be patient, something that was difficult for me. I wondered how the two murders were connected. Who would have a reason to murder both of these old women, and what was that reason? And what had happened to the three neighbors who had disappeared? Did Mrs. Reynolds and Mr. Silverman really despise each other, or was that an act? Had they murdered these two (or maybe three women) and gone away together when their discovery was imminent? Were they in hiding? Or had they been murdered, too?

I would let things rest until Monday. Maybe by then, someone would return home. Maybe the phone records would shed some light on some of what went on.

I called Lou to see what he was up to. He answered on the second ring.

"Hello, Cy."

"How did you know it's me? Did you get Caller ID?"

"I don't need it. No one else ever calls me except you."

"Would you like me to give your number to Heloise Humphert?"

The two of us enjoyed a good laugh as I recanted my most recent encounter with my next-door neighbor.

"So, Lou, what've you been up to since you got home?"

"Am I a suspect now?"

"I don't know. Have you done anything suspicious?"

"Does calling Thelma Lou count?"

"So, Lou called his sweetheart. Have you been talking all this time?"

"No, Cy. I just called to see if she'd like to go out this weekend in case I have some free time. After I hung up, I plopped down in front of the card table and worked on my latest puzzle. I've been neglecting it for the last few days."

"Well, Lou, at least you're a bachelor. You don't have anyone telling you to work your puzzle or put it away."

"No, I can leave the card table up as long as I like, which is most of the time. Anyway, I put together a few pieces. You know how exhausting that can be, so after a few minutes I ambled over to the recliner, let gravity have its way, and took a nap. I just woke up a few minutes ago. I'd just picked up my book to see what those wuthering people were up to when you called. So, Cy, did you solve the case or are you just calling to brag on your love life?"

"Just to let you know that I'll call you if we get any breaking news."

+++

Talking to Lou had inspired me, so I leaned back in the recliner and took a nap. While I slept, I dreamed I was Wile E. Coyote, and my next-door neighbor was that dastardly Road Runner. While I dreamed, I envisioned the doorbell ringing. I hurried to the door and found a shipment from the Acme Warehouse. With saliva dripping from the side of my mouth in typical Wile E. Coyote fashion, I uncrated each purchase and did something no man has ever done. I read the instructions.

As I continued to dream, I saw myself counting the minutes until it was dark enough to sneak next door undetected. Then, I eased out of the house, crept to the house next door, hooked up the explosive device, slithered home under the cover of darkness, and waited for the contraption to put an end to my problems.

Little did I know that Muffy had seen me make my delivery. Silently, Scruffy Muffy sneaked out of her house, disconnected the device, lugged it back to my house with her formidable teeth, and hooked up the device, again.

I suspected nothing when the doorbell in my dreams rang and went to see who was calling. I opened the door, was horror-struck as I looked down at the ticking device, and woke up just before the apparatus ticked down to zero. It was then I realized that I needed to find a new home for the dog before I eliminated the neighbor.

It was still early when I woke up, so I sifted through my DVD collection and found one Lou had given me. It was filled with commercials from my childhood. I took a chance and watched some of them.

A few minutes in, I was so disappointed. Instead of commercials I remember, like the Speedy Alka-Seltzer commercial, Johnny the bellboy hollering, "Call for Phillip

Morris," or seeing a man falling from the sky to let Hertz put him in the driver's seat, I saw a mishmash of repeats of a few commercials that were made in the '70s. I was so disappointed I went to bed.

39

I'd had a little more rest the night before, so I woke up a little earlier on Saturday morning, rubbed the sleep from my eyes, and read my daily devotional before I took a shower. I smiled as I envisioned Lou doing the same. There weren't many times when I got up at nearly the same time as my friend. I read, then reflected on what I'd read, as I watched darkness change into daylight.

So this is what a sunrise looks like.

I eased into my day and headed to the shower. I'd just stepped out of the shower when the phone rang. I hurried to the phone to see who was calling. The ringing phone meant the time had come when I needed to change from ordinary citizen Cy Dekker to Lt. Dekker.

"Lt. Dekker, this is Officer Davis. I thought you might want to know that one of the parties has returned to the street."

"Are we going to play Twenty Questions or are you going to tell me who it is?"

"It's the next-door neighbor, Irene Penrod, or at least it's somebody who went into her house. She just stepped out of a taxi, gave me a furtive look, and then lugged her luggage up to her house."

"Thanks, Officer Davis. You've done well. Stay there and Sgt. Murdock and I will be there as soon as we get through with our preliminaries. If by some chance she leaves, follow her."

As soon as I finished my phone call with Officer Davis, I called Lou to let him know there might be a break in the case.

"I'll be there in thirty minutes," I informed Lou. Even though I couldn't see his face, I could envision the surprise that must be on it as he looked at his watch and realized that I was ready so early.

My mind wasn't so focused on Irene Penrod that I forgot to ask Lou what message God had given him that morning. Because it brought back pleasant memories, Lou let me know.

"Carnac the Magnificent."

"Carnac the Magnificent?"

"Yeah, you know, the character Johnny Carson played on his show, the swami who could tell what message an envelope contained before he opened it."

"I know who Carnac was. I stayed up later in those days. I was younger then."

"So, Cy, what do you think it means? Will we run into some guy in a turban or someone with a boatload of envelopes?"

I hung the phone up, got ready to pick up Lou. I kept thinking of the latest development. Would Irene Penrod be able to shed some light on the case and provide the clue of the day?

+++

Lou and I hurried to Hilltop Place. We parked behind Officer Davis's cruiser and got out to see if there had been any new developments. As we sauntered up to the cruiser,

Officer Davis got out and greeted us. We said our hellos, and the three of us turned and looked up at Miss Penrod's house. The red brick exterior looked no different than any other time in the last week, but the house's lone resident had returned, and Lou and I were eager to question her. Officer Davis filled us in with what little he knew.

"As far as I know, she's still in there. At least she didn't come out the front way, and I haven't seen anyone else. The rest of the street is as dead as it has been."

"Thanks again, Officer Davis. We'll go up and talk to her now. We'll stop on our way out." My voice cracked as I mentioned going up and talking to Irene Penrod. I didn't relish another climb of that magnitude.

"Say, Lou, what do you say we stand at the bottom of the steps and call out to her? Do you think she'd come down and talk to us on the street? Or better yet, what did Romeo have on us. How about 'Irene, Irene, wherefore art thou, Irene?'"

Even though Lou had grown accustomed to my sense of humor, it still brought a smile to his face.

"I don't mean anything by it, Cy, but I can't see you being anyone's Romeo. And I doubt if Miss Penrod will come down to us. The only one I know who came down to His people was Jesus. Everyone else expects you to climb up and bow down to them."

"Good point, Lou. We don't know her yet, but she's definitely not Jesus."

"No, and while it may be a long way up to her house, that's not heaven up there, either."

"No, but it's higher up than the Tower of Babel ever got."

Eventually, we quit stalling and reached for the railing. How many steps was it again? Too many. That's how many. Surely, the Washington Monument had fewer.

Lou and I wheezed in unison as we climbed a little, rested a lot, and climbed a little more. Eventually, we arrived at the front porch with the sun still high in the sky. We were about to meet the elusive Irene Penrod.

40

I punched the doorbell and waited for Miss Penrod to answer. In a few seconds, I was relieved to see that Miss Penrod had not been murdered, nor had she disappeared with the Reynoldses and Silverman. It was comforting to know that not everyone on Hilltop Place had been abducted.

"Miss Penrod?"

"Yes, I'm Irene Penrod," the woman answered quizzically. Miss Penrod wore a beige knit top and camel-colored pants. She appeared to be around five-six, had light brown hair, and was slender. I guessed her to be somewhere in her early to mid-thirties.

"I'm Lt. Dekker and this is Sgt. Murdock. We're with the local police department. We're detectives."

"Is there something wrong, Lieutenant?" I noticed that the woman remained calm, at least on the outside.

"I'm afraid there is, Miss Penrod. Have you been out of town?"

"Yes, Lieutenant. I left last Saturday and I just got back a little over an hour ago. What can I help you with, Lieutenant?"

"And where have you been, Miss Penrod?"

"Visiting relatives." Miss Penrod was straightforward with her answer. She didn't seem to have Mrs. Reynolds's belligerent attitude.

"Miss Penrod, I want to show you something. Tell me if you've seen it before."

With that, I reached into my coat pocket and extracted the envelope we'd found underground. I handed it to Miss Penrod, and she opened it and looked at it.

"Yes, Lieutenant. This is the note I received from my aunt whom I've been visiting. How did you get it?"

I avoided her question and continued.

"Miss Penrod, are you aware that there are tunnels under the houses on this street?"

"Of course, Lieutenant. Everyone on this street knows about them."

"Well, Miss Penrod. I found this envelope lying in the dirt in one of those tunnels. Do you have any idea how it got there?"

"I have no idea, Lieutenant. Mr. Hartley, our mailman, delivered the note just before I left. I'm pretty sure I left it on the table in the hall. But I guess I couldn't have. Otherwise, someone would have had to have broken into my house and taken it. There would be no reason for anyone to take the note, and as far as I can tell, there's nothing missing."

"Miss Penrod, did you know Mrs. Nelson and Mrs. Jarvis?"

Miss Penrod seemed visibly shaken.

"Y-y-you said 'did I know.' Did something happen to them?"

"Yes, Miss Penrod. Both of them were murdered."

Miss Penrod grabbed the door facing.

"I think I need to sit down. Would you like to come in?"

Miss Penrod used the wall for assistance and helped herself to the nearest chair. I looked for somewhere to sit and noted that most of Miss Penrod's furniture appeared to be antiques. Either they were handed down, or Miss Penrod spent a lot of money furnishing her home.

"I can't believe this, Lieutenant. No one would've wanted to murder either of these dear old ladies. Everyone loved them."

"Everyone, Miss Penrod?"

"Everyone who knew them. How did it happen, Lieutenant, and when?"

"Mrs. Nelson was murdered last Saturday morning."

"But that was the day I left, and I saw her Saturday morning."

"Tell me about the last time you saw her, Miss Penrod, and the last time you saw Mrs. Jarvis."

"I saw Mrs. Jarvis Saturday morning, too. Mrs. Nelson called me and asked if I was coming over before I left town. You may or may not know that Mrs. Nelson had fallen recently and had just gotten out of the hospital. She was incapable of doing anything for herself, so I went over a few times each day to empty her bedpan and fix her something to eat. I was concerned about her, but Mrs. Nelson told me not to worry, that her granddaughter Angela would be back that same morning and would come to check on her.

"I had tried to get hold of Angela to let her know that her grandmother had fallen, but she was away because of her job and I was unable to reach her.

"Anyway, Mrs. Nelson asked me if I had time to run over to Mrs. Jarvis's house and pick up something and bring it to her. I told her I would be glad to. She told me that Mrs. Jarvis was expecting me. When I got to Mrs. Jarvis's house, she hollered for me to come in. Mrs. Jarvis was confined to a wheelchair, so I stepped inside and Mrs. Jarvis handed me an envelope and asked me to take it and give it to Mrs. Nelson. Then, Mrs. Jarvis told me 'goodbye.' She seemed so afraid. Now that I think of it, it's just as if she knew she was going to die."

"What did you think of Mrs. Jarvis?"

"She was a nice lady, but I felt sorry for her."

"Sorry enough to put her out of her misery."

"Absolutely not, Lieutenant."

"Miss Penrod, someone overheard you say something about not having to take care of Mrs. Jarvis much longer. What did you mean by that?"

"Mrs. Jarvis didn't want to leave the house where she had lived for such a long time, but it was difficult for her to take care of herself and the house. In the last few years, she'd had to hire someone to come in and do her cleaning, but still, that didn't seem to be enough. For some time Mrs. Jarvis had been contemplating having a young person move in with her, and give her free rent in exchange for helping her whenever she needed some assistance. She told me that next week she was going to contact an agency to help her find someone."

"Did anyone else know about this, Miss Penrod?"

"I'm sure Mrs. Nelson did, but I don't know of anyone else. Mrs. Jarvis didn't confide in a lot of people."

"Just you and Mrs. Nelson?"

"You act like you don't believe me, Lieutenant. I loved those ladies, and both of them were alive the last time I saw them."

"I didn't mean to insinuate otherwise, Miss Penrod. Carry on. Pick up with when you left Mrs. Jarvis's house."

Miss Penrod was not as calm as before, let out an indignant breath, and then continued.

"Anyway, I told Mrs. Jarvis goodbye and hurried off to Mrs. Nelson's house, since I didn't know how much help she would need and I had a bus to catch."

"Did you catch that bus, Miss Penrod?"

"You ask that as if you know I didn't, Lieutenant."

I didn't give away whether I knew or not, so Miss Penrod continued.

"Just after I got to the bus station my cousin drove up. He gave me a ride to his mom and dad's house. Not only did it save me the price of a bus ticket, but we didn't have to stop in every little town along the way."

"And you're just now getting back from your visit?"

"That's right."

"Sorry to interrupt, Miss Penrod, but I have another question. Did you see anyone between the time you left Mrs. Jarvis's house and you got to Mrs. Nelson's?"

She took a minute to think.

"Yes, I did. Mrs. Wilkins was sitting on her front porch. I didn't have my cell phone with me, so I asked her what time it was."

"And what time was it?"

"I don't remember, but I remember that I didn't have much time to spare before I got to the bus station."

"Please continue from the moment you went to Mrs. Nelson's house."

"Well, I went up and rang the bell and Mrs. Nelson let me in."

"I thought you said she was disabled."

"Sorry, I'm a little nervous, and I'm getting ahead of myself. I rang the doorbell and Mrs. Nelson pushed a button above her bed to let me in."

"So, you didn't have a key?"

"Oh, yes, I had a key, but as you probably already know, Mrs. Nelson's front door was double bolted. You could unlock one lock with a key, but you still couldn't get in until Mrs. Nelson pushed that button. Say? Wait a minute. How could anyone get in and murder Mrs. Nelson? She would've had to admit them, and she would never admit anyone she didn't know. Do you think someone murdered

Mrs. Jarvis first, and then went down into the tunnel and came up through Mrs. Nelson's house that way?"

"I don't know, Miss Penrod. You're the detective."

"You don't think I did it, do you, Lieutenant? I know how it must look since I admit I saw both women on Saturday morning, but someone had to have entered those houses after I left."

"So, Miss Penrod. Do you know who else has a key to Mrs. Nelson's house?"

"Most of the neighbors and who knows who else."

"So what did you do when you arrived at Mrs. Nelson's?"

"Well, I turned the key and spoke into the intercom to let her know it was me. She buzzed me in, and I immediately went up to her bedroom. She asked me if I had been to Mrs. Jarvis's, and I started to hand her the envelope. She waved me away, and said, 'just put it on top of the other one.'"

"There was another envelope?"

"Yes, Lieutenant, but I suppose you already know that, too."

I didn't reveal that this was news to me and continued with my questioning.

"Where was the other envelope?"

"On the table beside her bed."

"Describe the envelopes to me, Miss Penrod."

"Well, both of them were long envelopes. Both of them were white. There's nothing much to describe."

"Do you have any idea what was in either envelope?"

"Of course not. I didn't open them. Neither lady confided in me, and I didn't ask, but Mrs. Nelson said something that frightened me."

"What was that, Miss Penrod?'

"She said, 'Irene, I want you to take these envelopes when you leave, and if anything happens to me, I want you to give them to the police.'"

"So, will you get them for me?"

"I, uh, don't have them. I forgot and left them on the table."

"I see, Miss Penrod. Well, from the size of the envelope, did it appear to be paper inside or something else?"

"Oh, I'd say both of them contained paper, probably two or three sheets from the thickness of them."

"So, did you put Mrs. Jarvis's envelope on top of the other one?"

"Of course, Lieutenant. Why wouldn't I?"

"And what did you do after that, Miss Penrod?"

"I emptied her bedpan, washed my hands, and asked her what she'd like for me to fix her to eat. She told me not to bother, that Angela would be there before long."

"Miss Penrod, when you visited Mrs. Nelson, did you ever fix her something to drink?"

"Not usually. Prior to her fall, she was able to take care of herself, but I did fix her something to drink on the day she came home from the hospital."

"And what did you give Mrs. Nelson to drink?"

"Grape juice. She asked me if I would be willing to pick up some purple grape juice for her, and so I did."

"As far as you know, was Mrs. Nelson in the habit of drinking grape juice?"

"I have no idea. I don't think I saw her drink it before, but usually, I wasn't around Mrs. Nelson when she was eating or drinking. Normally she dined alone unless Angela was there."

"But on the day she died, you fixed her a glass of grape juice."

Miss Penrod seemed visibly shaken. To keep her hands from shaking, she gripped the arms of her chair.

"No, I said I fixed it the day she came home from the hospital. Why do you ask? Did someone poison her grape juice? It wasn't me, Lieutenant. Remember, she died after I left on Saturday."

"She did die on Saturday, Miss Penrod. As to whether it was before or after you left, I have no idea. In any case, no one is accusing you of poisoning her. I'm not in a position to accuse anyone right now."

Miss Penrod seemed a little relieved, but not much. She took a moment to recompose herself and replied to my statement.

"I'm sorry, Lieutenant. It's just that this is difficult for me. I thought the world of Mrs. Nelson, and Mrs. Jarvis, too."

"Miss Penrod, did Mrs. Nelson appear to be sleepy on Saturday morning?"

She looked puzzled. "No," she answered.

"Well, did you give her any medication or anything to help her sleep?"

"No, did someone give her something?"

I avoided the question and continued.

"Miss Penrod, during the time you were at Mrs. Nelson's, did you see anyone else other than Mrs. Nelson?"

"Yes, Mr. Hartley stopped by with the mail, and I saw Mr. Silverman watching all that went on from across the street. Oh, and I saw that messed up young man down the street."

"Do you mean Jimmy Reynolds?"

"That's right."

"Where was he?"

"He was hiding on Mrs. Overstreet's porch when I went to see Mrs. Nelson. I know it's not his fault that he has problems, but he still scares me. He came running down the steps when he saw me. I thought he was coming after me, but he went back to his own house."

I made a mental note, wondering why Mr. Silverman did not say anything about this. Then, I remembered that the Overstreet house is the only house where a tree blocks Mr. Silverman's view of it.

I looked back up at Irene Penrod. She looked nervous. I continued my questioning.

"Back to Mr. Hartley. Did he stay long at Mrs. Nelson's?"

"A few minutes, but not long."

"So Mr. Hartley left before you did, Miss Penrod?"

"I assume so."

"Did you actually see Mr. Hartley leave the house?"

"No, I was still with Mrs. Nelson in her bedroom. I was telling her goodbye and told her I'd see her when I got back. She gave me a big hug. That seemed strange because she wasn't used to hugging me. Of course, she was not bedridden before, and I'd never gone away, so that might have had something to do with it."

"Miss Penrod, did you notice whether or not Mr. Hartley saw the envelopes?"

"I couldn't say."

I leaned forward and calmly asked my next question.

"Think for a moment, Miss Penrod. Did Mr. Hartley by any chance set his mail down while he was there?"

"You know, now that you mention it, it seems like he did, but I think he put it down on the bed, not on the table. Still, he might have put it on the table. Do you think he put the mail he was to deliver on top of those two envelopes and then picked them up without realizing it? Do you think he might have delivered them to someone else by mistake?"

Miss Penrod looked at me and read my mind.

"I know, Lieutenant. I'm the detective, but I'm more inclined to think of myself as a concerned neighbor."

This time Miss Penrod could not help but crack a little smile.

"Anything else you might be able to think of that might be helpful to us?"

"Well, just as I was about to leave, Mrs. Jarvis called. I answered the phone, so I knew who it was. I handed the phone to Mrs. Nelson, and evidently, Mrs. Jarvis asked Mrs. Nelson if I gave her the envelope, because she said, 'Yeah, she brought it.' Mrs. Nelson hung up, I said goodbye to her and hurried home to call a taxi."

When Miss Penrod mentioned the taxi, it gave me another idea.

"When the taxi picked you up, did you notice whether or not Mr. Silverman was sitting at his window?"

Miss Penrod stopped and thought for a moment.

"I don't think he was."

"Well, Mr. Silverman said he saw you leave. Are you sure he wasn't sitting at his window?"

"To tell you the truth, I was more concerned about getting away than I was looking to see who knew I was leaving. Still, if Mr. Silverman was sitting there, I didn't notice him."

"What about Mrs. Wilkins? Did you see her when you left?"

"I was more concerned about making sure I didn't fall down the steps with both hands full of luggage. I couldn't tell you where Mrs. Wilkins was, or anyone else for that matter. I can tell you only that the taxi driver never bothered to get out until I got to the bottom of the steps."

I thanked Irene Penrod for her help, got up, and headed for the door. Lou followed. As Lou and I left, we stopped by Officer Davis's cruiser to ask him a question. It was just as I thought. Officer Davis didn't see any envelopes on the table beside the bed, but then that morning he was not in a frame of mind to notice anything.

As Lou and I walked back to Lightning, I wondered whether or not it meant anything that Stanley Silverman said one thing and Irene Penrod said another. For some reason, I remembered the dust I had seen on Silverman's shoes that day. Now, that I think of it, the dust resembled the dirt in the tunnel. Was it because he had visited his mother's grave? Or did Silverman give us a play-by-play of the day's proceedings merely to give himself an alibi? Was he watching everything from inside Mrs. Nelson's house, rather than his own? Or was Miss Penrod so preoccupied with getting away with murder that she paid attention to little else? I wondered which facts to discard, and which ones to use to find a murderer.

41

As Lou and I pulled away from Irene Penrod's house, some of what Sam told me came back to me. Irene Penrod was known for lying, had once gotten even, and had been overheard saying that she wouldn't have to take care of Mrs. Jarvis much longer. Were there two envelopes, and if there were, were these two women afraid something was going to happen to them? Or was this one of Miss Penrod's lies in order to divert suspicion away from herself?

If Irene Penrod was telling the truth, why would those two women give the envelopes to her? It seemed reasonable that Mrs. Nelson would give them to her granddaughter, or to her attorney. Could it be that she didn't trust one or both of them? Did the latest development mean that all the other suspects had been eliminated? If there were two envelopes, had someone destroyed them? Or was it possible that someone is using those envelopes to blackmail someone else? If so, was the money we found in the rented house blackmail money? We found the money in the house Hartley had rented. Could he have seen someone murder one or both women? He did say something about becoming better off financially.

Lou and I pulled away and headed off to find Hartley. After driving up and down several streets, we finally located the post office's version of Speedy Gonzales. Hartley said he didn't see any envelopes on the table in Mrs. Nelson's bedroom, but then I would've been surprised if he had said otherwise.

Lou and I turned away from Hartley. I stood at the car door for a few moments before I opened it. Raincoats, magnets, envelopes. How many of these things were evidence, and how much was clutter?

I opened the door, got in, and started the car before Lou's curiosity got the best of him.

"Do you have any idea what was in those envelopes, Cy, or do you even think there really were any envelopes?"

"I'm not sure."

"You're not sure of what?"

"I'm not sure whether there were any envelopes, and even if there were, I'm not sure what was in them."

"Let's assume there were two envelopes. What would they contain? The logical explanation would be a will, but Hornwell has Mrs. Nelson's will. It doesn't make sense that there would be a second will, and if there were, it would supersede the other one, wouldn't it?"

"It depends upon when the wills are dated."

"That means that whoever took the will would have to be either Miss Penrod, which doesn't make sense, Hartley, Miss Nelson, or whoever owned those footsteps Officer Davis and Miss Nelson heard running from the house. If the envelope contained a will, it would've made sense for Angela Nelson to have taken it if it had been a will that disinherited her, but the one that pretty much disinherits her is the one that was found. Besides, what she told us was in the will was what was in the will."

"None of this makes sense, Lou. If there were two envelopes, why would the old lady have given them to Miss Penrod? She knew her granddaughter would be there shortly. She should've given them to Angela unless she was afraid Angela might try to kill her, or she wanted to disinherit Angela. However, as you said, the will we have pretty much disinherits Miss Nelson, so that doesn't seem to be a reason. Besides, Miss Nelson has an alibi for the entire morning. First, she was on a plane. Next, she was in a cab. Then, Silverman saw her get out of a cab, and he continued to watch her until Officer Davis arrived. Even Mrs. Wilkins claims to have seen her. She might've wanted to kill her grandmother, but didn't have an opportunity. And her attorney was two hours away at his cabin, and someone saw him there twice. That leaves us with Miss Penrod, but that doesn't make sense, either. Hartley interrupted her visit. I don't think she had time to give the old lady the medication and then give her the poison thirty minutes to an hour later."

"Maybe the two of them were in it together. Maybe Miss Penrod gave the old lady the medication, and Miss Nelson gave her the poison."

"And maybe Officer Davis held her hand while she did it."

"Oh, I forgot that part."

"This thing would be a lot simpler, Lou, if we could forget a few parts."

"Cy, I'm assuming that the poison was added to the glass of grape juice, and not the container."

Before Lou finished his comment, he could see a different look in my eye.

"No, Lou, it was in the container. Mrs. Jarvis wheeled up to Mrs. Nelson's, the two of them had a drink together, and then Mrs. Jarvis wheeled home so she could die in her own house."

Lou continued with my humorous fable.

"How fast was Mrs. Jarvis going when she wheeled up the hill in her front yard?"

"Fast enough that Officer Davis almost pulled her over before she could get in the house and lock the door."

Lou interrupted my vision of a cruiser chasing a speeding wheelchair with a question about our other favorite subject.

Steve Demaree

42

Sunday morning Lou and I attended church, sat in our pew on the back row. We learned years ago that we can hear the sermon just as well from that distance. After church, we stopped and ate lunch before each of us went to his home. The next thing on my agenda was to take a nap. Before I lay down, I unplugged my phone, so no one would interrupt my much-needed sleep.

In the middle of the afternoon, I received a call from Officer Davis. He had been trying to get me since the night before. Harry Hornwell had been on the street on Saturday night when Officer Davis was doing surveillance. He delivered a package to Stanley Silverman's house and left a few minutes later with two envelopes.

When I hung up from talking to him, the questions began to flow. Did Silverman take the envelopes from Mrs. Nelson's house? Could it be he watched everything that went on Saturday morning from inside Mrs. Nelson's house instead of inside his own? If so, did that make him the murderer, or did he know who the murderer was? And was Silverman at home when Hornwell visited or did Mr. Hornwell let himself in? Each new happening led to more questions. I hoped the phone records I planned to pick up the next day would help me gather some answers.

+++

Around 6:40 Sunday night, Lou pulled up in front of my house in his red and white 1957 Chevy. I dashed out the door, well I moved as fast as someone my age in my condition could move and slid onto the front seat of Lou's fine automobile. We were off to pick up the girls. Lou and I were lucky to have friends like Betty and Thelma Lou. Not every woman is willing to go out on short notice. Most of them fall into one of two categories. The category Betty and Thelma Lou are in, and the category Heloise Humphert is in. I'd choose the first category anytime.

The four of us had a nice time. The food was good, and Lou and I enjoyed spending time with people who were not on the verge of rigor mortis or on our suspect list. If either Lou or I decided to settle down, Betty and Thelma Lou were women we would want to settle down with. The only problem was that I'd been by myself so long that I had resigned myself that I had done all the settling I planned to do. Besides, I was still in love with Eunice.

+++

Monday morning the phone rang. I stumbled from my bed and went to answer it.

"Oh, hi, Frank. I assume you have identified the body you dug up the other day."

"That's right, Cy, and I have nothing hair-raising to report. The body was Mrs. Olivia Silverman, and she died of natural causes. No poison this time. As best we can tell, she's been dead for about three months."

"Thanks, Frank. I'll try to lighten your workload."

"You do that, Cy."

Steve Demaree

I hung up the phone and pondered the facts Frank had relayed to me. Evidently, Silverman didn't kill his mother. Did this mean that he didn't murder Mrs. Nelson or Mrs. Jarvis, either? If so, how would he explain those two envelopes, or were they the same envelopes? Or did Irene Penrod ever have two envelopes? Could it be that she found out that Hornwell was going to Silverman's to deliver a package and pick up two envelopes and wanted to cast suspicion away from herself? Or did Mrs. Nelson have a reason to suspect her granddaughter or Mr. Hornwell of wanting to do away with her?

For the time being, I forgot about what might be true and thought about what I knew to be true. Actually, I knew nothing to be true, except the fact that two elderly women were murdered, but I decided to believe anything confirmed by two or more witnesses. Two witnesses, Silverman and Mrs. Wilkins, confirmed that no one entered the front door of the Nelson house from the time that Irene Penrod left until the time Angela Nelson entered with Officer Davis. Did that mean that either Irene Penrod murdered Mrs. Nelson or the murderer entered the house through the underground passageway? I wish I knew.

43

After I talked to Frank I got ready to pick up Lou. I was on my way to dial his number when the phone rang.

I chuckled when he answered.

"You must be feeling good this morning, Cy."

"Yeah, I've been thinking about going out and working on my golf game today."

"You've never played golf, Cy."

"Then I'd say my game could use some work."

"There are a lot of things about you that could use some work."

"You're a piece of work yourself, Lou. I'd rather save all this for another time. Are we going to spend all morning on the phone whispering sweet nothings to each other, or are we going to get on with our day?"

"Boy, Cy, you sure are feisty this morning."

"What can I say? I'm just one of those people who's grumpy when I think I'd rather be resting than investigating."

"Birds of a feather."

"See you in fifteen minutes."

Lou was waiting out in front of his apartment building when I pulled up. "You know something, don't you, Cy?"

"A little bit, but what I don't know is God's message for today."

"Alexander Graham 3:00 A.M."

"Aha! I know that one, Lou."

"You should. How many times did we see *The Parent Trap* when we were kids?"

"At least a dozen. We had to. You were in love with Hayley Mills."

"And what was the name of that TV star you liked?"

"Lori Martin. She played the daughter on *National Velvet.*"

"Oh, yeah. Remember how we used to go up in our treehouse and pretend those girls were in love with us."

"Yeah, I remember, but don't let it get around the department. George and Frank would have a field day with that one."

"Oh, to be young again."

"We're still young, Lou."

+++

A few minutes after we left the Blue Moon we had copies of the phone records for all the suspects except Don Hampton, who had no phone. I'd planned to give all of them a good going over, but I was particularly interested in the records of four people. In some cases, I was interested in who was called. In other instances, I wanted to know if any calls were made to or from a certain number. Not only did the records show all incoming and outgoing calls, but how long each call lasted.

It took a few hours for the two of us to go over the records. We'd gathered some helpful information. Where it would lead, we didn't know.

No one made any calls to or received any calls from the Reynolds house. Someone had made a couple of calls from the Silverman house after Silverman's alleged disappearance. If Silverman made those calls, why did he continue to hide?

Angela Nelson had lied to me when she told me she didn't know her grandmother had been hurt. She made some calls to the hospital and one to her grandmother's house the day before she died. Why did she lie to me? Did she think it would make her look bad because she was unwilling to cut short her buying trip, or was there more to it?

I also learned that at 9:35 on the morning of the murder someone from Mrs. Jarvis's house called Mrs. Nelson's house. The phone call lasted only a couple of minutes. A short time later, at 9:48 Irene Penrod called the local cab company from her own home. Both of these agreed with the information Irene Penrod had given us. We continued perusing those phone bills until I felt I had them memorized.

+++

Lou's night was his own. He told me he planned to go home and lower himself into his folding chair. It was time to work some more on his jigsaw puzzle.

Both times I went out that day I returned and noticed the absence of my neighbor. I wasn't sure how much longer Miss Humphert would avoid exposure to my "illness," but I hoped she'd stay away for a while longer. While I wished it would keep her away for a year, I planned to take it one day at a time and be thankful for each of those days.

+++

While Lou played, I had work to do. I placed a phone call to Angela Nelson.

"Hello."

"Miss Nelson, this is Lt. Dekker. How are you this evening?"

"Uh, fine, Lieutenant."

"Miss Nelson, I told you that I would let you know if we found out anything else about your grandmother's death. I've uncovered some new evidence. Could Sgt. Murdock and I drop by tomorrow morning sometime?"

"I was supposed to work tomorrow, Lieutenant, but I don't have anything urgent. I can call and let them know that I won't be in until tomorrow afternoon if that's okay."

"That'll be fine, Miss Nelson. We'll drop by somewhere around 10:00 if that's all right."

+++

I planned our strategy for the next day. The next morning we planned to question Angela Nelson to see why she lied, locate Stanley Silverman, even if it took a search warrant, and talk to Harry Hornwell, if necessary. If we didn't discover our murderer by that time, we planned to look inside the house Hartley rented for a month to see if the money was still there and do whatever was necessary to find the Reynoldses. I felt we were getting close to solving the case. All we had to do was talk to the right people and push the right buttons.

+++

Shortly before I went to bed, it hit me. My brain had been sorting so many clues, I had forgotten one of the most important ones. I needed to place another call. I had only one question I needed to ask a certain witness. If that witness gave me the answer I expected, I figured I had the case wrapped up, or at least I was well on the way to doing it.

I made the call and confirmed what I expected. It was the only way the case made any sense. Too many people had too many alibis and not enough motives. I still had people to see the next day, but at least I expected to wrap up the case before the day was over. It should have been enough to make me smile, but there was something about realizing one person murdered another that kept me from smiling. Besides, I felt like kicking myself for not solving the case sooner.

Steve Demaree

44

I awoke Tuesday morning, rolled over, and looked at my old-fashioned alarm clock. The hands pointed to 7:23. That gave me time to hop in the shower, get dressed, read my daily devotional, pick up Lou, before our appointment with Angela Nelson.

As I showered, my thoughts drifted to the two women who had died. Even though I'd spent many years on the police force, it still pained me each time I discovered another body. At least this time both women were well up in age and in poor health. One of them had no family. The other had only one granddaughter.

As the water turned cold, I realized my thoughts and I had lingered a little too long. I jumped from the shower, or at least as much of a jump as someone my age and physical condition could manage and dressed hurriedly. I had no desire to rush. Once I'd dressed, I called Lou to let him know that I was on my way.

Just as I was about to leave, the phone rang. It was someone in the department telling me about some new evidence that just came in, evidence that would solidify our case. I made note of the information, hung up the phone, and prepared to leave. It was then that something happened that had never happened to me. I reached in a drawer and found something that could be helpful, then closed the door, and left to pick up Lou.

+++

Lou opened the car door and was about to get in. As he ducked his head and looked at me, he froze.

"Cy, you look like you've had a head-on collision with the Cheshire cat. What gives?"

While I always like to bring each case to a close, each time it pained me to know that someone had murdered another person. A full-faced grin was something Lou never saw unless we were having fun.

Lou sat down and repeated his question.

"What gives, Cy?"

I puffed up and said, "Guess who God spoke to this morning?"

"You don't mean He spoke to you, do you, Cy?"

I grinned from ear to ear and nodded my head.

"Now, don't get me wrong. The house didn't shake. I didn't even hear anything, but the thought was clear enough. Is that kind of how you get your messages, Lou?"

"Pretty much. So tell me your message, and I'll tell you mine."

I stopped smiling. I was disappointed that Lou had a message, too. I'd hoped that my message was the only message of the day. Nevertheless, I shared my message with my friend and hoped his didn't cancel mine.

"My message was, 'Lightning,' and I even know what it means."

"Oh, you do, do you? Well, let's see. It has nothing to do with your speed."

"Or yours."

"Don't interrupt. I assume it doesn't have anything to do with a pedestrian being struck by Lightning."

"No, and I'm not going to tell you what it has to do with. Just watch me operate today."

"Yes sir, Dr. Dekker."

"So, Lou, what's your message of the day?"

"My message for today was, 'Listen to your partner, both of them.'"

"That's what I've been trying to tell you for years. You should listen to whatever I tell you."

Lou laughed and then replied, "I don't know, but since this is the first time I've had this message, and this is the first time God has trusted you to get a message right, maybe this is the first time you've said anything worth listening to. Plus, you're forgetting one thing, Cy."

"What's that, Lou?"

"My message said 'both of them.' Know what that means?"

"Yeah, it means Jesus and I agree on whatever this is, and you'd better listen to us."

"Well, I promise you I'll do my best to listen to the One of you who's never wrong."

45

I eased Lightning in front of Angela Nelson's house. Lou and I stepped out of the car and looked up to see Miss Nelson peering through the blinds. I counted the steps I needed to mount before reaching the front porch. I refrained from smiling when I noticed there were only three. After all, this was not a moment to smile.

I climbed those three steps, knocked on the door. Angela Nelson opened the front door and admitted us.

"Why don't we have a seat in the living room. I think we'll be more comfortable there."

I nodded and Lou and I followed Angela Nelson. The living room contained facing couches and a couple of chairs. Miss Nelson took a seat on one couch, and Lou and I plopped down on the couch across from her. No one spoke for a few seconds, and then Angela Nelson broke the silence.

"You said you have some information about my grandmother."

"That's right, Miss Nelson. We've uncovered some new information about your grandmother's death."

"I thought you said she was poisoned. You mean she wasn't poisoned?"

"Oh, she was poisoned, all right, but not the way and the time that we had originally thought."

"Oh?"

"See, when I originally looked over the evidence, I couldn't see anyone with a motive for murder except you."

"I assume you mean that you thought I would be inheriting my grandmother's estate."

"That's right, Miss Nelson."

"But I told you at the time I wouldn't inherit."

"I know that Miss Nelson, but many years on the force have taught me not to believe everything I hear someone say. It was only after Mr. Hornwell made the will public that I knew that you'd told the truth. That was when you lost your motive.

"Anyway, I studied the evidence trying to find out who killed your grandmother. The next day I found out that it took the poison somewhere between fifteen and twenty minutes to work. So, I began to muddle through what I knew at the time."

"We know that Irene Penrod went over to see your grandmother that morning and that Mr. Hartley was there, as well. Could it be that one of them poisoned your grandmother before he or she left? We also know that someone else was in the house because both you and Officer Davis heard this person. As far as both of you could tell, this person ran out of the front door. At any rate, even if the intruder continued to hide in the house if this person was the murderer, he or she would've had to have murdered your grandmother prior to this point because either you or Officer Davis were in the house from that time on."

Angela Nelson interrupted me.

"Plus, Lieutenant, Officer Davis and I had already discovered my grandmother's body by that time."

"I'll get to that in a minute, Miss Nelson. We aren't sure when Mr. Hartley or Miss Penrod left your grandmother's house. Supposedly, Mr. Hartley left first, but he could've been the person you and Officer Davis heard leaving. However, that's doubtful, because Mr. Hartley had already delivered mail to everyone on the street.

"So, we have Mr. Hartley, Miss Penrod, and the person who ran from the house, who could've been anyone. Plus, we have one other person, Miss Nelson."

"Who's that, Lieutenant?"

"You, Miss Nelson."

"But, I wasn't there yet."

"I'm not talking about who was there yet, but who was there at all."

"But I never saw my grandmother until the officer arrived."

"I know that, Miss Nelson. We even have witnesses. Mr. Silverman said he saw you, and Miss Penrod confirmed that he was watching. Even Mrs. Wilkins had her eyes on you from the moment you arrived until you gained entrance to your grandmother's house, assisted by Officer Davis. Mr. Silverman also said you never entered the house until Officer Davis arrived, and we have every reason to believe him because if not, we would have to assume that you were lying, Mr. Silverman was lying, Miss Penrod was lying, and Mrs. Wilkins was lying. That's just too many liars to suit me.

"Not only that but according to the time the taxi driver said he dropped you off and the time Officer Davis said he arrived, you didn't have enough time to murder your grandmother. That is, you didn't have time unless you murdered her after you and Officer Davis discovered the body."

"But Officer Davis would've known if my grandmother was still alive."

"Not necessarily, Miss Nelson."

"I don't understand, Lieutenant."

"I think you do, Miss Nelson. It's called assisted suicide."

"You think my grandmother and I planned her death in the few seconds I was alone with her before Officer Davis came in the room."

"No, I don't, Miss Nelson. When Mrs. Reynolds, her son Jimmy, and Mr. Silverman disappeared, I decided to subpoena everyone's telephone records to see if there were any phone calls made from either house. I was getting their phone records, so I decided to look over the records of anyone else connected with this case.

"Miss Nelson, you told me that you didn't know that your grandmother had been hurt in a fall until you arrived at her house, but our records show that you talked to her. We have records of phone calls that were made from various hotels across the country where you were staying at the time. Some of those were made to your home, evidently to retrieve whatever messages had been left on your answering machine. Others were made to the hospital where your grandmother was a patient.

"Plus, we have a record of calls made from your cell phone to your grandmother's number. One of those calls was made the day before your grandmother died. I think that was when your grandmother pleaded with you to help her die and to help Mrs. Jarvis escape her wheelchair for good. I think there's evidence of this in two envelopes that Miss Penrod told us about. I think you have those two envelopes, Miss Nelson. Why don't you go get them for us?"

"I don't know what you're talking about, Lieutenant."

I never played poker, but I knew how to bluff.

"Oh, come on, Miss Nelson. I know you have them. I could get a search warrant, but I know you don't want me to do that."

Lou and I tried not to get involved emotionally as tears began to flow down Miss Nelson's cheeks, but it became more difficult as those escaping tears changed to sobs. I wasn't in a hurry. I remained silent and planned to give Angela Nelson as long as it took.

A few minutes later, Angela Nelson took her hands away from her face and looked at me.

"I'll be right back," she said, as she stood up and walked out of the room. She returned carrying two envelopes and a tape recorder. She handed them to me.

"What's this?" I asked, looking at the tape recorder.

"There's a tape, too," Angela Nelson responded.

46

I sat the tape recorder between Lou and me and laid the two envelopes on top of it. I picked up the top envelope and motioned for Lou to pick up the other one. The two of us opened and read silently as Angela Nelson sat across from us. When both of us had finished reading, we exchanged envelopes. When Lou and I'd finished reading the contents of both envelopes, we faced Angela Nelson who broke the silence.

"The tape recorder has batteries in it. Just push the 'play' button."

I turned around the tape recorder, pushed the "play" button, and looked at my watch.

"Hello, Grandmama. It's me, Angela. Are you feeling better now that you're home?"

"No, Child. I told you the other day that the doctor said my old bones are too brittle to heal."

"Maybe you'll feel better when I get there. I'll be home tomorrow."

"Angela, I've already told you what the doctor said. Remember what we talked about the other day?"

"I don't want to do it, Grandmama."

"Please, Angela, you don't know how much it hurts. I don't want to hurt anymore. You're the only one who can help me."

"But Grandmama, it's not right. Besides, I don't want to lose you."

"I don't want to lose you either, Child, but I just hurt so much. Help me, Child. I want to go to be with your grandfather. Please."

"I'm afraid, Grandmama. I'm really afraid."

"Just listen and I'll walk you through it. I've written down that it was my idea, and Mabel Jarvis has done the same. I'll send Irene down to pick up Mabel's envelope tomorrow. The envelopes will be on the table beside my bed. You pick them up and put them in your pocket as soon as you see them. Understand?"

"Yes, Grandmama."

"Okay, here's what I want you to do. Irene will be here in the morning. She'll be leaving town, so she'll be leaving a few minutes before you get here. Nosy old Mr. Silverman will be watching as always from his house, so he'll give you an alibi. Just come up on the porch as if nothing's wrong and ring the bell. I won't answer, of course, but ring it anyway. Then, go over to Irene's, as if you don't know that she's already left town. When she doesn't answer, come back over here and make sure that Mr. Silverman sees you using your cell phone.

"Call the police. They'll probably send some tenderfoot who doesn't know what he's doing. When he breaks in, go to the back of the house first, so he won't know anything, and then come up to my room. Make sure that you get here before he does and pick up the envelopes. Then, go into your act. Chances are he won't know enough to check and see if I'm dead. He'll have to go out to the cruiser and call in. That'll be your cue to hurry to the refrigerator and get a glass of grape juice. Bring it up and go to the medicine cabinet and get me the poison. I'll put the poison in the juice and drink it. If the officer isn't back yet, we'll say our goodbyes and you can go back downstairs and delay the officer until I'm gone. Chances are he won't come back upstairs until the medical examiner comes.

"Wait around until they leave, then sneak through the underground passage and take some juice and poison to Mabel Jarvis. You got that?"

"I wish you'd change your mind, Grandmama."

"I can't, Child. I just can't. I need to catch up on things with your mom and dad and your grandfather."

The sound of a doorbell came through on the tape.

"I've got to go now, Child. Irene's here. I love you, and I'll see you tomorrow."

"I love you, too, Grandmama."

I pushed the "stop" button and looked at my watch again. Only Angela Nelson's flowing tears kept her from knowing that she was not the only one who had shed a tear.

"What happens now, Lieutenant?" Angela Nelson asked in a choked-up voice.

I paused and composed myself.

"I know it's been rough, and it'll continue to be, but as best you can, I'd recommend you do your best to try to get your life back together."

"Does that mean you're not arresting me?"

"Miss Nelson, the last time I checked there was no charge against giving a thirsty woman something to drink. In a world where everyone is eager to get his or her hands on every relative's money, you declined your grandmother's estate. You were coerced into doing something you didn't want to do. I see no reason to ruin the life of a woman who's already struggling, nor do I see why we should deprive the American Heart Association and the

American Cancer Society of your grandmother's money. However, I do have a couple of questions, Miss Nelson."

"What's that, Lieutenant?"

"Were you the person in the raincoat?"

"Yes, my grandmother came up with that when she first told me about her idea. She wanted to muddy the waters as much as possible, hoping that the police would give up on trying to solve her murder. I guess she never expected someone as good as you."

"So, how were you able to answer your home phone just after eluding Sgt. Murdock and me?"

"Have you heard of 'call forwarding?' That night I had all calls forwarded to my cell phone."

I had never considered 'call forwarding.' It was the price I paid to live in the past as much as possible.

"And where did you go when Sgt. Murdock chased you?"

"The only place I was sure I was safe, Irene Penrod's place. I knew she was still out of town and no one would think of looking for me there."

"There's one other thing, Miss Nelson. Tell me about Mrs. Jarvis."

"I had planned to go directly from my grandmother's to Mrs. Jarvis's, but of course you ruined that plan. So, I had to go back after you left the street. Before I gave Mrs. Jarvis her grape juice, we talked for a few minutes. She told me that because of her wheelchair she had never been able to see the underground, and she asked me if I would wheel her down there. I agreed to grant the dying woman her last wish. I held on as I wheeled her down the basement steps, and again when we headed down the secret passageway. I stood beside her and listened to her share about her life until she nodded her head and was gone. I shed a few tears, asked God to take good care of my grandmother and Mrs.

Jarvis, leaned Mrs. Jarvis back in her wheelchair, and I walked back up the stairs and left."

"But what if we never found the passageway?"

"Oh, everyone knew about the passageway. Someone was going to let it slip before too long. Besides, I left enough clues for you."

"Does that include the newspaper date and the galoshes in the pantry?"

"Yes."

With that, Lou and I got up, hugged Angela Nelson, and told her to call us if there was ever a need we could fill. Then, Lou and I walked out in silence.

47

As Lou and I got to the car, I turned and saw that Angela Nelson stood in the doorway. I waved. She waved back. Lou looked in the side-view mirror and told me that the young woman continued to lean against the door watching us as we drove away. I had already informed the sergeant about my plan. Now, it was time to see if Lightning II, my bugging device, would pay off. I turned on the receiver and turned up the volume. I smiled as we heard the sound of a door closing and something that sounded like someone clapping.

"A magnificent performance, My Pet."

"Thank you, Harry, but I couldn't have done it without you."

"Obviously, My Pet, but you were the one who imitated your grandmother's voice on that tape."

"It looks like all my years of acting lessons finally paid off."

"Not to mention what a wonderful job you did copying your grandmother's and that Jarvis woman's handwriting. And who can dispute that the handwriting was theirs? Who can they come to? You were your grandmother's only relative and the Jarvis woman had none. They can come only to me for verification."

"Plus, you covered for me when that lieutenant almost ruined things by sending me away before I could kill Mabel Jarvis. That old woman would have assumed the worst and would have contacted the police when she saw them carrying my grandmother out. It's a good thing you were there to put her out of her misery."

"Also, it was a good thing I was here to give your grandmother the medication that put her to sleep. Otherwise, she would've cried out. Even that wet-behind-the-ears rookie cop would have been able to figure that one out. And it was a good thing Irene Penrod left those envelopes behind. If the police had gotten them, they might've have gotten even nosier. Before that, we weren't sure that your grandmother suspected we were up to something. And Stanley Silverman gave me an opportunity to show that rookie cop two envelopes stuffed with blank paper when I left his house. No one could tell that they weren't the same envelopes that Penrod woman had. And even if he'd stopped and searched me, envelopes with blank paper couldn't incriminate anyone."

"I couldn't have done it without you, Harry. You even knew we could let them know about the one will as long as we had another one dated later that we can use."

"Yeah, but you were the one who found all that money that Jarvis woman had hidden in her house."

"But you were her attorney and knew she had money hidden somewhere."

"Plus, I knew she died intestate. In time, we'll release your grandmother's other will plus the one you wrote for that Jarvis woman."

"Yeah, that lieutenant had no idea those two were worth millions. Of course, I was a little scared when he called about coming by. Good thing we had a back-up plan."

"Come here, My Pet. It's best if we don't see each other for a while. Then, we'll collect our money and meet on the beach in Fiji."

Lou and I had heard enough. We turned the car around and headed back to Angela Nelson's. Too bad my bugging device doesn't include a hidden camera. I would've loved to have seen the look on Angela's face when I rang her doorbell a second time.

"Oh, hi, Miss Nelson."

"Er, uh, did you forget something, Lieutenant."

"I did, Miss Nelson. This will take only a moment. Mind if I step in?"

"Uh, sure, Lieutenant."

Angela Nelson stepped back as Lou and I entered the house.

"Oh, here it is, Miss Nelson," I said as I bent over and reached between the couch cushions.

"Here's what, Lieutenant."

"I call it Lightning II. It's a bugging device. I don't want to lose it. Do you know that it was still picking up loud and clear even after we turned the corner?" I turned away and raised my voice. "You can come out now, Mr. Hornwell. Oh, by the way, Miss Nelson. You might want to consult an attorney before you say anything else, but I wouldn't recommend Mr. Hornwell. I'm afraid he'll be too busy to handle your case."

+++

We read Angela Nelson her rights, confronted her with her taped confession. Angela confessed to what she and Harry Hornwell had done.

287

"Angela, don't do it. That recording will not be admissible in court. They can't use it. Understand?"

"Harry, I didn't want any part of this to begin with. I'm finished listening to you, and I'm willing to pay for what I've done. Maybe you should do the same."

When questioned alone in another room, Angela said Hornwell had enlightened her as to how much her grandmother had salted away, and how her grandmother had talked about changing her will. I doubted that Mrs. Nelson planned to change her will, but Hornwell needed an accomplice and would make up whatever story he needed to accomplish his objective. On that occasion, a seasoned attorney seemed so credible to one so young.

After officers had transported Miss Nelson to police headquarters, she opened up. She told us how she had met Hornwell at her grandmother's house one day, how she saw him a couple of days later when she was eating lunch at a downtown drug store. He asked her to meet him for dinner that night. He wanted to discuss some ideas for her grandmother's estate with her. She declined at first, but he convinced her that these possibilities were good for her grandmother and that her grandmother would be more receptive to a suggestion if it came from her. As Hornwell and Angela finished dessert that night, she realized that the subject of her grandmother never came up. Instead, Hornwell related to her about how lonely he was since his wife became an invalid and was confined to bed. He pleaded with Angela Nelson to meet him a couple of evenings a week for dinner, nothing else. Again Angela declined, but the persistent attorney convinced the young woman that there was nothing wrong with meeting for dinner.

Miss Nelson related that over time the attorney began to come on to her. He began to give her money and buy her gifts. Also, he started telling her how miserable her grandmother was and how she would be better off if she died peacefully. Miss Nelson never agreed until after her grandmother's fall. This encouraged Hornwell to format a plan for getting rid of Mrs. Nelson and Mrs. Jarvis. As the attorney for both, he knew how wealthy both women were, but then Angela needed no convincing of that. Her grandmother kept no secrets from Angela about her wealth. Plus, Angela had discovered the secret and location of Mrs. Jarvis's wealth. Still, Angela was unwilling to go along with Hornwell's scheme until she heard what condition and state of mind her grandmother was in the first time she talked to her in the hospital.

As the plan became more of a possibility, Angela and Hornwell communicated only by personal ads in a metropolitan newspaper. If either of them wanted to meet, he or she placed an ad in code, always paid cash, and the two of them met to discuss Hornwell's plan. Finally, Angela agreed to go along. Unless either of them foresaw a complication, they agreed to follow through upon Angela's return. The plan was open-ended. It called for Hornwell to sneak over to the house he owned at the other end of Hilltop Place in the middle of the night on Friday night, before the lookouts arose. Without being seen, he prepared to keep watch on the neighborhood's proceedings and Angela's arrival. As soon as Irene Penrod's taxi left Hilltop Place on Saturday morning, Hornwell hurried underground and raced to Mrs. Nelson's house, where he gave her a sedative. Then, he waited inside Miss Penrod's house to see if Angela would be able to commit both murders. If not, he would take care of Mrs. Jarvis. Everything went well until Hornwell hurried underground to Mrs. Nelson's house. He was almost tackled by a deranged man. When Hornwell realized that the police were taking Angela away, he hurried to Mrs. Jarvis's house. This time the deranged man was nowhere to be seen.

Angela Nelson continued her confession until we knew everything. Sadly, Lou and I turned away. It was not the first time we had seen a young person waste his or her life by committing a terrible crime. The two of us walked out and decided that it was over.

"Cy, you never cease to amaze me."

"I couldn't have done it without you, or without all the help we both had."

"But how did you arrive at Angela Nelson and Harry Hornwell as our murderers?"

"Well, I admit it took me a lot longer than it should've. There were too many clues, many of which had nothing to do with the murder. Each of them made things more complicated. Nothing seemed to make sense, so I decided to try to narrow things down a bit. It helped when we got the phone records. Last night I was thinking about those two phone calls on the morning of the murder. The call Mrs. Jarvis made to Mrs. Nelson and the one Irene Penrod made to the cab company. It got me to thinking about the time issue and the most important clue we had.

"Frank told us that someone had given Mrs. Nelson something to put her to sleep forty-five minutes to an hour before the poison was administered. I had thought of that before, but only to try to figure out why someone would put her to sleep. What I needed to do instead was add the time needed to put her to sleep to the time it took to kill her and see where we stood. I added them together to see if I could eliminate any of the suspects. I looked over the clues and alibis we had been given for that morning and considered all of them gospel if they were confirmed by two or more people. It turned out that I could eliminate almost all of our suspects.

"Supposedly, Angela Nelson and Officer Davis found Mrs. Nelson dead at around 10:45. Using the quickest time period Frank accounted for, that means that someone had killed her by at least 10:30, but probably a little sooner, and had administered the sleeping tablet by at least 9:45. Irene Penrod could have administered the sleeping tablet after Hartley left, but she couldn't have killed Mrs. Nelson. Hartley was off the hook too, because he was seen delivering the mail after he left Mrs. Nelson's house, and when I checked, he went immediately to an adjacent street and continued his deliveries. So, that eliminated him.

"With the two of them eliminated, I decided to see who else I could cross off my list. I checked on Mrs. Murphy, the maid. She was feeding the homeless at her church. Witnesses accounted for her being there from 6:30 until after 11:00. Bobby couldn't have done it, because witnesses confirmed that he had delivered groceries at 9:45 and 10:05. He couldn't have entered the Nelson house before or after. The only way to enter the house was by way of the front door, which was being watched the entire time, or by underground, which no one could do unless they were already inside one of the houses on the street.

"Other than our ultimate murderers, that left us with only the people on the street. Mrs. Wilkins confirmed that she saw Jimmy, Mrs. Reynolds, and Silverman often enough that none of them had time to hurry through the tunnel, kill Mrs. Nelson, and hurry back to establish an alibi. The only time they were unaccounted for was after Angela Nelson arrived. That left me with only Angela Nelson and Harry Hornwell as possible murder suspects. The problem was that Angela didn't enter the house until she and Officer Davis discovered her grandmother, which presented another problem. I had already confirmed that Angela's plane arrived at 9:17 and that she left the airport in a taxi at 9:52. That taxi pulled up in front of Mrs. Nelson's house at 10:20, or exactly an hour before we arrived. Two witnesses kept her in their sights the entire time until Officer Davis arrived.

"There was only one possibility. I called Officer Davis, and luckily, he admitted his shortcomings. When I asked him if he confirmed that Mrs. Nelson was dead, he told me that he was too scared at the time to do so. All of us assumed that Mrs. Nelson was dead when Angela and Officer Davis entered the house. All of us assumed wrong. As soon as Officer Davis left to report the murder, Angela went to work. She poisoned her grandmother and hoped she would die before we arrived to confirm the death. The only problem was that while Angela could have murdered her grandmother, there was absolutely no way she could've put her to sleep. She had to have had an accomplice, and Hornwell was the only one who could've done it."

"But what about his alibi that he was at his cabin?"

"The only time anyone could confirm that Hornwell was in the vicinity of his cabin was when he stopped at the general store on Friday afternoon and Sunday morning. Hornwell left his home on Friday afternoon, all right, drove to the general store to establish an alibi, then drove back to Hilldale, waited until dark and sneaked undetected into a house he owned on Hilltop Place. A magnet he carried gave him access to any house on the street by way of the underground tunnel. Except for the time that he left to commit his crimes on Saturday morning, he remained in his house until after dark on Saturday night, at which time he hightailed it to his cabin to establish another alibi. The Thursday night rain gave him the tracks and footprints he needed to establish that he'd been at the cabin. To make sure he had an alibi for the entire weekend, he stopped by the general store on Friday and Sunday."

"But how did you know things didn't happen as Angela said?"

"Two things. One, the woman had to have been given a sleeping tablet an hour or so before she was murdered. Irene Penrod denied giving her a sleeping tablet, and both Irene Penrod and Fred Hartley said the woman was not groggy when they talked to her. Also, we have the tape Angela gave us. I timed it. The tape was longer than the time of the phone call she made to her grandmother that morning. Besides that, the doorbell that rang at the end of the tape did not match the one at Mrs. Nelson's house, but the one I heard as I rang the bell at Angela's."

"Of course I didn't know anything about the tape until we arrived at Miss Nelson's. Luckily, once I arrived at my conclusion, I memorized everything I could about any of Miss Nelson's phone calls. When I narrowed my suspect list and decided who murdered Mrs. Nelson and Mrs. Jarvis, I had to devise a plan to capture her. It was then I thought of the two, white envelopes that Miss Penrod told us about and the two envelopes Hornwell made sure Officer Davis saw. Our murderers knew Miss Penrod might tell us about the envelopes, so they had to have a story ready in case we confronted them with it. After some thought, I came up with the idea of trying to get Miss Nelson to agree to assisted suicide. If we could get her to agree to that and catch her in a lie, I felt we could get her to break.

"In addition, we got a search warrant for Hornwell's cabin. Just before I left the house this morning I received a phone call telling me that the rest of Mrs. Jarvis's money had been found. Yesterday afternoon, a Mr. Anderson contacted the department. He said Mrs. Jarvis knew someone found out where she had hidden her money, and she thought that person or those persons would try to steal it. She confided in Anderson, who isn't known to anyone else on Hilltop Place. Mrs. Jarvis gave Anderson a list of all the serial numbers of the bills and told him that under no condition would she allow the money to leave her house before her death. An officer picked up that list and Mrs. Jarvis's note from Anderson last night. Some of the serial numbers matched the money we found in the house Hartley rented from Hornwell. The others matched the bills they found in the safe in Hornwell's cabin.

"But that's not all, Lou. We found some samples of Mrs. Jarvis's handwriting. I believe we will find that tests will prove that the note about the money is actually her handwriting, while the "will" Hornwell has is a forgery. And one more thing, the guys up north did some more checking today. They located the people who have the cabin next to Hornwell. They arrived at their cabin around noon on Friday and left Monday morning. They said Hornwell wasn't at his cabin at any time on Friday, but arrived sometime late Saturday night. Hornwell had not arrived by the time his neighbors walked their dog around 10:00 Saturday night, but his car was there when they took the dog for a walk early Sunday morning. The couple even commented that they were surprised to see Hornwell's car on Sunday morning, because on the weekends Hornwell uses his cabin, he arrives sometime early Friday evening and leaves Sunday afternoon. Other than the weekend of the murder, his neighbors have never known him to vary from this routine. While his neighbors didn't see Hornwell arrive, they did see him leave Sunday afternoon. They were sure it was Hornwell. He waved to them as he left. Our boys up north had already determined that there was only one set of tire tracks and one set of footprints leading to and from the cabin. Evidently, Hornwell only went to the general store on Friday, then hightailed back to Hilltop Place and never set foot in his cabin until late Saturday night when he called his wife from the cabin phone to establish an alibi."

"Cy, you just never cease to amaze me, but there are a couple of things I still don't understand."

"Such as?"

"First of all, why didn't they just strangle Mrs. Nelson? Why such a production?"

"Miss Nelson said Hornwell called the shots. First of all, Hornwell is the kind of guy who wants to match wits with the police, to show that he is smarter. Second, Miss Nelson said Hornwell thought with all the modern technology we would've been able to prove murder anyway. If he choked her, marks would show on her throat. If he used a towel, we might've been able to find fibers in her throat. Plus, Hornwell was so afraid that Mrs. Jarvis would talk and cast suspicion on one or both of them, so he felt they had to do away with her, too. He didn't figure anyone would believe two deaths by natural causes so close in proximity and time."

"But why didn't Hornwell kill Mrs. Nelson instead of taking a chance on Miss Nelson being able to do it?"

"This is all conjecture on my part, but I believe that Hornwell wanted Angela Nelson in as deep as he was. I don't think Hornwell would've committed either murder unless he had to. When we sent Angela away, Hornwell had to make a decision. Either he had to let Mrs. Jarvis live, or he had to kill her."

"Well, like I said, Cy, you never cease to amaze me."

"I should've amazed you sooner."

"Or I should've amazed you. After all, I was privy to most of what you knew."

"So what are we going to do now?"

"I'm not sure there's anything to do. We just need to wait for the trial, if there is one."

"No, I mean now."

"Oh, you mean now now. Well, it looks to me like we're free as a bird again."

Lou and I were happy to conclude another case. A closed case meant more time for eating, dating, reading, and watching TV. But who knew when we'd get called in on another murder case? As it turned out, another murder has already taken place. I'll fill you in later.

Printed in Poland
by Amazon Fulfillment
Poland Sp. z o.o., Wrocław